SMILE, HO

When she was photographed, she smiled. Not just any smile: the famous, enchanting, hopeful, provocative, innocent Honey Markham smile, a token of uncritical affection freely given.

The smile had shaped her life. When she was six her mother secured the child's first part in a film, gossip had it by sleeping with the producer. Better informed sources knew this to be slander. Florence Markham slept with anyone, but for pleasure, not profit. Six-year-old Honey could just learn her lines and could just hit her marks, but to achieve both these feats simultaneously was beyond her. So Florence stood behind the nearest camera. 'Smile, Honey,' she called; when sound was running she mouthed the words. 'Smile, Honey, smile!'

Honey smiled her way into a career.

**Also by the same author,
and available from Coronet:**

HANNAH AT THIRTY-FIVE
POOR DEAR CHARLOTTE

About the author

Born in India, Anabel Donald 'established her
credentials as an acute observer of the Battle
of the Sexes in a brilliantly accomplished first
novel, HANNAH AT THIRTY-FIVE, or HOW TO
SURVIVE DIVORCE' (John Nicholson). Her
second novel, POOR DEAR CHARLOTTE,
exploited her knowledge of life in an exclu-
sive girls' school. SMILE, HONEY shows the
culmination of a splendid comic talent with,
like the best of comedy, a thoughtful and
thought-provoking undertone.

SMILE, HONEY

ANABEL DONALD

CORONET BOOKS
Hodder and Stoughton

First published in Great Britain in
1988 by Hodder and Stoughton
Limited

Coronet edition 1989

British Library C.I.P.

Donald, Anabel
  Smile, honey
  I. Title
  823'.914   [F]

  ISBN 0-340-50609-1

Printed and bound in Great Britain
for Hodder and Stoughton
paperbacks, a division of Hodder and
Stoughton Ltd., Mill Road,
Dunton Green, Sevenoaks, Kent
TN13 2YA (Editorial Office:
47 Bedford Square, London
WC1B 3DP) by Cox & Wyman Ltd.,
Reading.

Chapter One

Most of her friends thought Honey had recovered very quickly.

At first, of course, none of them knew the extent of her disaster. She had broken up with Steve, her live-in lover; that was common knowledge. "The decision was absolutely mutual. Yes, eight years has been a long time. I hope there are no hard feelings on either side. They were good years. You can't win 'em all." She said this to her friends, to reporters from the women's magazines, to the man from the colour supplement, and to the British public on the Wogan show.

The public was interested because Honey was a Personality; the prettiest girl in England, according to the tabloids.

Like most Personalities, she didn't do much. She hadn't made a film since *The Daughters of Captain Bridge* in the late sixties. But *Captain Bridge* was a classic, almost as popular as *The Wizard of Oz*, more popular than *The Railway Children*. It was shown every Christmas on British and American television; it sold steadily all over the world. She still appeared intermittently on celebrity quiz shows and chat shows. She opened fêtes, did commercials, and was photographed arriving and leaving at public functions and airports.

When she was photographed, she smiled. Not just any smile: the famous, enchanting, hopeful, provocative, innocent Honey Markham smile, a token of uncritical affection freely given.

The smile had shaped her life. When she was six her

mother secured the child's first part in a film, gossip had it by sleeping with the producer. Better informed sources knew this to be slander. Florence Markham slept with anyone, but for pleasure, not profit. Six-year-old Honey could just learn her lines and could just hit her marks, but to achieve both these feats simultaneously was beyond her. So Florence stood behind the nearest camera. "Smile, Honey," she called; when sound was running she mouthed the words. "Smile, Honey, smile!"

Honey smiled her way into a career. Even Vernon Cole, the well-established character actor then in his forties and consuming a bottle of Glenlivet a day, noticed it. "That little bitch has the most erotic smile I've ever seen," he confided to one of his ex-wives, who was also working on the picture.

"Nonsense, Vernon, she's only six. It probably just coincided with your annual erection," said the ex-wife. However, he was right and the box-office returns proved it.

So, even though Honey had broken up with Steve after eight years, which would generally incline people to sympathise with or gloat over her as a woman spurned, she was so clearly in a strong position to find another man that the break-up was merely regarded as intriguing rather than disastrous.

In any case, most of her friends had never thought Steve good enough for her. He was only a documentary cameraman building a reputation. True, he was considerably younger than she – how much younger depended on your estimate of how many years Honey had spent as a child actress rising fifteen – and attractive, if you liked men tall, muscular and bearded. But Honey was Honey.

The split occurred just before Christmas; Honey and Steve went to Vienna together and returned separately. For a week or so Honey saw no one. Then she emerged and went on with her life. Lunches and dinners out, shopping, and the gruelling ritual of exercise, massage and skin-care originally imposed by her mother and now refined and modernised by the very professional Honey.

In mid-January she was invited to dinner by Tom and Maggie Wyatt. They lived only three doors away, up Campden Hill Road; they had known Honey for nearly twenty years, ever since she married her late husband. Tom was a publisher and Maggie's life was devoted to finding too much to do. In pursuit of this aim she had produced five children, followed a demanding career, acquired a large house in London and a weekend cottage with six bedrooms in a particularly inaccessible part of Suffolk, entertained regularly and kept the household topped up with au pairs and dogs who, obligingly, soon developed time-consuming problems and afflictions.

Tom Wyatt was becalmed in the eye of his household storm. His manner was politely bemused, his grip on proceedings vague. Fifteen minutes before the guests were due to arrive he stood amiably in the drawing-room watching the younger lurcher being sick behind the sofa.

"Why are we giving a dinner-party?" he asked.

Maggie, occupied at the drinks tray mixing a cocktail, was touched by this unusual token of interest on his part. "Why do you ask?"

"It just occurred to me – " he said wistfully, "just an idea – that since Christmas is over and we did have rather a lot of people to stay for nearly two weeks down in Suffolk – and then Candida's twenty-first last week – "

"It was *Camilla's* twenty-first, Tom. Candida's only nineteen."

"Good for her," said Tom encouragingly. "But we've been doing more than our share of entertaining, haven't we, and very few people give parties in the middle of January. There's a tacit agreement, surely, that everyone can recuperate . . ."

"The party's for Honey," said Maggie. "Poor darling Honey, at a loose end since that swine Steve dumped her, though if you ask me it's the best possible thing. So I decided to give a *Captain Bridge* party."

Tom looked puzzled. The lurcher, having licked up most of its vomit, ambled towards the kitchen. "A *Captain Bridge* party?"

"Just a little joke," said Maggie. "A party for people from the film. You remember the film?"

"Certainly," said Tom. "It was made twenty years ago. Is now the time to celebrate?"

"It'll be nice for Honey," said Maggie firmly.

"Remind me who's coming."

"Pandora and Ben Considine. She played one of Honey's sisters, remember, and he wrote the script. Then there's Madeline Cabot Goldberg."

"Who had nothing to do with the film, surely."

"Of course not, Tom! I asked her for two reasons. One, she rents part of Honey's house, so she's a neighbour; and two, she's taken up with Jacky Hamzavi, that gigolo friend of Honey's who was also in the film. He's on to a good thing if he can hold on to Madeline. She's incredibly rich."

"And incredibly mean," said Tom who did remember that he and Maggie had entertained Madeline at least six times whereas she had asked them back once. To tea.

"And lastly, Vernon Cole."

"Good God! Is he still alive?"

"He seemed to think he was when he accepted the invitation."

"Have you checked the stock of whisky?"

"Of course, and we've plenty in hand."

Tom sipped at the cocktail Maggie pressed on him. "And you'll have asked Matilda, of course."

"Certainly not!"

"Explain," said Tom wearily. He didn't like cocktails and he wanted a pink gin. He also wanted to be left alone in his study to read.

"She couldn't come anyway, because she's in Canada, but if she had been in London we couldn't have asked her with the Considines. Surely even you remember the affair Matilda had with Ben Considine?"

"Of course I remember. It was hardly a secret. But I thought it was an Edward the Seventh affair, where everyone knew and no one minded."

"That was during his first marriage, when his wife spent her time in psychiatric clinics. Now he's married to Pandora and she's kept him away from Matilda. As far as anyone can tell. Matilda's always a dark horse."

"I like Matilda. At least she's literate, which is more than one can say for the rest of your line-up."

"Ben Considine is literate."

"He's a playwright. Not necessarily the same thing."

The doorbell rang, Maggie dashed upstairs to tidy her hair, Tom went to answer it. Honey stood there, seven minutes late as Matilda had once told her was polite, looking to Tom's eyes like a laundry-basket of extremely seductive black washing. They kissed and Tom felt an unexpected shiver of pleasure. He led her into the drawing-room, talking to cover his surprise. He was the most faithful husband in London, everyone knew that. Not that he hadn't had his opportunities. He preened himself in the hall mirror as he passed. Not bad for fifty-four. His features were as regular as ever, his blue eyes as startling, his skin smooth even if he did grow more and more like a waxwork drained of blood. "So how's Steve?" he asked.

"We've split up," said Honey.

"Oh God," said Tom. "Have a drink."

"You must have one of my amazing new cocktails," called Maggie. "My hairdresser brought the recipe back from the Seychelles."

"That would be lovely," called Honey, who would have preferred orange juice. "Don't worry about Steve," she went on more quietly, "it was absolutely mutual. Just one of those things."

The bell rang again and Tom went to answer it. The younger lurcher re-entered from the kitchen, loped twice round the room, and was sick behind a chair. Honey turned away and looked expectantly towards the hall.

Ben Considine came in. So did Tom and Pandora, but in Ben's presence others were insignificant. He was tall, rangy, and strikingly attractive, rather than good-looking. His face was lop-sided, his thick toffee-coloured hair tousled, his dinner-jacket rather too big. This must have been an illusion, thought Honey, as Pandora would certainly have had it made for him. He hugged her; Honey withdrew gracefully as soon as she could. Pandora wouldn't like it.

Pandora stood behind him not liking it. She was averagely pretty herself, slim, of medium height; this year her hair was short and blonde. Her eyes had a slight tendency to cluster round her rather long nose. She was, officially, one of Honey's closest friends. They greeted each other with cries of delight. "*Love* your outfit. Japanese?"

Honey nodded. "Love yours. Italian?"

Pandora nodded.

"You must have one of my marvellous new cocktails," said Maggie. Pandora and Ben looked without enthusiasm at the pinkish liquid.

"Not for me," said Pandora. "Just a little white wine, please. And Ben would like some Perrier water."

This announcement caused a minor sensation. "Pandora thinks I drink too much," said Ben. In silence, they all agreed with Pandora. "I think it's a mistake to keep me sober," he went on. "I'm more unpleasant sober."

"You don't hit so many people," Pandora pointed out brightly and proprietorially.

"But I inflict deeper wounds."

The doorbell rang. Maggie called from the hall, "What fun, all our last guests!"

Honey murmured warmly. Pandora and Ben sat down on a sofa, dislodging the elder lurcher. "I think you all know each other, except for Madeline and Vernon." Maggie introduced them. Madeline, a woman preserved by determination and money between fifty and seventy, peered distastefully at Vernon Cole.

He was decaying but sprightly, wearing a wig which looked, for him, unusually realistic. "Darlings!" he embraced the room at large. "Do you like the rug? One of the best perks from my last film! An epic! The film and the rug! Both masterpieces in their kind! Like precious Honey, still beautiful after all these years, and darling Pandora, such a trier! Like the hair! Blonde is so wise after thirty-five!"

"I'm thirty-four," said Pandora.

Behind Madeline stood Jacky Hamzavi. He was as beautiful as Honey, half-Persian, half-French. He had thick creamy ivory skin, a mouth carved with attention to detail, a straight high-bridged nose and large hazel eyes, which were fixed on Madeline, his current employer.

"Isn't it fun to see Jacky again?" continued Vernon, brushing aside Maggie's proffered cocktail and seizing a tumbler to fill with whisky. "It's been twenty years since I laid eyes on his deliciousness, though he'll have been laying other things since, I've no doubt! What is it this week, Jacko, boys or girls?"

With a graceful gesture Jacky laid his hand on Madeline's arm. "I'm fortunate enough . . ." he began.

"Jacky's with me," interrupted Madeline, also rejecting the cocktail and opting for white wine. "So you're an actor, Mr Cole?"

"Dear lady, Sir Vernon! The Queen has distinguished me for services to the thee-atah!"

Ben stood up to shake hands with Madeline; the lurcher resumed his place on the sofa; Ben sat on the dog, who bit him.

"Tell me how you all know Jacky," said Madeline, displaying stoic indifference to Ben's injury. Tom hustled the dog out into the hall and shut the door behind him. The dog whined.

"I'm not going to ask Honey again for a while," said Maggie, pulling back the Early American patchwork bedcover, present from an author to Tom, and thrusting her exhausted feet between the Irish linen sheets.

"I like her," said Tom examining his scalp in the mirror, remembering the touch of Honey's cheek as they kissed goodnight. "Do you think I've lost more hair?"

"No. You've got far more hair than most men your age. The party was going so well – "

"It went *very* well," said Tom, massaging his barber's special preparation into the remaining roots. "The food was splendid."

"So it should be." Maggie was a professional cook. She wrote steady-selling books with titles like *The Fruits of Summer* and appeared on television at odd times of the day, when only the unemployed, the retired or the ill could watch. She was pleasant to look at, with a faded rose-leaf quality that made people say, "She must have been so pretty once." Honey, a constant assessor of women's looks, doubted it. Maggie had small eyes and pouchy hamster cheeks; her children looked like younger, fresher hamsters. She looked ruffled and crumpled now. Tom, who was guiltily fond of her – he knew that after thirty years of loyal marriage he didn't love her as much as she wanted or deserved – abandoned his scalp and joined her in bed.

"I don't see what you thought went wrong," he said. "Everyone joined in and tried to answer Honey's questions. It was a lively evening."

"Lively! I'd say disastrous! Take abortion, for instance. 'Is abortion ever justified?' I ask you! The idiocy of the girl. When Pandora, who's supposed to be one of Honey's best friends, has had two to my certain knowledge – "

"She didn't take it personally. She carried it off well."

"She needed to. Then we had 'the importance of chastity'. Apart from Honey, none of the guests would recognise chastity if it bit them on the leg. And she was so *serious* about it, so moralistic. She sounded like a Catholic."

"Nothing wrong with Catholics."

"Not if you know they are and can take avoiding action. Honey's never been Catholic and it's unreasonable of her to start at my dinner-party. Then she moved on to homosexuality – "

"That was a little tricky," admitted Tom. "Jacky Hamzavi is more than a touch AC/DC. Madeline didn't like the subject at all. Do you think she was annoyed on her own behalf or his?"

"His. She's heterosexual in spades."

"Jacky has plenty of hair for his age," said Tom. "He didn't seem upset. He seemed to be enjoying himself specially, I thought."

"That's how he earns his living, by seeming to enjoy himself specially. How can we tell what goes on behind his eyelashes? Mind, not that I care. He's not important."

"Except in human terms."

"Of course, except in human terms."

A pause, while they respected their liberal humanist principles.

"It's so – adolescent. This pursuit of truth. Why, why, why, like a parrot, when we all *explained* to her."

"She didn't accept our explanations."

Maggie wasn't appeased. "She *should* have. She's only invited to look beautiful and smile. She *disturbed* everyone."

"Surely she can talk if she wants to?"

"Not at dinner-parties. That's not what they're for. Not to talk about ethics."

"You don't mind if we discuss South Africa."

"No, because we're all on the same side. But to talk about right and wrong when it makes people at my table eating my food—"

"The food was excellent—"

" – feel uncomfortable, feel – bad – and now you're taking her side!" Maggie began to cry quietly. Tom

13

slipped his arm under her shoulders and she half pulled away, preparing to be comforted.

"Shh, shh," he said. "You've been doing too much. You're tired. Honey loved your cocktail."

Maggie sat bolt upright, wrenching Tom's shoulder as she went. "You – STUPID man!" she hissed. "People say you're vague but I think you're just plain STUPID! Why did you have to mention the cocktail? NOBODY ELSE DRANK IT!"

The Considines were in the car on their way home. Pandora was driving; it was a town car, her choice, black, smart and much too small for Ben, who shifted irritably in the designer seat. He wanted a drink, a whole hand of good whisky. Or just whisky. Or any alcohol that would barricade him from Pandora: her possessiveness, her concern, and the deadly room she called his study with its silent word processor, the stacks of untouched paper, the sharpened pencils.

It wasn't that he hated her. At times he had hated his first wife, her bursts of wilful madness, her jealousy, the destruction she had made of their shared hopes. He had also loved her. But Pandora didn't rate such emotion. She was a nonentity, he thought, looking at her presented profile. A nonentity in herself, but a member of a usefully powerful theatrical family. In marrying Pandora, youngest daughter of Sir Leo Pardoe and his wife the playwright, he had entered the charmed circle of Pardoe actors, reviewers, script writers, directors, television producers, who reviewed each other, backed each other, cast each other and, every BAFTA or television awards or *Evening Standard* drama awards evening, presented prizes to each other.

The Pardoes were his safety net. His two plays had been so often produced by Pardoes that it appeared he had written ten. Under the Pardoe aegis he had contributed scripts to every British soap opera, had been interviewed on each TV channel and on radio; it was a dim and collateral Pardoe working for an examining board who had chosen his plays as an O-level text thus ensuring solid sales for years. Ben's Jewish instincts could not ignore this. Both his passionate desire to make a success of at least one major relationship and his innate caution kept him with Pandora.

The Pardoes were pleasant people. They did not bear grudges or deliberately do others down. They merely took the best for themselves, and since they were talented, confident actors and entertainers, they got on. They were not intelligent but they didn't know it, and they shared with their public the illusion that an actor possesses the qualities he can project. If a Pardoe was currently playing a doctor they went first to him for medical advice.

"Did you enjoy yourself, Ben?" she asked, braking sharply for a red light. She was a terrible driver. He tried not to remember Matilda, who was an excellent driver, who had never, ever sharpened pencils or asked him if he had enjoyed himself.

"Are you thinking about Matilda?" said Pandora.

"No," said Ben.

"She's in Canada," said Pandora.

"Oh," said Ben.

"She was looking very old the last time I saw her," said Pandora.

Ben wanted to slap her. He shifted in his seat and said, "Odd that Jacky Hamzavi turned up again. I haven't seen him since *Captain Bridge*."

"I have," said Pandora. She always liked to know more than her interlocutor. "He's been knocking round London off and on, always in tow to some rich older woman. That's when he's not losing his money at the roulette table."

"He used to play superb poker." Making conversation with Pandora irritated him almost beyond bearing. He should have stayed drunk.

"That woman Madeline could be useful to us. She's got lots of money and she wants to be an angel."

"Oh foolish Madeline," said Ben.

"Daddy's looking for backers for a musical version of *Macbeth*."

Ben started to sing. "Hello, Banquo. Well hello, Banquo. It's so nice to see you back where you belong."

"No, Ben," said Pandora patiently. "It has new tunes, of course. I'll ask Madeline to dinner. And Vernon; she liked him."

"And your father."

"Of course, Daddy and Mummy. We might as well have Circe and Salome too."

Ben closed his eyes to shut out the prospect. In his jacket pocket, he thought, was his address book. In his address book were numbers. He ran over them in his mind. When Pandora went to bed he'd go to his study, make use of the only virile implement in there, and telephone someone. Someone unmarried; it was past midnight. Someone who knew nothing about modern playwrights beyond the fact that he was an eminent one. Someone young and uncritical, with flesh that didn't move when she turned over, and a brain that was satisfied with compliments and groans and sleep.

When Honey got back from the Wyatts' party she cuddled the cat, who didn't protest. Madeline and Jacky had walked back with her. Madeline rented the upper three floors of Honey's large house; she kept a flat in the basement and sole use of the garden. For the eight years of her tenancy Madeline had struggled to make a friend of Honey, but so far Steve had kept her at bay.

Inevitably, when they reached the house, Madeline pressed Honey to come up for a drink. Her dark eyes were avid. Honey knew she wanted to pump her for details of the break-up with Steve and her future plans. Honey kept refusing, but Madeline only desisted when

Jacky, fond of Honey and recognising his cue, added his voice too enthusiastically to the invitation. At this Madeline accepted the refusal and hustled Jacky up the front steps.

Honey went into her flat, cuddled the cat. The flat was familiar but not a refuge. She had no territorial refuges. She felt safe where her man was.

She had only ever had two men. The first was her husband. She married him when she officially reached eighteen; before that, she lived with her mother. Her husband was fifty-five when they married. He was an eminent and fashionable surgeon, a widower with two sons grown and gone, one to Canada, one to Strasbourg where he still worked for the European Parliament. They would inherit the trust fund Honey now benefited from, when she remarried or died. Her husband had settled all his affairs tidily before he, tidily, killed himself. He hadn't warned her, but wrote a considerate final letter, explaining that he was ill, would otherwise die at length and sordidly. He had never asked more of her than that she looked beautiful. He explained once that he was tired of decaying female bodies, that he loved her healthy, perfect one. She gave herself entirely to his life, his friends, his house, and loved him as much as he would accept.

When he died, Steve replaced him. They met at the funeral, which he was covering for the BBC, whose news resources were stretched that day. Immediately, he coveted her; after a few weeks he moved in and she gave herself entirely to his life, his friends, his work, and loved him as much as he would accept.

She hugged the cat tighter and it protested, leaping aloofly away and licking its paws. The silence of the flat swamped her. She was appalled by her own despair; the more appalled because she was so successful at disguising it. Since Steve had left the gap between what she said and what she felt widened daily.

Not even her mirror comforted her. She had been

beautiful so long she took it for granted. What use was it when her looks couldn't even keep a man to love her, a father for her child?

She hadn't expected his reaction. She should have, she could see that now. He'd been talking for months about her career, how she shouldn't wander round the world as a camera assistant with him; she should make a come-back in a feature film. She thought that was consideration, touching loyalty. Whenever she mentioned marriage he pointed out that she would lose the income from her trust. She had plenty of money, she said. She'd saved capital of her own and she earned well; the house was hers outright and it was worth half a million.

When they got back from the United States before Christmas she was pregnant. Probably the pill hadn't worked because she'd had stomach upsets, the doctor said.

Now he'll marry me, Honey thought. He'd said often enough that they'd have children one day. She was thrilled; she hugged her secret to herself and thought about names and schools and how happy he'd be when she told him. She hesitated to do this, wanted to pick the right time.

The trip to Vienna had been a mistake. She'd wanted a romantic atmosphere to tell him about the baby and in the early days of their relationship he'd said he would like to see Vienna. She wanted to see the Prater Wheel. The scene with Orson Welles from *The Third Man* was one of her favourites; she watched it on video again and again.

They stayed in the Hôtel de France on the Ringstrasse. It was luxurious, full of Italians in fur coats and boots. "Another fucking hotel room," said Steve dumping his case on the bed. He was wearing clean jeans, soft leather boots, a flannel shirt, a cashmere sweater. He'd be a perfect father, thought Honey. In some ways, added a shrewder, recent, maternal voice.

18

"What aren't you happy about?" asked Honey. She trembled when he was annoyed, which annoyed him more.

"Forget it," he said. "I've had it to the back teeth with travel, that's all."

"You could have told me when I said I was booking the trip."

"Does it matter? I'll probably enjoy it."

"You always wanted to see Vienna."

"No, I didn't."

"You did, I remember, you said—"

"Who the hell believes what a man tells you the second time he takes you out? What kind of innocent are you, Honey?"

"And you said it again, in bed. When we were on location in Kenya. You said it the first night, in the Nairobi hotel, and then you said it again in a tent near Lake Turkana . . ."

"Forget it, we're here now. What do you want to do?"

What Honey wanted was to tell him about the baby and hear him say the right things; responsible, affectionate things about marriage and a future, or just a future. Looking back, she saw she had been inadequately naive, but hormones and hope were singing in her blood, and there were men, surely, who would have responded like that? Often she suspected that Steve categorised as naive feelings that were inconvenient for him, but she didn't think she was competent to judge.

She knew she was ignorant, uneducated. She hoped it was a secret that she could hardly read, though Till and her mother knew, and probably other people had guessed.

Words baffled her. She was acutely dyslexic. Her childhood had been spent learning lines read to her by her mother, hitting her marks and smiling. Intermittently, she attended a stage school in Ealing. It hadn't been hard to disguise her ignorance from them. Her mother was her chaperone and tutor; she believed that reading would just give Honey ideas, and she colluded with her to hide her disability.

Honey had developed strategies over the years. She claimed to be short-sighted, and had always forgotten her contact lenses when she had to read unexpectedly in public. Her mother dealt with business letters.

Honey felt her illiteracy keenly. She never stopped wanting to read and to know. She ordered any books reviewed in the *Sunday Times* or the *Observer* and then stumbled her way through the blurb, the description of the author and any reviews printed on the dust-jacket. Her book bill almost approached her clothes bill, though it never topped it; clothes were work and Honey was professional.

Everyone she knew, even Steve, was better informed than she was, despite all her efforts. When she was in England, she managed most of the news and opinion pages of *The Times* every day, but she could only remember what she had read, not process it. She lacked a framework of understanding, and most of all she lacked vocabulary. She looked words up in the dictionary and found them defined in terms of other words she didn't understand. When one correspondent's view was contradicted by the letter pages or the leader, she couldn't reconcile them. She believed both simultaneously. Then one day she sat at lunch next to a Cabinet Minister who said he didn't believe a word he read in *The Times* any more, the paper had gone to the dogs, and her tenuous grasp of current affairs vanished before her still smiling eyes.

So if Steve said she was naive and unreasonable, she probably was, and when they sat on a damp bench in a children's playground near the Prater Wheel, which was shut, and he made her promise to have an abortion, she agreed. He seemed frightened behind his bluster. She tried to make him see it wouldn't be his problem, she had enough money to look after the baby, but every time she said "baby" he shuddered as if she were applying a red-hot poker to the soles of his feet. He liked having his feet tickled, she thought. When he asked her why she was smiling she told him, and he said, "You're not just naive, Honey, you're idiotic. Talk about dumb blondes! What kind of mother would you make? Think about that. We're responsible adults, surely."

Honey felt but could not express his inconsistency, and they were not in any case involved in a logical argument. They came back from Vienna with Honey's promise firmly given. Steve was reluctant to go back to San Francisco; he wanted to stay with Honey and check that her promise was carried out. He called it "standing by her". But one of the characters in the documentary film they'd been making for the past three months was on the point of death; the chance that he might die on camera was too good to be missed, so Steve went.

That was a month ago and, despite increasingly agitated phone calls from San Francisco, Honey had still done nothing about it. She knew that, soon, she must, but she was waiting for Matilda to come back from Canada. There was a postcard from her propped against the mirror on the mantelpiece. It read:

> NO SIGN OF A MAN
> IN SASKATCHEWAN:
> HERE'S HOPING FOR THREE
> IN TENNESSEE

Till always printed when she wrote to Honey. Honey held the postcard for comfort, hoping that Tennessee had only been included for the rhyme, and that Till was coming straight back from Canada at the end of the week as she'd planned.

Chapter Two

Jacky Hamzavi lay in Madeline's bed thinking about his mother. It was six months and three days since her death; he had thought of her every day during her lifetime, and couldn't break the habit now.

Madeline was in the bathroom. The whirr of her electric razor punctuated his thoughts. She had very dark, coarse body hair. To keep her legs and underarms smooth was a constant battle, fought like all Madeline's battles by pre-emptive strikes. He had tried suggesting that European women thought body hair attractive. "We all know about European women," she said in her characteristic tone of contempt, and the razor continued to whirr.

Jacky's mother had brought him up to be kind to older women. Now he lived by it. He did not find it undignified or humiliating since he had to an advanced degree the capacity to ignore other people's opinions. What his mother thought had originally mattered to him. Then he came to share most of her views and to expect her approval even when she did not agree; Jacky was very much loved.

Because he was so accustomed to happiness, he had no idea how happy he was. Most of his waking hours were spent enjoying himself. He liked food and drink and clothes and houses and sex and most people for short periods of time. Now he wished his mother were still alive so he could gossip with her about Madeline. He stretched in the satin sheets. He preferred linen, but he liked satin too. He was counting his blessings. With

Madeline, he had free board and lodging. She bought him clothes, and his wardrobe was dating fast so that was useful. She was sexually demanding but he was used to that; she liked extended performances, but he was used to that too, and as he desired women only moderately, he could perform and perform and perform. Boredom was the drawback, but he had accepted that long ago as the major disadvantage of his chosen career. Pumping up and down inside rich women was not nearly as bad as real work.

"D'you reckon little Honey'll keep her baby?" said Madeline sitting on the foot of the bed.

"Are you sure she's pregnant?"

"Yes. All that stuff about right and wrong – her eyelids only flickered when she mentioned abortion. She's got great control, that one, but I spotted it years ago. When she's really upset her eyelids flicker. And she's upped her milk order. Three pints a day."

"I expect she'll keep it, then," said Jacky. "She hates killing things – rescues spiders and slugs, you know." He flexed his feet and rubbed his toes together. He had long, flexible toes. Never used those on Madeline. Perhaps next time.

"I do admire her. She dresses real well. That black outfit – Kenzo?"

"Isey Mayake," said Jacky. "Are you finished with the bathroom?"

"Yes, but keep talking to me. Leave the door open. I want to know about Pandora. Who is she?"

"Child actress. Least talented of three daughters of a theatrical family. The others are called Circe and Salome."

"My! She earns enough money to keep that husband?"

"Yes. She presents a television programme called *Cupid*. Millions of people watch it. They find lovers who were split up by accident and then reunite them. The longer they've been split up, the better. War-time sweethearts if they can find them. Pandora squeaks and squeals in pretend excitement and sings a song. The programme's been running for five years and I don't think it'll ever stop."

"Just turn off the bath water a while, please. I can't hear you. And Ben writes plays?"

"Did. He hasn't for years. Not since he and Matilda split up."

"And I haven't met Matilda?"

"No. She's in Canada. She was the eldest sister in the film."

"Should I meet Matilda?"

"Everyone should. She's an experience. Can I run the water now?"

"Not yet. Cream your face, it's quieter. This Ben. Do I gather he likes girls?"

"Very much."

"What age girls?"

"Under forty," said Jacky, adding fifteen years to his actual estimate.

"No chance for me?"

It flattered Madeline to be spoken to with what passed for frankness. "No," said Jacky. "You're too much of a woman for him."

"Too old."

"Age cannot wither you, nor custom stale your infinite variety."

"I like that. You sure have a turn of phrase."

"That was Shakespeare. About Cleopatra."

"She must have been something. Before HRT and all. You can run your bath now, and I'll wash your – back."

"Men don't like children," said Florence Markham. "Not men like Steve with their future in front of them. Such as it is. You've handled this all wrong, Honey. If you

24

wanted him you should have grabbed him in the first year. Got any gin about?"

"It's only ten in the morning," protested Honey. It was a small defiance of her mother's chilling worldliness. Often Honey listened to her mother's cynical assessments and wished there was another world for her, a place where tenderness and consideration were possible, where self-interest did not rule and she could find herself a niche.

"Just give me the gin," said Florence. She was a big, still impressive woman in her early sixties with a ravaged face and an assortment of brightly coloured clothes draped about her in an artistic manner. She had decided to be raven-haired and curls escaped from her usual silk turban. She had outlined her eyes in kohl and her lips in scarlet with a generous assessment of the size of these features. She looked ready to step on stage as Madame Arcati, a part she had just been playing in a tour of Australia, New Zealand and the Far East.

There was awkwardness between mother and daughter. Though Florence was protective and fought fiercely for Honey's interests, her perception of those interests and Honey's own seldom coincided. She thought Honey half-witted and she increasingly disliked her as one does someone to whom one has done a serious disservice. For here Honey was, obviously unhappy, and since Florence had directed her career and life it must be at least partly her fault. Her guilt was exacerbated by the knowledge that Honey was continually grateful to her.

Honey delivered the double gin. "You should have stuck to gentlemen," said Florence. "At least they walk out on you tactfully."

"How can you be tactful about that? He didn't want to marry me and he did want to get rid of the child."

"I don't know why you waited so long to tell me about the baby," said Florence. "Pass me the Yellow Pages."

"No, Mother. I haven't decided what I want to do

yet." Honey hadn't expected any other reaction; from Florence there would be no emotion, no sympathy except of the roughest practical kind. But she longed for it, and thought this immediate flight to the Yellow Pages un-grandmotherly.

"You mean you want to have it? A child is a hell of a bind."

Honey remembered the days of her own childhood, which had, despite intermittent awfulness, been a time of closeness and co-operation between mother and daughter, of hours spent keeping each other's spirits up in dingy bed-sitting-rooms between a succession of "uncles" and the joy when Honey's earnings had swollen from a trickle into a flood; moved, she kissed her mother.

Florence was never slow to capitalise on advantage. "How about another gin?"

"Did you ever regret having me?" Honey asked.

"You were a terrible baby. You cried all the time. It was hard, Honey."

"I know. But it won't be hard for me. Not in the same way."

"The money won't, but what about the loneliness? A child needs a father, someone to be there to comfort you when the child goes."

Honey listened with increasing despair. Her mother always offered the thoughts women had refined and dis-tilled over generations of love and betrayal and stupidities committed out of naivety and trust.

"I also thought, maybe if I got rid of it, I could get Steve back." The hope, unspoken for so long, sounded absurd as soon as she voiced it.

"Not a chance," said Florence. "Once they've gone, they've gone. Cut your losses."

"Men do come back."

"I suppose so. And films *are* finished according to the shooting schedule and under budget. Just not the ones

I've had anything to do with. I speak as I find, Honey. Whatever you do must be because you want to do it. And whatever you do your mother will be behind you all the way." Tears, part gin, part motherly feeling, were meandering their black course down her face. "Do you want me to put off my week in Tunisia?"

"No. I'll be fine. I'm a big girl now."

Florence looked at Honey and wondered what else she should have done. The child seemed to have no defences.

Pandora was sorting through the invitations on Honey's mantelpiece and came upon the postcard from Matilda. "How like Till," she said scornfully, turning it over, reading it, tapping it with enamelled mandarin nails. "She's over forty: you'd think she'd give up this man nonsense."

"Why?" asked Honey, pouring coffee.

"Isn't it obvious? She'll make more and more of a fool of herself. She wasn't much to look at even back in the days of *Captain Bridge*. Now, really. Last time I saw her I was quite shocked, she'd let herself go so much. Put on weight, abandoned her hair, scuffing round in those baggy skirts and sweaters."

"I didn't know you still saw her. What with Benjamin—" Usually Honey kept clear of this subject, but she resented Pandora's bitchiness.

"Benjamin has nothing to do with it. She's a complete back number as far as he's concerned: you know what a snob he is about women's looks. Benjamin is married to me."

"I know," said Honey, utterly out of charity with Pandora and all women safely ensconced in a marriage. "He was married to Jane for years, and that didn't stop him seeing Till. Where did you meet her, anyway? She didn't tell me."

"That doesn't surprise me. You know how devious she

is. I met her at a party. She was trying to get some work in television. Can you imagine the stupidity of it? After all these years as a shrink, trying to get back into acting. She'd precious little talent in the first place."

"I don't agree," said Honey. "I watch *Captain Bridge* quite often, and it seems to me she was very good."

"But plain."

"Expressive face," said Honey.

Pandora was surprised by her stubbornness. "Of course you always hero-worshipped her. Are we going shopping, or not?"

Honey looked out of the window. It was a chilly day; the pavements were deep in slush and grimy water sluiced down into the basement area in front of her flat. "I think I'll stay in," she said. "Sorry, Pandora. I've got things to do."

"You might have thought of that before I slogged over here from Hampstead."

"Stay and have lunch. Let's neither of us go," offered Honey. She seldom intentionally gave offence. "We can watch *Death in Venice*."

This was a recognisable peace-offering. Pandora refused it, and went away balked. She'd wanted to discuss Honey's future, the Wyatts' party, and Ben.

When she'd gone Honey sipped half a cup of low-fat milk and looked round for the cat. It was somewhere else. Honey would have been somewhere else too, if she could have thought of somewhere comforting to be. As it was she thought about last night's dinner-party. Each of the women there – Maggie, Pandora, Madeline – was much less pretty than she. Each had children. Maggie had five. If you had a child, you would never have to look round for a cat. Not for at least eighteen years.

She stroked her stomach reflectively.

She had promised Steve, promised him absolutely. That at least was clear.

She could wait and ask Till for advice. But it was time

28

she took her own decisions. Steve's observation about responsible adults had cut and scarred her. What kind of mother would she make, if she couldn't even decide an issue like this?

She took out the Yellow Pages, crossed to the desk, sat down. She printed PERGANCY and ABROTIN and started to search. Eventually she amended the first syllable of pregnancy, copied down the numbers printed in large type, and dialled the first.

"Good morning, Save A Life here, can we help you?" The woman sounded middle-aged and as if she had just been to the hairdresser.

"I don't know," said Honey. "What do you do?"

"We try to help girls in trouble. We try to give you time to consider." By this time Honey had a vivid mental picture of the woman, her forehead still pink from the drier, with one or two deep indentations where the rollers had been.

"It's an abortion I want."

"My dear, have you *thought*?"

"I promised, you see."

"Promised who?"

"The father."

"What kind of father would want to kill his own child?"

Honey gave the question serious consideration. "It depends, I suppose, on how frightened he is."

"Frightened?" The woman was disconcerted. This was out of her script. "Who could be frightened by a poor innocent baby?"

"It isn't a baby, is it? Just a could-be baby. And if the father doesn't want marriage or children—"

"So he won't marry you?" This was familiar. "Believe me, my dear, in this day and age, the stigma is *nothing* any more. If it's money that's worrying you, we can help. We have sympathisers who offer funds and honest work . . ."

"You're not an abortion agency, are you?"

"No, haven't you read our advertisement? We offer an alternative, a choice. It's quite clearly set out in our advertisements."

Honey rang off. She felt thoroughly foolish, a frequent sensation for her, particularly undermining now. She couldn't even, it seemed, correctly identify an abortion clinic in the Yellow Pages. She rotated her head to relax her neck muscles and dialled the next number on her list.

"Women's clinic services," said a female voice which Honey immediately identified as youngish, left-wing and belonging to a girl with a razor-cut and dungarees.

"Hello," said Honey. "Are you trying to save babies or do you provide abortions?"

"We help," said the voice. "We believe in a woman's right to choose."

"Choose what?"

"Choose anything."

"Even high heels and nail varnish?"

"Sure, if that's what she wants. Are you kidding me?"

"No. I think I'm hysterical."

"That figures. If you want an abortion, honey, come see us."

"What did you call me?" said Honey, alarmed.

"I called you honey. I lived in the States for a while. Sorry if you find it degrading. How about sister?"

"Sister is fine. What's your address? I don't have my glasses with me."

"No hassle. We're at 23A Pole Street. That's POLE, just off Oxford Street. We close at five. Will we see you later?"

"Probably."

The pregnancy advice clinic was up two flights of stairs in a shabby building largely given over to travel agencies. Outside the door, an Oxford Street trader sold balloons,

T-shirts and souvenirs, and the brassy music from a hamburger joint seeped up the stairs after her.

Tom Wyatt hated going to the office. He hated the management of the firm, the books they published; he hated board meetings where he was always in a minority of one, standing alone for a humanism and aestheticism which was steamrollered by the editorial staff with their horror novels and coffee-table books ostensibly written by people famous for things other than writing. He thought the fiction they published mindless, pornographic and violent, the travel books meretricious and puffed far beyond their worth, the religious books superficial, tub-thumping and saccharine.

It had been a family firm. His grandfather had started it: good novels with some best-sellers; poetry, well reviewed, steady-selling; books of philosophical self-improvement for artisans. His father had continued with a sharp Jewish partner; it had made more money. They had the crime writer who wasn't quite Agatha Christie. She kept them turning over nicely in the thirties, forties and fifties.

Then they had expanded and in the seventies were bought up, together with the publisher next door in the quiet Bloomsbury square, by an American conglomerate. Oil company, video, film, leisure pursuits – he refused to ask himself what these could be.

When he and Sammy Steen had agreed to sell the injection of capital was necessary. Educating five children was expensive. There were the houses to keep up. He didn't want to retire, he was only forty-eight. So he stayed with a seat on the board and a vaguely PR responsibility, and when he didn't go in to the office no one noticed.

He sat glumly at his desk. His office was still a good one, on the first floor of the house, looking over the gardens at the back. It had framed illustrations by

Victorian artists, an impressive Regency desk, a thick carpet, an eighteenth-century mirror and bookshelves heavy with past successes. He had added nothing commissioned to the bookshelves since the takeover.

He was thinking about life. He spent most of his time doing that. He was reflective and serious; he had high principles. "I grow old, I grow old. I shall wear the bottoms of my trousers rolled because I have more hair on my calves than on my head," he murmured. He thought about his children. He wished he could like them more. They seemed arrogant, spoilt, and mediocre. It they were spoilt, it was his and Maggie's fault. He wished he could love Maggie more, and desire her at all. He wished he had not sold Thomas Wyatt to the conglomerate. He looked out of the window, swivelling his chair round, propped his feet on the radiator, watched the stark trees and the melting snow and wondered what he should do. "I have measured out my life in coffee spoons," he said.

There had been a board meeting earlier that day. He had missed it. He looked at the agenda, pushed it away. He buzzed his secretary through the intercom. She was an amiable, punkish girl in her early twenties who had been educated far beyond her interests. Roedean and Cambridge had given their all and now she spent the lunch hour snorting cocaine. So gossip had it. If snorting was the right verb. Today she wore black clown trousers and a metallic sweater with pink giraffes grazing it, some upside down.

"Good morning," said Tom.

"Hi, Tom, how ya doin'?"

"What is the best-selling title this month?"

"Probably still *Mucus*."

She was possibly a nice girl, he thought. Why shouldn't she be? Just because she looked so awful and spoke in that casual way shouldn't condemn her. She could still be well meaning. She was quite efficient. His last secretary he'd had for twenty years. She'd retired last month. They'd given her a video machine, presumably for her leisure pursuits. She'd known more about publishing than the giraffe-spotted creature was likely to learn. She'd marry an aristocrat and snort cocaine in Wiltshire before she actually had to learn anything. Had she ever read a proper book? Surely one could not take an English degree from Cambridge without reading books? Not even nowadays.

"Have you read *Mucus*?"

"Yes. It's terrible."

Tom made up his mind. This lack of responsibility couldn't continue. All over the country, readers were ingesting *Mucus* as purveyed to them by a publishing house to which he was still connected, of which he was still titularly a part. "Bring me a copy."

"Of course," said his secretary.

The cover wasn't promising. It showed two contorted human faces, one male and adult, one female and child. The adult might have been molesting the child. Green matter, raised to fingertip-touch, oozed across the cover. "From the darkness of the human psyche to a nightmare of hellish degradation came the MUCUS," it said. Tom sipped his freshly ground Kenya coffee. His secretary had learned, at least, how to make coffee.

He thought about Honey. Now she didn't have a man, not, of course, that that mattered to him. Her questions, her intellectual earnestness had stirred him. He had touched her arm when he helped her on with her coat. She was wearing silk and the silk had moved on her skin. She'd smiled that touching smile. She'd asked about the meaning of life.

Tom approved of such concerns. Maggie's concentration on the success or failure of her party was small-minded. Maggie was altogether uninterested in general issues, concentrating on the logistics of her proliferating responsibilities. Once, long ago, she and Tom had discussed morality, ethics, aesthetics. Then they decided what they believed and now Maggie was smug. Possibly, so was he.

Once, at dinner with the Wyatts, Matilda Livesey had told Tom that she always enjoyed visiting their house because they were such good-hearted Pharisees. She'd smiled as she spoke. Tom had never forgotten the smile or the remark. He liked Till. She was a clever woman, easy to talk to, attractive despite her plainness because she had the unmistakable aura of one to whom bed was familiar. There'd be no trouble with Till, he felt. Not that he wanted an adventure.

Back to *Mucus*. The plot was straightforward; if he had been acquainted with the genre, he would have found it familiar. It was set in New England, where a lonely Gothic house had been deserted after a father, mother and teenage daughter were found axed to death, here an arm, there a head. The teenage son of the family had gone missing, was presumed to be the culprit. There followed an outbreak of graphically described corruption in the family life of the township: incest, drug-taking, suicides.

He stopped reading, buzzed for his secretary. "I've got to the corruption in the township," he said. "Can you tell me the rest of the plot, briefly?"

"There's a fungus in the walls of the house which infects the mucus of anyone who goes in there. It releases the darkest impulses of the human spirit. These are usually perverted and sexual. Lots of lascivious horror, a mysterious scientist discovers an antidote which he produces in a nasal spray, the horror ceases, the end."

"Ah," said Tom. "Is the style consistent throughout?"

"If anything, it gets slimier."

"A marriage of form and content."

"All the way to the bank. Shall I take it away?"

"No. I'd better finish it. Later."

Honey was used to people looking at her naked body. When she was in London, her masseuse worked on it three days a week. Honey had decided years ago that massage was ineffective but she was attached to her masseuse, as she was to most people she met over an extended period of time. So, unembarrassed, she whipped her silk camiknickers off when instructed to do so by the female doctor, raised her legs, adjusted her pelvis to allow the plastic-covered hand easy access.

"Can you see my appendix scar?" she asked and the doctor, withdrawing her hand, obligingly looked.

"It's a very small one," she said tracing it with a finger.

"My late husband did that. Before we were married. That's how we met."

"Do I know you?" said the doctor, while Honey dressed.

"I used to be an actress."

"Under your own name? Sarah Markham?"

"Of course not," said the receptionist Rachel, giving Honey a cup of coffee. She had recognised her and was pleased with her discovery. "You're Honey Markham! One of the *Daughters of Captain Bridge!* I really loved that film when I was a kid. It's so happy, with that lovely ending where you run into your father's arms. I realise now the false paternalistic fascist values it expressed – but I used to cry with happiness when I was a kid."

Honey remembered the scene as a nightmare of spoilt takes, Vernon Cole's fury, Pandora's hysterics and the fight over Honey's nipple caps.

The scene was in a bedroom; the four girls, sleeping in their camisoles and petticoats, wake up in the sun-kissed double bed as their father opens the door. "I want that bed SUN-KISSED," Vernon shouted at the lighting cameraman.

"If it's any more sun-kissed it'll MELT," he shouted back. When it was settled, Honey was first up from the bed. She sat up, registered delight at finding her father at last, got out of bed and ran through the beams of sunlight to hug her father. The studio was cold, it was a chilly October day, and even the heat of the lights didn't stop her nipples from peaking. Florence stopped the shooting after the fourth take. "I want my girl decent," she insisted to Vernon.

"She's decent, she's decent." Vernon looked through the camera and loved what he saw. "All she has to do is run across the room, then we shoot over my shoulder and she smiles," he said. And not a loose pair of trousers in the house, he thought.

"Nipple caps or Elastoplast, I don't care. Honey's a child and I don't want her exploited."

"If she's a child she doesn't need nipple caps," said Vernon.

"She's past puberty," said Florence flatly.

"You admit it?"

"Shut up, Vernon." Once, long ago, Florence and Vernon had had a brief affair and it had left little goodwill between them. Florence had found Vernon unsatisfactory and he knew it. "She's not going on till this is settled."

Honey got back into bed and pulled the covers over her. She was between Pandora and Till; Flea was on the other side of Till. Flea was only eight and easily upset, frightened of Vernon, frightened of making a mistake. "What's the matter?" she asked anxiously.

"Don't worry about it," said Till. "Technical stuff." Till was twenty-one and had fallen into the habit of looking after Honey and Flea. Pandora looked after herself.

"It's Honey's nipples," said Pandora. She was fourteen and still enjoyed saying rude words in her childish moods; she swung between sounding eleven and sounding twenty-five. "Vernon wants to film Honey's nipples and Florence doesn't want him to."

"Will he want to film my nipples?" said Flea, looking for them.

"Nobody wants to film your nipples yet," said Pandora scornfully. "You're too young to have *interesting* breasts. My breasts are interesting, and Till's would be if she was prettier—"

"If you bitch at me I'll slap you," said Till, and Pandora subsided. Till did slap. It was the only way to make any impression on Pandora.

"Honey Markham to wardrobe," said the assistant director. "Take fifteen, everyone."

Rachel and the doctor were still talking about the film. It had that effect on many people. Honey could answer the questions in her sleep. She wondered sometimes if Judy Garland had taken to drugs because she was incessantly cross-examined on the *Wizard of Oz*.

"I'm not sure about the abortion," she said to drag the conversation back to the vital point.

"There's not much time to play with," said Rachel. "You must be sure, though."

"Are people ever absolutely sure about anything so important?"

The other two women ignored this. Honey would have liked an answer.

"Why don't you want to have the baby?" Rachel asked.

"I promised the father."

"It's your body, and – how old are you, thirty-eight? – the old biological clock is ticking away. You're already old for a first baby."

"I promised," said Honey.

Honey hated her flat, particularly the spaces where Steve's equipment had been. Every last metal Sammy box had gone, every cable, light meter, soldering iron.

There were some sweatshirts and shorts, some unmatching socks in the bottom of a cupboard. She sent them to the laundry and, when they came back, stacked them neatly in a drawer.

When she returned from the pregnancy advisory service, she looked at her diary. It had been a duplicate of Steve's. She had handled his bookings, acted as assistant cameraman. Towards the end she thought she was a better cameraman than he; her visual sense was more imaginative. She could have made a career of her own, but she didn't want that. She wanted a man to love and build her life round, and she wanted his child. Now her diary traced his alien movements through the year. Three days in Manchester – February. She crossed them out. Two months in Kenya – May and June. She crossed that out. Then she turned back to make an entry for her one significant commitment. Tuesday, January 28th: 10 a.m. Abrotin, Nitingal Clnic.

Chapter Three

"Honey's recovered very quickly," said Pandora. "A bottle of the house white, please."

Pandora and Till were having lunch at San Lorenzo. Pandora was paying. Till's flight from Montreal had landed only that morning and she was missing a night, otherwise she wouldn't have agreed to the lunch. She was feeling tired and dislocated. The gentle light and shabby streets of London were unfamiliar, her flat was a mess because her undergraduate son was staying there with friends who were sleeping in heaps, some on beds, some on the floor. She had dumped her cases in the bathroom and prowled through looking at bodies. All young men look the same, she thought wearily as she chose one familiar-seeming shape and challenged the sleeping head. "Are you my son?"

"I don't think so," said the youth politely, lapsing immediately into still deeper slumber.

She abandoned her quest, listened to the answering machine. Three calls from Pandora, the last one sounding upset; one quiet request from Honey, "Please ring me when you have a minute," took priority, but there was no answer from Honey's number. She had a bath, ironed some clothes, pushing aside a body to set up the ironing board, and left a note propped up against the kettle, certainly the first resort of the youths after the lavatory. "I am the owner of this flat and I have returned. I expect to find order when I return about three or there will be MURDER DONE."

San Lorenzo, even with Pandora, was an appealing alternative.

"What was the matter with Honey, then?"

"She broke up with Steve, no one knows why. How was Canada, ghastly?"

"I enjoyed it. The parts were good. Lady Macbeth, Cleopatra, Gertrude."

"A Shakespeare tour."

"You guessed."

"How many in the company?"

"Six. Shakespeare in education."

"Aaah," said Pandora. She managed to convey scorn, relief and pity in one sigh. "How much were they paying you?"

"Expenses. It was a co-operative venture."

"Meaning you paid them?"

"More or less. I'm lucky to get any parts at all. Considering I'm virtually an amateur."

"Do you still hold an Equity card?"

"Yes."

"If I played Lady Macbeth, I'd make damn sure I was well paid."

"If you played Lady Macbeth, you'd lose." Matilda was not ruffled by Pandora's inquisition. She was a tall, solid, untidy-looking woman, with wispy brown hair in an undisciplined perm. She ate pasta, drank wine and waited for Pandora to tell her why she was there. Pandora would not have spent any money at all on Till, much less a San Lorenzo lunch even with stern hostess piloting towards the cheaper end of the menu, unless she wanted something badly. As far as Till could calculate, she had nothing Pandora wanted.

"Maggie Wyatt had us all to dinner last week – the *Captain Bridge* survivors," said Pandora. "Honey was there, and Vernon, and Jacky." And Ben, thought Matilda.

"Good party? How was Maggie?"

"Same as usual. Wearing a Laura Ashley number, all patterned with frills. You couldn't tell her apart from one of her sofas."

"Surely the dress wasn't encrusted with lurcher vomit?"

"Honey was very cheerful. I think she should get a millionaire next. Or a Royal."

"She can't have been cheerful."

"She was. Very. I'd have known otherwise – she's completely transparent."

"No one who successfully lies into a camera lens while technicians fart and scratch themselves is completely transparent."

"That's *acting*," said Pandora scornfully. "I always know what Honey's thinking. When she's thinking, that is."

Silence. Till finished her pasta and looked wistfully at the pudding trolley. Pandora saw someone she knew; she waved and kissed and squeaked and chattered. Till understood that this was a professional necessity. Her own inability to do it was one of the reasons she earned her living as a psychiatrist and paid people to let her act.

The last thing she expected happened next. Pandora said, "Have you seen Ben lately?"

"Not for six years," said Till.

"Are you lying?"

This was not an offensive question, even from Pandora. Till was well known for her indifference to fact. She made things up. Not necessarily things to her own advantage; she just found fantasising less dull. Anyone who knew her well would signal their intention for a serious conversation by asking just such a question.

"No. Why?"

"We're very happy together," said Pandora. Till didn't draw the obvious conclusion that Pandora was about to burst into tears and describe the breakdown of her marriage. She waited.

"This has got to be kept between us. Promise?"

"You'll owe me," said Till.

"I've bought you lunch at San Lorenzo."

"I'm not interested in lunch at San Lorenzo. Your paying is a fact, not a favour."

"I'll owe you. But not much."

"I promise."

Pandora opened her little leather bag, put a piece of paper on the table. "I found this on Ben's desk."

It was a complete page of A4 typing, consisting of the same words repeated. "I wish I was dead I wish I was dead I wish I was dead . . ." The page brought Ben back so clearly that the wounds Till had thought were well healed tore open and left her sick. He used paper of a particular grey, expensive paper made to order for him; the sight of grey paper would always bring back the years and the fights and the last painful parting.

Pandora was waiting, silent. She must be seriously worried. "What do you want from me? A diagnosis?"

"Anything."

"Is it part of something he wrote? It reminds me of *Lolita*, where Nabokov says, 'Lolita – repeat printer till the page is full.' Has he turned to novels? It's unlikely for a speech from a play, unless – of course Beckett—"

"Forget literature. You know I don't read it."

"But Ben tries to write it."

"Not any longer. Not since – not for years. He tries, but he just tears it up. He won't even touch the word processor I bought him. The wastepaper basket is always full, the desk always empty. You don't want sweet, I suppose."

"No, thanks," said Till. "If he's not writing, he'll be miserable. Is he drinking?"

"He was, heavily, on and off. He's sober at the moment."

"So he wrote this sober."

"Probably."

"And left it for you to find."

"Not exactly. It was in a stack of fresh paper. But – there's – something else." It was sticking in her throat. Till gave a psychiatrist's non-committal nod. "After the Wyatts' party, he stayed up, working, he said. He didn't come to bed and he must have gone out. He came back before lunch. He said he'd been walking all night."

"I sometimes walk all night, and morning too."

"Everyone knows you're eccentric. Ben doesn't. I suppose – he was with a woman."

"Probably. Why does that worry you? It's his first, second and last resort."

"He's been faithful to me since our marriage. I made him promise. I can't stand infidelity, Till, I'm not like you. I'm normal."

"Then you're the first normal person I've ever met. This is an important moment for me. Can I use you as the subject of a paper?"

"Be serious. He's been faithful, I tell you."

"Balls."

"Don't be crude." Pandora was dabbing her eyes to prevent her mascara running. "He treats me so well, and he says he's happy."

Jealousy gritted Till's teeth. She drank wine to wash it down. "What do you want me to do?"

"I don't know," wailed Pandora. "I hate to ask you. But you know that. You're supposed to *understand*."

"I thought you didn't believe in psychiatry."

"I'd try a fortuneteller if I thought it would help."

Till hadn't supposed Pandora capable of such deep emotion. She herself wanted to keep out of this, keep away from Ben. Their roots went back too far and too deep. They always hurt each other, sometimes with pleasure, joy and comfort added, sometimes not. Now, as Till was manless and middle-aged, Ben would be a disaster for her. He would be in too strong a position. "Has he been getting into fights?"

"Now and then."

"Losing them?"

"Usually. That's when he was drinking, of course."

"But he might have been drinking to fight, not fighting because he drank." This was beyond Pandora. "He should talk to someone," said Till, clearing an exit.

"Who?"

"A professional. Someone he doesn't know."

"Surely it would be better with someone he does know?"

"He usually screws people he doesn't know," Till pointed out. "It's often easier. It would be easier for him."

"There's nothing *wrong* with him, not like that. He doesn't need a psychiatrist."

"Keep saying that and he might need an undertaker."

"You're a *bitch*," said Pandora.

"And he'd have to want to go."

"You take this seriously? This 'I want to die' stuff?"

"It's not as direct as that. 'I wish I was dead' is one step away from 'I want to die'. But I do take it seriously, yes. He's always been violent."

"I want you to talk to him."

"No," said Till loudly. The occupants of the next table turned to look. They were three women, dieting. They were eating salad and drinking Perrier water and a fight would have been a welcome distraction for them. They looked as if they had spent hours getting dressed to come to the restaurant, where they couldn't eat.

"But I want you to," said Pandora in the tones of one who usually got what she wanted. "I think – I think – he'll talk to you. You've always been friends."

"No," said Till. "He used to break my ribs now and then. We were lovers, but never friends. He doesn't like women."

"Ben?" squeaked Pandora. "He adores women!"

"No. Could I have some coffee?"

"He used to break your *ribs*? On *purpose*?"

"I don't think that was his specific purpose. He got angry and hit me."

"You must be a masochist," said Pandora proudly; she was proud of the word and the put-down.

"I'm not. That's why I'm not married to him," said Till. "Thanks for the lunch."

When Till returned to her flat, Honey's number was still not answering.

The flat was the basement and half the ground floor of a double-fronted house in a street off Ladbroke Grove. The street was a cul-de-sac, ending in a council housing estate. Most of the remaining Victorian houses had been gentrified and bristled with anti-burglar devices. The smart residents complained that the people who parked there didn't have the residents' parking permits they were supposed to buy from the council.

Several Mercedes, often occupied by swarthy Mediterranean men, double-parked in the small street. Children played; in the tottering unimproved houses there were elaborate lace curtains and window-boxes; in the summer women hung out of the windows or sat on the steps.

Till loved it, the life of Ladbroke Grove, the dirt and smartness side by side, the blacks and the Turks and the Spaniards and the Irish and the atmosphere, half menace, half opportunity. The best Pandora had ever managed to say for it was that it was so close to everything. Till also thought it close to everything, but they had different things in mind.

The flat was tidy. Harry, Till's elder child, lay on the sofa. Too old to think of as a child, thought Till as she kissed him and caught the rasp of patchy shaving. "What are you reading?" she asked.

"Anthony Powell's autobiography. Some humanist left it behind so I thought I'd culture myself briefly. We scientists can't afford to miss what chances we get."

He was six-foot tall, nineteen, blond, elegant. Till was grateful he was so fair: Charles, her ex-husband, was also fair and if Harry had been dark he'd probably have been Ben's.

"What do you think of Powell?"

"You've never been in the Welch Guards or had a title?"

"Not recently."

"According to Powell, everyone else has. Do you want tea?"

"Lapsang, if you lot haven't scoffed it." .

"You've been away for four months. It would be stale anyhow. How was the tour?"

"I'll never be Vanessa Redgrave."

"Would you want to?"

"Where's Amanda?"

Till's other child, Amanda, was still a source of anxiety. Harry was off and flying, Amanda still uneven and uncertain. The family had heaved a collective though divorced sigh of relief when she too had managed to get into Oxford. She was altogether more unpredictable than the solidly clever Harry. Till had hung on to the telephone from Canada evening after evening while they awaited Amanda's results. She suspected Amanda thought her disloyal for not cancelling the tour to be with her; currently the fiction she had chosen was that Till was a devoted, interfering mother, whereas Till, though devoted, seldom interfered in anything, even her own life. She preferred to let the river of chance and circumstance tumble her along.

"Staying with Daddy. She'll ring tonight. Here's the tea. Earl Grey is the best I can do. I expect he was in the Welch Guards."

Till had seized the sofa and put her feet up. She closed her eyes, sipped the tea, and enjoyed one of the moments of perfect happiness that made life endurable. Back safe in her own flat; in the company of one of the

46

two people she loved beyond doubt and beyond disappointment; in a place which hadn't yet become boring. Boredom was Till's constant scourge.

"How long are you staying, Harry?"

"Term starts next week. I'll go up tomorrow, catch up with some essays. Unless you want me for something?"

"We could go to a play."

"That'd be good." Harry liked to please his mother, who he thought was to be protected, even pitied, now that he was at university and bursting upon the world with all his talents, ambitions and immortal perfections. Till resolved not to appear to notice as each successive failure and humiliation ground him into an adult. "Shall we take Honey?" said Harry.

"Sure. If she ever answers her phone, and if she isn't busy."

"She's split up with her man, have you heard?"

"How do you know?"

"She was talking about it on *Woman's Hour*. I was at daddy's and you know Claire listens to *Woman's Hour*. It's probably her highest intellectual achievement. I was doing the washing-up and Honey was talking about a charity she's fronting for. Leukaemia, it was. God knows how they got from leukaemia to Honey's love life."

"More interesting for the punters. If you haven't got leukaemia you don't want to hear about it and if you or you child has you specially don't want to hear about it."

"Odd how people don't like facing facts."

"Only odd when you haven't had to face unpleasant ones."

"Talking of which, I need some cash."

Honey had packed carefully for the clinic. It was expensive, much used by Arabs, just off Harley Street. She'd been there several times to visit friends after cosmetic operations. She knew it was well heated, so despite the freezing temperature outside – it would snow when it

47

warmed up slightly – she took only a silk kimono, a Swiss cotton nightdress and a pair of high-heeled slippers with feathery ornaments. The fifties overtones of the slippers seemed in keeping with the expedition. It was a Lana Turner part, she felt. Seduced and abandoned. She kept her mind occupied to avoid thinking about the proceedings of the day and their intention.

Before she left she dialled and dialled Steve's number in London. She listened to the Ansaphone message more than six times through. She stopped counting after the sixth and looked out of the window. A nanny walked past, up the hill, with a pram. On the way to Holland Park, probably. As opposed to down the sluice.

". . . please wait for the tone, leave your name and number, I'll get back to you . . . beeeeep . . . This is Steve Robson. I'm not in at the moment to take your call. Please wait for the tone, leave your name and number . . ."

It was reassuring to Honey to hear Steve's voice without needing to speak to him and hear the tone change. He was vain of his voice. It had faint Northern remnants in the vowels and in the slowness of speech, with film technician Cockney additions and a mid-Atlantic dash of pretension.

Detached, Honey knew he wasn't kind, strong or special. She loved the weak, on the whole. She belonged among them and whatever small benefit she could confer would be, she felt, more significant. She didn't think highly of herself. She had noticed the high value others placed on her beauty; but as it was so manifestly her good fortune not her merit, and as she traced daily its ultimate departure, she did not think it significant.

On the set of one of her early films someone had discovered that one of the carpenters could draw, freehand, a perfect circle. He was often asked to do it and watched while he did. The pieces of paper with the perfect circle were discarded. Honey collected them. Florence, packing to move, tore them up. When Honey protested she snapped, "Don't be silly, the circles aren't important. The interesting part is being able to do them."

Honey identified with the circles.

The front doorbell rang. It was the taxi come to take her to the clinic. No sign of Till yet. She would have liked to speak to her before she left. She put on her coat, an insignificant, grey flannel. She wore no make-up, her hair was brushed neatly. She didn't expect to be noticed at the clinic; it would have its share of newspaper informers, but she felt herself quite safe. Just as she knew how to be the famous Honey on demand, she also knew how to be a nonentity. So long as she didn't smile, and there wouldn't be much occasion for that.

It was a large room for a modern hospital, oblong, white-painted, with an enormous television set offering a video channel with Arabic films. The information about menus was in English and Arabic. She could understand the English one better, but only just. She ordered supper, perversely, from the Arabic menu. She put on the paper gown, the disposable airline slippers, the shower cap. She put away her clothes. She agreed with the nurse that the weather was bitter, but what you would expect for January. The nurse was sturdy, Irish, competent. She nipped in and out, gave Honey instructions; Honey obeyed them.

After half an hour's waiting the nurse was back. "Follow me, there's a good girl." She marshalled her little flock outside the lift. There were two teenage girls and one woman in her late thirties, heavily overweight, wearing a wedding ring well sunk into her finger and the expression of one from whom the last bus has departed.

The operating theatres were on the ground floor. Honey was led to a room with the others, instructed to get up on a trolley. She, and the others, did. Honey was the furthest away from the door. The Irish nurse had gone and two other nurses were gossiping. One was

Asian, one Mid-European. They were talking about the sales and describing the clothes they had bought.

Honey listened. It sounded, from their account, as if they had been rooked, buying not only out-of-date styles but last year's colours.

Above her head was a clock with a prominent second hand. It swept round like a Formula One car. How long, Honey wondered, before the fade, the dissolve, the cut to her back in her bed upstairs, while it was still snowing? She could see snowflakes tumbling down the area through iron bars on the windows in a corner of the room.

Outside, the squeaking wheels of a departing trolley. Then the front trolley went from her room. She could see the white cap of one of the young girls as it whisked away round the corner.

It was eleven-fifty – five, ten, fifteen, thirty – eleven-fifty-one. It would be the early hours of the morning with Steve in San Francisco. Steve would probably be asleep. They usually stopped work about two, when the street kids went to bed. The sound recordist would still be up, doing his sheets for the day's work. No, San Francisco was further behind than that . . . the sum was beyond her.

The second trolley was going. Twenty minutes had passed. Then the third, a quarter of an hour later. Now Honey was alone and the remaining nurse patted her hand, which was clutching the covering sheet. "It doesn't hurt," she said in a London voice, incongruous from her almost purple Asian lips. "Soon be back to normal, dear."

"Thank you," said Honey.

"Do you live in London?"

"Yes."

"That's nice."

"Yes."

"Not too far to go home."

50

"No."

"You've got a very good surgeon."

"Oh."

"He's the best. Don't tell anyone I said so. It's not done for us to comment on the surgeons."

"No," said Honey, sitting up.

"Lie down again, there's a dear. Nothing to worry about," said the nurse soothingly.

"I'm going home," said Honey. She had griping pains in her stomach. She wanted to get out and away. She knew that no promise on earth would hold her to killing her child. She didn't know how long she had known this and whether she had ever thought, even when she walked into the clinic, that she intended to go through with the operation.

The nurse was alarmed. "Won't be long, dear, really. Just lie back. Ah . . ."

"Next, please," said the other nurse returning and gripping the trolley.

Honey headed for the lift with both nurses scampering after her, protesting. "Thank you, you're very kind, but this is my business," said Honey, crying with relief.

"You realise no refund is possible?" said the Mid-European nurse. "Just come back here, it'll be all over soon—"

Honey stood beside a trolley bearing the unconscious form of the fat woman; her escort had called the lift. "Please let me go," she said firmly. "I've made up my mind." The sensation of decisiveness was unfamiliar but invigorating.

"A bit late, if you ask me," said the Asian. The anaesthetist, gowned and masked, appeared in a doorway. "Can we have the next patient, please? We're waiting."

One of the nurses explained to him in an undertone. "Really, nurse," he snapped. "Pre-op nerves." He approached Honey with a hand outstretched, speaking soothingly as to a racehorse who refuses to enter the starting stalls. "Now, now, Miss er . . . hospitals are frightening at first and no one likes the thought of an op but think how much happier you'll be when all this is over. Come on now, be a brave girl—"

"I'm thirty-eight," said Honey. "Don't call me a girl and don't talk to me as if I was half-witted. I'm going home. I think abortion is murder and I'm going home."

"You're just upset, it's natural you should be." The anaesthetist produced his trump card. "Hormones!"

"Upset."

"Come now."

"Hormones," chimed in the soprano and contralto of the nurses, and the baritone pressed on with the recitative. "Just come into this room here and we'll soon have you settled. Just a little prick in the arm, just a little prick in the arm . . ."

"Just a little needle."

"You'll hardly feel it."

"Don't you think abortion is murder?" demanded Honey.

"Now is hardly the time to discuss it," said the baritone.

"Not the time."

"Hardly the time."

"NOBODY EVER ANSWERS MY QUESTIONS!" screamed Honey, and the noise made them all fall back briefly. The lift doors opened, an impassive nurse pushed the bulky, unconscious woman into the lift on her trolley, and Honey stepped in after her.

The others stood irresolutely at bay. "Goodbye," said Honey. Then, as the doors closed on her, she smiled.

"My God!" said the anaesthetist.

She hesitated inside the front door of the clinic. Snow was still slurrying down. She had a painful stomach ache. The prospect of the silent flat daunted her. She wanted to talk to someone about her condition, her decision and her future. Florence was in Tunisia. Pandora would fuss and say worldly practical things, and be on the telephone to half London as soon as Honey left.

She walked along the pavement. She was in the heart of medical country. Large, expensive cars were parked at the extra-long meters. An entire Nigerian family, father, mother, seven children, straggled out of a taxi. The mother was in native dress, the others in European clothes. The bright blotches of red, orange and black on the imposing mother were dampened by the English light, but she still seemed energetic, buoyant, capable of producing any amount of children. Too late for me to catch up with her, thought Honey, proud of the life inside her stomach. Perhaps another one after this. If there was to be no father there should be another child.

She ducked into a telephone box. It was, at least, warm. Honey held her wrist to her nose, smelling scent rather than urine, and dialled Till's number. The Ansaphone was no longer connected – a good sign – but the number rang and rang without reply.

She signalled a taxi and directed it to Steve's flat near Shepherd's Bush. She still had keys to the flat, let herself in.

It was silent, cold and stuffy. The cases Steve had moved out from Honey's flat were stacked neatly in a corner of the living-room. It was a media flat. One cork-covered wall contained a photographic record of Steve's career, stills from pictures he had worked on, snaps of himself on location, and Honey, Honey, Honey. He photographed Honey so often that Till had once said, "I don't know why he doesn't just take the camera to bed with you and cut out the middlecock."

The living room was in the starkest of derivative taste. Beige carpet, brown sofa and chairs, probably Habitat; souvenirs from location in Iraq, India and Kenya. The bedroom had cupboards built by Steve, a bed with a bachelor-pattern duvet bought from John Lewis, a bed-side table with anti-malaria tablets and a camera catalogue. No trace of his origins in Bradford, no echo of his affectionate, dowdy parents. On the walls two framed publicity posters for films he had worked on.

In the kitchen, also built by Steve, nothing out on the surfaces. In the refrigerator, cans of film.

Honey felt faint. She lay on the brown sofa. The flat was not encouraging. The pain in her stomach was worse. Then she started to bleed. She could feel the warmth between her legs, the gouts of matter. Better on the sofa than the floor, she thought dizzily. It would never come out of the carpet.

She called Till. This time there was an answer. "Honey here. I'm at Steve's flat."

"I heard you'd broken up—"

"We have. He isn't here. I'm lying on the sofa and I'm bleeding. I think it's a miscarriage. What should I do?"

"Don't move. Keep warm. I'm on my way."

Honey lay in the cold flat, the chill inside her greater than the ambient temperature. She knew she had miscarried. She wasn't going to look. Until she knew for certain what had happened, she refused to feel.

When even running through last night's Channel Four Fellini film frame by frame ceased to distract her, she looked round for books. There were none. Steve wasn't interested in anything except his work. He had often been annoyed by Honey's conversation, her attempts at literary discussion. "Shut it," he used to say, at first fondly, as to a small child; later, more impatiently. "Don't bother with that kind of stuff. You're too pretty to think. Leave that to dogs like your friend Till."

"Till isn't a dog," protested Honey.

"She is. Women like her have to think. They have to earn their living. But girls like you don't. Let's go to bed."

When Till rang the flat doorbell – she had managed

to get in through the front door of the house – Honey dashed to the door, then back to the sofa. She was even wetter now but there was no trail of blood on the beige carpet.

Till pulled up Honey's skirt, pushed apart her unprotesting knees. "I'm going to pull down your pants," she said briskly, and did so. "You have miscarried," she said. Her tone was neutral.

Honey said nothing. Her tears, silent, just pinkening her eyes, were affecting. "We'd better clean you up," said Till sitting down beside her. "I don't suppose the hot water's on? I'll boil a kettle."

"Like in westerns," said Honey bleakly.

Till had never seen Honey so hopeless. It worried her. "I'll ring for a doctor, shall I?"

"Don't bother. There's nothing a doctor can do. You're a doctor, come to that. I was looking forward to seeing you. And now – it doesn't make any difference, it's too late. There's nothing we can do, is there? Not put it back, like a tooth?"

"No," said Till, not smiling.

Honey sat stupefied. She felt her significance, a small flame briefly rekindled in the future of her child, now absurdly puddled between her legs. She was more than ever convinced that there was a trick to the universe which she hadn't mastered.

"Don't tell me if it's a boy or a girl. I don't want to know."

"Okay."

"What would you normally do now? With the foetus?"

"Put it down the loo."

"We could bury it, of course."

"If you like."

"Do you think it's true what they say, that when one door closes another opens?"

"In my experience when one door closes another swings back and takes your toenail off," said Till. "The answer is to take evasive action. I'm going to boil a kettle, clean you up, and take you back to my flat."

"I want to go to sleep."

"You can. Back at my place."

"Is there room for me to stay? Aren't your children there?"

"Only Harry and I'll chuck him out. He can stay with another gilded youth."

"You're the kindest person I know."

"Only to those I love."

Honey sat while Till coped. She had been for so long looking forward to seeing Till; she wanted her advice, her company. Now her own sense of identity had gone and with it her wish for human contact.

"You don't mind that I'm beautiful, do you?" she said.

"Not in the least. You are a bird of paradise, delighting all who gaze on you."

"That's fine for the gazers. Not so good for the bird of paradise," said Honey.

"That's better. I like the astringency."

"I've grasped irony," said Honey. The concept had eluded her for years despite Till's best efforts to explain. "I've even got an example for you. I think."

"Let's have it," said Till. "I've brought you a pair of Amanda's pants, some jeans and a sweat shirt. Shall I put them on?"

"Do," said Honey, lifting her pelvis, raising her arms to be dressed. "Listen to the irony and tell me if it's right. This morning I went in to have an abortion. I decided not to. Then I miscarried. Is that irony?"

"You've grasped irony," said Till. "Or it's grasped you."

Chapter Four

Honey spent the night in Harry's bedroom. It was a tiny rectangle, nine feet by six, coffin-like and appropriate, she felt. She didn't sleep; she lay with the curtains open watching the late-night activities in the street. By three o'clock the passers-by were few, though at four two girls tottered home on high heels and alcohol, discussing their shared boyfriend. He sounded active, if spoilt.

Apart from listening to the street she thought of nothing. She felt empty. She hadn't asked Till if the miscarriage could have been brought on by the stress and conflict over the abortion. She preferred to assume it had been, and blame Steve. Her body blamed Steve. It had been an absolute betrayal. She would pay him back. The lust for revenge was satisfying.

At seven o'clock she got up, bathed, wandered around Till's flat. Till woke up late. She made coffee and they drank it in silence. Eventually Honey said, "Where did you put the foetus?"

"In one of Steve's 35mm film containers. It's in the fridge, wrapped in a plastic bag."

"Would you mind if we buried it?"

"Where?"

"In my garden. This morning. Then it'll be over."

"Not yet," said Till. "It won't be over yet."

Honey didn't answer. She wore a particularly compliant expression which Till knew of old as a refusal to accept what had been said. Then she melted into agreement. "It won't be over until I've paid Steve back," she said. "I lay awake all night, planning revenge."

Silence from Till.

"Don't you think it was Steve's fault?"

"It's easy to miscarry. There may have been something wrong with the baby."

Honey rejected this observation. It did not match the shape of her thoughts.

" 'Come to his aid, O Saints of God: Hasten to meet him, Angels of the Lord: Taking up his soul, Presenting it in the sight of the Most High,' " read Till. Honey gently lowered the tiny box into the hole hard won from the frozen earth in her garden, just inches away from the back wall; a spot that was sunny in summer. " 'Eternal rest grant unto him, O Lord, and let perpetual light shine upon him.' " The pages of Till's old missal were stained by damp; she could hardly make out the words in the dim light.

"Is that all?" said Honey, scraping earth back into the hole. "Read something else. Something hopeful." Till could see, over Honey's shoulder, Madeline watching interestedly from the back window of her drawing-room.

" 'May the Angels take you into Paradise, may the Martyrs come to welcome you on your way and lead you into the holy city, Jerusalem. May the choir of angels welcome you and with Lazarus who once was poor may you have everlasting rest.' "

"Any problem?" called Madeline, opening the French windows. "Can I help?"

"No, thank you," Honey called back. "What can we say we're doing, Till?" she hissed.

"We're just taking soil samples," called Till.

Madeline watched them all the way up the garden. "Do you *have* to be poor?" said Honey anxiously. "Is that vital?"

"I'll explain later," said Till pocketing her missal. Honey clutched the plastic bag, into which Till had

58

quickly shovelled some loose soil, and the trowel. The garden was a long, narrow one. It was still under snow; patches of frosted earth were revealed here and there. Honey was wearing Katharine Hamnett black. She was sincere about the occasion and though Till saw the episode as, in one sense, absurd, she pushed the absurdities from the front of her mind out of affection for Honey. If Honey wanted a garbled form of the Catholic burial service then Till would provide it, though she retained no trace of her Catholic faith. "They always seem so much more convincing than the Church of England," Honey had said. "So certain of themselves."

Honey stopped walking, gripped her hands into fists. "It's so cold, Till. So cold. How can the baby just be buried there in the cold?"

"Only its body is buried. Its soul, the angels are leading into Paradise."

"Do you believe that?"

"How can we know?"

"So it could be true?"

"Absolutely."

"I don't believe it," said Honey. "I think people like me made it up for comfort."

"What book were you reading?" called Madeline. "I just love books."

"Have you met Matilda Livesey?" said Honey. "Madeline Cabot Goldberg."

"The Cabots of Boston?" said Till, hoping to start a compelling hare.

"My second husband was a member of a cadet branch of that distinguished family."

"I don't believe it," murmured Till in Honey's ear. "I think she made it up for comfort." Madeline, standing one level up, was just too far away to hear.

"If you want some redesigning and landscaping for the garden, I'll be happy to pay for a gardener," she said. "I would prefer to have part use of the facility, you know. Come in and have a drink – no, I insist. There's just one or two things I'd like to talk to you about, Honey."

"I'm sorry. We must go," said Till firmly.

"Isn't it funny," pursued Madeline. "I got the impression – you were at a funeral. Just shows how wrong you can be. Maybe it's the English winter. Makes me morbid."

Till, wishing at all costs to distract Madeline from a subject which was evidently shrinking and bleaching Honey, said, "How's Jacky?"

"Ah," said Madeline bridling. "He's moved in, you know."

"Really?" said Till.

"It's easier for him, as my social secretary."

"It would be."

"And it's a delightfully spacious house."

"Plenty of beds," said Till.

"You must come to – tea. And Honey, of course. It is so exciting living above a real live film star."

This gambit was so familiar that years of training carried Honey through. "I'm hardly still a film star," she said.

"Oh yes. One of the immortals. That movie – entirely delightful. A most touching story with a happy ending. I do so admire a happy ending. So rare. You know the film, of course, Martha?"

"Matilda," said Till. "I was in it. I played the eldest daughter."

"The main part," said Honey.

"The main part but not the starring part," said Madeline. "So you were the eldest daughter? My, doesn't time pass! And yet Honey looks even more beautiful."

"Do you believe in life after death?" said Honey, looking down the garden.

"Why, of course," said Madeline. "My family have always been Episcopalian."

"What's Episcopalian?" said Honey as soon as they reached her flat.

"Same as Church of England in America. I wish you'd stop smiling, Honey. I hate it when you smile."

"Most people like it."

"That's because they don't know why you do it."

"And why is that?"

"For them, never for you. Never because you're happy or pleased or amused. I'll have to go home soon, Honey. Amanda's coming up this morning. Come home with me."

"I'll stay here. I'd rather avoid children – just now. Besides, I have to decide what to do."

"Don't do anything for a while," said Till. "Give it time. Get better."

"I haven't got time," said Honey bitterly. "I want children, and I haven't got time. They said at the clinic I was leaving it too late already."

"You'll have to get a man first."

"No, I don't. Not a proper man. I don't want a proper man ever again. Just a child."

"You feel that now . . ."

"Don't psychiatrist me. I know what I want. Steve has done this to me. He killed our baby. I loved him so much, Till. I wouldn't have miscarried without the strain. I couldn't have done more for him. What more could I have done?"

"Less," said Till.

"Don't be clever, I'm too – annyhalted. Is that how you say it?"

"Annihilated," said Till.

"I'm that. Go home."

So Till went home.

Honey sat at her rear window looking down the garden. She knew she couldn't dig up and warm the capsule containing all that remained of her hopes. After a brief struggle, she captured the cat, hugged it to her, and thought.

Amanda lay on the sofa, young, tousled and fresh in black leggings and a huge red sweater. Till said the appropriate things about her success at getting into Oxford, about how proud she was. Amanda grunted. She had dark brown hair cut in feathery spikes and a sulky, discontented look. "I want to be a man," she said. "I want to be Harry."

"Well, you can't," said Till. "Are you hungry? Would you like lunch?"

"Just like you to talk about food when I want a serious conversation."

"I very rarely talk about food."

"And you think you're right all the time."

"Why do you want to be a man?"

"Because it's easier. I find men very difficult. I want to be pretty but I don't want to want to be pretty for *them*. It's humiliating."

"I agree. It was worse for me."

"Why?"

"Because I couldn't be pretty even if I tried. You can. You are."

Amanda grunted again and assessed her mother. She certainly looked unattractive – but why did men keep turning up? It made her sick. It had always made her sick. Surely everyone would soon realise the obvious fact that she, Amanda, was sexually attractive and her mother was not?

Till, unaware of her specific thoughts but unavoidably aware of her hostility, tried not to be irritated. Her baffled affection so soon became frustrated rage.

She was still simmering when, later that afternoon, she went back to work at the Psychotherapy Centre in Bayswater. Years ago, she had ceased to believe in the complete effectiveness of psychotherapy. All day long she would listen to vulnerable people reciting the dismal catalogue of their early hurts and later failures. It was her job. Few of her patients would ever recover. They had been too broken in too many significant ways; even more importantly, they believed this themselves. But they could improve, and she cherished each small improvement as the triumph it was.

Her first patient that afternoon was her least favourite. For the whole fifty-minute hour she nodded, prompted, re-interpreted, seeing only Amanda's apparently bone-less limbs sprawled over the sofa – her sofa. Surely a psychiatrist should be able to relate to her own daughter. Then she chided herself for such simplistic thoughts. "You feel your mother resented you?" she said, as the patient's flow of complaint paused. He was a middle-aged man, a medium-rank actor. He had been seeing Till for two years and showed no sign of change. What he appeared to enjoy was sitting in a chair and complaining. So long as he paid, she didn't mind.

"You don't think she did resent me?" he said anxiously. "You think I'm making it up. You think I'm paranoid, don't you?"

Till sighed inaudibly. What could she do about Amanda? To love and be loved – vital. And without a good relationship with her mother, Amanda's sex-life would . . . and from that she thought about Ben.

That evening she called Honey.

"I'm glad you rang," said Honey. "I've been worrying about the funeral service. I'm not particularly poor. In fact, I suppose I'm rich. Will that keep my baby out of heaven?"

"No. The bit about Lazarus being poor is just to cheer up poor people. It's also about attachment to material things – being hard to get to heaven if you love money more than God."

"My baby didn't have time to do that. So it's all right? Do you promise?"

"Word of honour," said Till. "Shall I see you tomorrow? Do you want to come over?"

"Not for a while. Thanks, Till. I'll be in touch, but I've got to think. I've cancelled all my engagements for a fortnight."

Florence, weary from Tunisia, was berating Honey. "Don't cancel engagements like that, without consulting me. You weren't ill, were you? The abortion went all right? No problems?"

"No problems," said Honey. She looked ordinary, in so far as that was possible. Jeans, a sweatshirt, trainers, no make-up, and most of all no charm. Worrying, thought Florence.

"So when will you work again?"

"Never. I'm retiring."

"You can't retire. You're only thirty-four."

"Thirty-eight. I was fourteen for four years."

"As far as I can see you still are. Get me a drink, poppet." She lit a cigarette from the stub of her last.

Honey already had. Florence gulped it.

"I'm retiring," repeated Honey.

"You could pass for thirty in daylight. Twenty-five on screen."

"I'm not going to work any more. I'm not going to exercise, except running. I like running. I'm not going to wax my legs and shave my armpits. My body can turn to – what's the word for great plains covered with grass?"

"Savannah."

"My body can turn to savannah with hair waving in the breeze. My tits can droop, my bottom can bounce on the ground as I walk, my face can be as lined as an Underground map."

"What about my commission?"

"Sorry, Mother. You've had twenty-five per cent of me for years. I'll help out if you need—"

Florence took another gin and thought quickly. "Is this Matilda Livesey's influence? It sounds just like her."

"This is nothing to do with Till. I'm thinking for myself."

"Then we're all in the shit."

Silence. Florence struggled for control, adopted her "I'm your mother who wants the best for you" voice. "I want to understand, Honey. Tell me what you're feeling, little girl."

"It's not easy," said Honey. "A story of Till's might help."

"I knew she was behind this."

"She isn't. This is a story she told me years ago, when we were making *Captain Bridge*. Pandora said I was too good to be true, always doing what other people wanted. Till said she'd read in a book about an American boy who didn't learn to speak. He said nothing for years. His mother took him to the best doctors and they couldn't find a reason for it. Then, when he was six, one morning at breakfast, he said, 'Momma, you burnt my toast.' His mother cried and laughed and kissed him and when she'd calmed down she said, 'Son, how come you never spoke before?' and he said, 'Momma, you never burnt my toast before.'"

"And?" prompted Florence, no wiser.

"Steve burnt my toast."

"So this is all about Steve! Honey, believe me, there are many more men where he came from—"

"I've made up my mind."

Later that day Florence phoned. "Can I announce your retirement, Honey?"

"And?"

"Then just a few personal appearances explaining—"

"No."

"No personal appearances?"

"And no announcement."

Tom Wyatt decided to walk home. It wasn't raining; it was chilly, but he liked the outdoors and he didn't want to take the bus. He left his briefcase behind – there was no work he wanted to take home – slid *Mucus* into his overcoat pocket, and tackled the walk home from Bloomsbury to Kensington with his recently acquired lively stride.

Mucus was his talisman. Since discovering *Mucus*, his life had changed. He *hated* it. The invigorating surge of feeling, similar to his excitement at Honey's touch but with a consoling moral element, had renewed his view of the world and his purpose.

Hyde Park was fresh when he reached it. It was dark; some people were walking their dogs, though it was too late for children. He watched the lights of the traffic on the road, listened to the swish of tyres through puddles, and hated *Mucus*. What a fool he had been to think that the old certainties had gone. He crossed into Kensington Gardens, walked past the bandstand, and picked his way through the bird droppings near the Round Pond. *Mucus*, he thought happily. That's all that matters. I don't need to part my hair behind (besides, the new lotion is helping – I'm sure it's thicker). By God I'll devour peaches by the pound, I'll resign, I'll start my own publishing company. I'll only publish work I respect. It's not too late!

Here he paused. "This is fantasy," he told himself; then felt *Mucus* hard in his pocket. His fingers ran over the raised cover. "Stamp out *Mucus*!"

Back in Campden Hill he stood outside the substantial stucco building that housed half his life and realised he had left his keys in the briefcase. Chances were that his wife or his youngest daughter would be at home; it was the au pair's afternoon off.

They weren't. It had now started to rain. His rheuma-ticky hip ached. He couldn't stand for ever in the rain.

Perhaps Honey would be in. Hesitantly, he moved down the road. Madeline's part of the house was brightly lit. He could always go there . . . but if Honey was in . . .

"I really want to be alone," said Honey, as near mutiny as she could manage. They were in Till's local off-licence, buying cigarettes; against all Honey's protests Till had insisted on bringing her over to her flat for supper.

"You have the wrong accent for that line," said Till. "Pick up some fruit juice, will you? It's over there, in the cold cabinet."

Neither of them noticed Vernon Cole. He was stand-ing at the video rack staring at a video of one of his Biblical epics. He was confused: because he was often drunk, because alcohol had damaged his brain, because he was getting old. He tried to remember who he was and what he was doing there. Surely he had enough whisky at home? Then he saw Matilda Livesey. She was a sensible girl. She would help.

"What am I doing here?" he asked.

"It's your local off-licence. You live close by. So do I."

"I know that," he said irritably. He didn't recognise Till's companion, a small, slim girl with undistinguished features, pale eyelashes and a glum expression.

"Did you come in for whisky?" Till understood his bewilderment, had met it before.

"No. I have whisky at home."

"But you came to buy drink? For someone else?"

"Yes! Yes!" Now he remembered. He had asked that American woman to drinks. With Jacky Hamzavi. Why had he asked her? Why had she come? What did she want to drink? "What do you suppose she drinks?"

"Who?"

"The woman who lives in Honey's house. And Jacky, but he doesn't matter. He'll drink what he's given."

"You mean Madeline," said Honey. "Madeline Cabot Goldberg."

"Howjerdo," said Vernon, nodding in her direction. Honey looked astonished.

Till said gently, "This *is* Honey, Vernon. She's not dressed up and in her war paint, that's all."

"Oh," said Vernon limply. "I'd just woken up when they came. Sorry, Honey, not myself. That woman did say white wine. I don't know why I invited her."

"Get some Perrier water as well," said Matilda briskly. "What wine would you like?"

"Pass me some of that rightly unassuming Muscadet. Three bottles, and some of that expensive French pee."

"Perrier?" Till lined up his choices on the counter.

"That's all, me dusky beauty," he said to the pregnant Pakistani woman serving. "You'd better come back with me, both of you. Sticky situation. I'm not well. Come and join us. Give me a hand."

"We're not dressed for a party," said Till.

"You're not coming to one."

"I don't want to," said Honey. "Till, I don't want to."

"Come on, Honey," said Vernon. "Remember the early days. I taught you everything I knew."

All Honey could remember of the early days with Vernon was his writhing thumb firmly inserted into her knickers. She hardly felt this warranted return favours of any kind.

"Go home and wait for me," said Till giving her the key. "I'll only be half an hour."

"Christ, I hope so," said Vernon. "S'long as you take that woman with you."

Vernon's flat was two streets from Till's, nearer Notting Hill and thousands of pounds upmarket. It was dark and crowded with furniture his ex-wives hadn't taken from larger houses. The drawing-room had a fitted carpet, worn through in places, and Persian rugs puckered and torn. It was difficult to walk over the rugs and round the furniture. That Vernon often failed to was evident from several splintered occasional tables, a broken mirror and yellowing bruises on visible sections of his flesh.

Madeline and Jacky were sitting in gloom lit only by a lamp and the sparkle of Madeline's diamonds. Jacky was telling a lively story, earning his keep. When he saw Till he hugged her, relieved at her presence. He knew the depth of Madeline's disappointment at Vernon's bewildered reception. She had been impressed by Vernon, a little excited by the invitation. She had put on her smartest, newest dress, her best jewels, had spent two hours getting ready. She had imagined a flat full of theatre people, or perhaps an intimate drink which would lead on to dinner. She was even prepared to pay for dinner. But when Vernon opened the door after repeated rings he had clearly forgotten who she was. When she was hurt she was often vicious. Till could help to share the burden of this potentially grim social event.

All the surfaces were covered with objects. Vernon looked round helplessly then swept the mantelpiece clear of trophies. "Bloody useless things they give one for acting," he said. "Modern design, sharp edges and no resale value." Till put the bottles on the mantelpiece, greeted Madeline.

"My!" said Madeline. "Did you get all that wine for little me?"

"Don't know how much you drink," said Vernon. "You don't have to finish it, we'll leave it in the fridge for my cleaning woman to steal."

"You have a cleaning woman?" said Madeline, looking round pointedly. The flat was very dirty.

"Shall I open the wine?" said Till and Jacky simultaneously. Jacky vanished into the kitchen and could be heard opening drawers, shifting piles of plates and glasses, looking for a corkscrew. Till caught Madeline's baleful eye and escaped into the kitchen too.

"*Not* the party of the year," murmured Jacky. "Thank God you're here. Great to see you."

"And you. Happy with Madeline?"

"I'm happy. And I'm with Madeline," said Jacky. "That's the way I'd put it. Here's the corkscrew. I'm worried about Honey. She's like a clock running down. Can't you help?"

"I'm trying. She's at my flat now."

"Has she told you about tomorrow yet?"

"Tomorrow?"

"I only agreed against my better judgement. Out of loyalty."

"Jacky!" called Madeline imperiously.

Jacky shrugged. "We must be nice to her. She had hopes of this," he said, and left. Till rinsed four glasses, dried them on kitchen paper as the only tea-towels were wadded into whisky-smelling heaps, and joined the others in the drawing-room.

Jacky was talking about Vernon's latest film. Vernon couldn't remember it. Till, who hadn't seen it, pretended she had. Madeline said nothing.

Jacky moved on to the weather. Vernon hadn't noticed it. Till tried London as a tourist city. Madeline said she wasn't a tourist, she lived there, and one of her sons lived there too. Till asked about the son. Madeline said other people's children were hardly an enthralling topic for the rest of the company. Vernon finished his drink and took another. Madeline said she must go.

In the car on the way back she was unusually silent. She felt angry, humiliated and lonely. She scrutinised her face in a mirror in the lights from passing cars, readjusted her diamond necklace. "I'll ring my son when I get in," she said.

"That'll be nice," said Jacky. "Shall I cook us a little

supper? You told the housekeeper we were eating out, didn't you?"

Further humiliation for Madeline.

"I'll make an omelette," said Jacky.

"Fat-free, please."

"Fat-free," said Jacky, shuddering inwardly. For him, omelettes meant butter.

"What'll we do after supper?" She was querulous. She sounded old.

"Whatever you like. We could watch television. We could play cards."

"Cards. We'll play poker for matches."

"Good," said Jacky. They were waiting at a red light. He took her hand, kissed it. "I was lucky to find you," he said. "You're marvellous company."

"Am I?"

"The best."

Much later that evening, Till and Honey lay on one of Till's ex-husband's old mackintoshes on a football pitch in Wormwood Scrubs, watching the stars. Till was depressed by Vernon's disintegration. She scanned the Milky Way, imagined travelling to the heart of the Galaxy, light-years away; imagined the red giant stars, the white dwarfs, the unknown planetary systems, some perhaps with life-forms she would not recognise as life. Contemplation of the size of the universe comforted her.

"Why are we looking at the stars, Till?" said Honey, misery making her impatient and warring with her natural instinct to trot beside Till picking up crumbs of wisdom.

Matilda was remembering a long-ago attempt to talk to Ben about stars. He hadn't listened; he was writing. "Shut up, Till. Stuff your stars. The scene's going well. Here, read this."

"Ben, there are stars unimaginably dense—"

"They sound like Honey. Read this speech. It's good, I know it is. Make coffee, there's my girl."

"I'm nobody's girl."

"Make coffee anyway."

"Till?" said Honey, almost sharply. "I'm cold. Talk to me."

"I was thinking of things from the point of view of eternity. The nuns always used to recommend that."

"Why?"

"Not to get earthly things out of proportion."

Honey was silent. Eventually she said, "I think that's stupid."

"Why?"

"Because we're not eternal. It's like saying think of things from the point of view of rocks or – or parrots. That would only be useful if you were a rock or a parrot."

"It's useful to me. I enjoy speculation."

"Does that mean thinking?"

"Yes. Processing ideas."

"Are they as real to you as things and people?"

"I suppose so."

"They're not to me," said Honey, standing up and stamping her icy feet. "I'm going home now. I need your help tomorrow morning, Till. Can you clear it?"

"How important is it?"

"Vital."

"Then I can. I only have one appointment and the patient isn't serious, I can reschedule it. What are we doing?"

"Stealing film."

"Who from?"

"Steve. I've been talking to his sound recordist's wife. The crew are flying back from San Francisco tonight. The boy they were filming has finally died. He died on camera. They're all very excited about it. That footage will make the film."

"And?"

72

"And it's my revenge. Destroying that footage. It'll SHATTER Steve."

"Are you sure you want to do this?"

"Positive." Honey explained her plan. The plane was due to land just after eight the following morning. When Steve cleared Customs he would take the cans of exposed film to the labs in Soho Square. Honey would then snatch them.

"What do I do?"

"First you help me by distracting Steve. Then you drive the getaway car. You're the best driver I know."

"Not good enough to get through Soho traffic on a weekday morning without Steve catching us."

"You'll just have to do your best. Jacky's going to help."

"He mentioned something at Vernon's. Why Jacky?"

"Because he's a fast runner and he doesn't mind helping."

"I think he does."

"Only because he's afraid. He doesn't disapprove. He doesn't have – he doesn't think it's wrong—"

"Ethical objections," said Till. "He doesn't have ethical objections. But you mustn't count on him for anything physical. He squeaks with fear at the prospect of violence."

"I know that," said Honey, impatience in her tone. "Anything physical, you'll do."

"Why me?"

"Because you're braver than Jacky and stronger than me."

"Yes, ma'am," said Till. She was a little irritated by her unaccustomed relegation to the role of sidekick muscle, but more intrigued by the signs of change in Honey.

All three wore tracksuits. They sat in Till's battered old car in Soho Square. Jacky was nervous: confidence tricks were more his line, or card sharping. His fingers itched for a pack of cards to shuffle. "I'm doing this out of loyalty," he kept saying.

"Thank you, Jacky. You look very good. Black suits you," said Honey.

"I've brought a Balaclava for the actual snatch. I don't want him to recognise me at a later date and smash my face to a pulp. Tell me again what I do, Honey. You grab the cans and pass them to me. I find the last can in the sequence . . ."

"The one labelled with the highest number," prompted Honey, "the last can they shot, the one with the boy's death on it . . ."

"And then?" said Jacky.

"You open it and expose it. Spill it out on the pavement."

Jacky had worked as an assistant cameraman, briefly, but long enough to recoil at the enormity of the statement. "*Expose* it?"

"Yes. Tumble it out on the pavement, scrabble it round, make sure it gets as much light as possible."

"I'll be liable."

"You've been liable for a lot more than that," said Till. "What happened to your second wife's jewels?"

"An unfortunate theft. Some heartless person stripped the flat while she was lying dead."

"I know," said Till.

"She cheated me. Her will was a complete farce. She left every penny to her family, nothing to me. She *promised*." Jacky was biting his nails in anguish. "It's unkind of you to bring it up, Till."

"I won't mention it again if you don't chicken out on us."

"For old times' sake. Out of loyalty I'm doing this."

Honey was anxious too, but determined. She had set her whole will on this enterprise; in conception and execution, it was hers. It represented a fundamental change of attitude to her life. She hugged her delicate hands between pink tracksuited knees and relaxed her neck muscles.

Till was enjoying herself. Bizarre as the enterprise was, it entertained her; she waited to see if Honey could carry it through. "How can you be sure that Steve will come alone?" she asked.

"He always does. It's like a superstition, he hates keeping cans of unexposed film about, especially important footage like this. He'll come straight from the airport."

"Steve's very strong. He'll be furious. I won't be able to hold him by myself."

"You won't be by yourself," said Honey. "You'll have me."

"Yes, ma'am," said Till.

"Do you mind doing this for me?" Honey turned to her in sudden apprehension. "It's perfectly justified. I backed the production so I probably own the footage. And what about the morality of exploiting a dying boy's last moments?"

"You don't have to convince me," said Till.

"Oh dear," said Jacky.

They sat in the car for an hour and a half. Till, tense despite herself, was beginning to snap at whining Jacky. Honey appeared calm; she was describing a film she had seen on television two nights before when she broke off and gripped Till's arm. "There he is! It's the Range Rover! Jacky, you go and stand by the lab doorway. Come on, Till."

Jacky pulled the Balaclava over his face; Till and Honey walked towards the Range Rover, which was parking thirty yards beyond the lab entrance. "Only Steve in it. Good," said Till.

"I told you," said Honey calmly.

Both women watched as Steve got out, went round, took a box and cans strapped together with camera tape from the front seat, and walked towards them carrying it.

"Right," said Honey. "Here we go."

He had almost reached them before he recognised Honey. "My God," he said, "you look different." Till's hands were shaking. She wiped them on her tracksuit top.

"No make-up," said Honey. "Oh Steve, I've missed you so much." She sounded weak, woebegone, entirely unthreatening. She threw her arms round his neck, kissed him. He staggered, off balance. Till grabbed the film. He gripped it tighter. Honey spat in his eyes. His grip slackened and Till ran with her prize, thrust it at Jacky.

"Go for gold!" she hissed. Jacky squeaked plaintively and skipped away, stripping camera tape off the cans, separating them. Steve charged towards him, Honey clinging to his shoulders. Till went for his knees in a rugby tackle. All three writhed on the ground, Steve swiping at random with his fists, Honey squeezing his neck, Till holding his ankles. Round them people passed, shooting cautious glances, unwilling to be involved. Jacky, twenty yards away, had found the vital can. Rip rip went the sealing camera tape. His shaking fingers scratched at the can, failing to open it, slipping with his terrified sweat.

Steve's first bewilderment had passed and he could see what Jacky was doing. He moaned with rage and fury and tried to run forward. Honey's arms were locked around his neck; Till clutched wildly at his knees again and brought him down, then threw herself on top of him, her weight, unusually, an asset. Her nose was bleeding; she could taste salt. Her face was wedged over his; he was turning an ominous colour and gasping for breath. "You're choking him, Honey," she said, alarmed. Honey, gripping his throat with all her strength, watched Jacky open the can and tip it up on the pavement. The film sprawled off the spool and glittered in the pale sun.

Honey left Steve, dashed to the film, seized the end

of it and ran away through the traffic, Steve's precious footage unwinding behind her. Steve's fist clubbed Till's head and while she was stunned he wriggled away in pursuit of Honey. Jacky shut himself in the car.

Till heaved herself up, shook her head to clear it, leant against the car watching Honey thread in and out of pedestrians in a lap of honour round the square. Behind her, Steve ran, futilely scooping up the film and tangling it in his arms.

"You all right, love?" a van driver inquired of Till. "Need any help? Mean-looking sod, in't he? What's he want the film for, then?"

"It's all right, thanks," said Till getting into the car and starting it. As soon as Honey opened the passenger door she gunned the engine; they were moving as Honey's bottom hit the seat.

Steve, festooned with ruined film, jogged beside the car thumping on the roof. "You bloody bitch! I'll kill you if this is the last reel! I'll get you for this, Honey! You'll never work in films again! Stupid, stupid bitch! And you, Matilda Livesey! I'll charge you both, see if I don't!"

"Sorry, Steve," said Honey sweetly. "I've killed your baby." And smiled.

Honey was too excited to sit still. She wriggled in the seat, knelt upright facing backwards watching Steve's receding figure dance with frustration. By the time he collected the remaining cans and started the Range Rover, the traffic behind Till's car had jammed solid.

"Any regrets?" asked Till.

"No," said Honey. "I'd made up my mind. I wanted to hurt Steve as much as he's hurt me. I never have. I never stood up for myself all my life through. I never even had a self to stand up for. I've been pathetic and vulnerable and clinging."

"Everybody's those things sometimes."

"I've made a career of it. Do this, Honey. Act, Honey.

77

Show us more leg, Honey. Cuddle up to him, Honey. More tit, Honey. Cry, Honey. Don't cry, Honey. Stand still and be buggered, Honey." She slapped her hand on the dashboard. Till noticed her unpainted nails. "Kill your baby, Honey. It's better for both of us, Honey. I don't even have a proper name. How many people know I'm called Sarah?" Honey didn't talk easily. The words globbed out under pressure like ketchup from a bottle. "I have nothing, Till. Nothing. I am nothing, only what other people want."

"Will revenge help?"

"Yes. It's an *action*. It's something I decided to do, me on my own account. I wrote the script and carried it through, all by myself."

"I broke two nails," said Jacky.

"With your help, Jacky. And, of course, Till."

"Of course," said Till, feeling the blood seep into an incipient black eye, wriggling her body to locate bruising.

"He nearly hit me," said Jacky. "Did you see the look in his eyes when he ran for me?"

"Yes. In close-up, *and* his fists. You can stop fishing for sympathy, Jacky," said Till.

"Oooh, you're so *butch*. Twice the man I am," said Jacky. "It must be hard for a guy to live up to. Have you seen Ben lately?"

"Steve will feel like death," said Honey. Her companions broke off their squabble and stared at her. She wasn't listening to them; she was only thinking of herself. *Honey?*

"He must feel like death. I did. I did. For Steve, that footage is just like my baby."

"I understand that," said Till.

"But you don't approve?"

"I don't think it's a moral issue. You can't actually compare even a foetus to a can of film."

Honey was confused. "Why did you help me, then?"

"Out of loyalty," said Jacky.

"Because you are my friend and Steve isn't," said Till. "Because you were hurt. Because I enjoy daft enterprises."

"I thought I was doing *right*," said Honey plaintively.

"I think you were doing *satisfying*," said Till. "It's amazing how right that can seem."

"I don't want to discuss it," said Honey. "Stop outside a bookshop, will you? W. H. Smith will do. I want to get a copy of *Mucus*."

"Why?"

"Tom Wyatt dropped in the other day. He was locked out from his house. He said *Mucus* had changed his life."

"Did he say *why*?" inquired Till cautiously.

"No, someone rang and then he left. Here's a Smith's, stop!"

Honey sprinted in, bought the book, ran back. She flopped into the car. "It's amazing not dressing up," she said. "No one notices me, no one cares, and I can run. I used to be good at running. I won the hundred-yard sprint at school three years in a row. Mind you, for two of those years the other fast runner was in a summer show at Blackpool." She knotted her fingers together, cracked the joints. "I don't like your view of the world, Till," she said. "It's too full of – of – what's the word for saying things aren't as simple as that, nothing is quite like that?"

"Qualifiers?" suggested Till.

"That's it. You take away my edge. You won't let me feel things simply. I *want* things simple; I want to do what's *right*."

"Want doesn't mean have. I *want* to be an internationally famous actress, I don't *want* to be plain, I *want* an ideal lover. The trick is to narrow the gap between what you want and what you can have, and learn to live with it. The gap is usually a yawning chasm. That's what you could use your smile for, to bridge the gap and acknowledge the irony of existence."

"That's too ambitious," said Honey. "I don't have those – things to fall back on—"

"Resources."

"I don't have those resources."

"You'll have to find them or go under. It's no good stamping your foot and shouting. If you can't have, then you can't. Only children can get away with that."

"There's a lot of ageing children about, then."

"Those are the ones who want your smile as a transformation. Perfect sexual love is possible, some people are entirely good, the intensity of the moment can transform home-coming disappointments and the dullness of accustomed things. That's all very well now and then, like getting drunk, but it doesn't build life."

"What does?"

"Everyone's answer is different."

"What's yours?"

"Live in the moment," said Jacky. "Enjoy what you can, praise what you can, take what you can . . ."

"I'm not telling," said Till. "You're too suggestible, Honey."

"Don't count on it. Anyway, I'll read *Mucus*. If it changed Tom's life it might change mine."

Chapter Five

Ben was dreaming. He dreamt that Pandora was strad-
dling him in oyster silk camiknickers. He woke to find
that she was, and knew it was Sunday morning, hellish
Sunday morning, what Pandora called Our Time. Latterly
she had decided to revive their flagging sexual relationship and had equipped herself with expensive under-
clothes and a book on sexual technique.

Ben wished harm to the author of the book. He
fantasised about catching him alone in a dark alley; better
still, calling him from the coaching bench and sending
him in as a substitute to see if he really enjoyed being
suffocated by a silk-clad rump while Pandora stimulated
his genitals with her mouth and his nipples with her
fingers.

"Urggghh," said Ben.

"Oh, lover," crooned Pandora encouragingly.

Thank heavens, he had an erection. He dreaded the
inevitable day when he wouldn't. This particular morning it was vital as he had refused, the night before, to
accompany Pandora to a Pardoe party and had visited an
accommodating BBC production assistant instead. He
suspected that Pandora suspected this.

If he was to breathe he had to act. Masterfully, he
turned Pandora and rolled over her, crushing her lips
with his, then gulped air. Her breath smelt of toothpaste.
On Sundays, she got up first, washed, brushed her
teeth, did her hair, put on touches of make-up that
wouldn't be disturbed by the encounter that Ben was to
provide. The toothpaste smell reminded him of this; he
found it touching. All that futile endeavour.

Like many promiscuous, attractive men, Ben made little effort in bed. He relied on women being sufficiently aroused by desire. This hadn't troubled Till who had accommodated herself to quick arousal. But for Pandora the thrill of sex was the anticipation and indulgence of being desired. Conscious of this, determined to behave decently for once, Ben approached her systematically. He stimulated the obvious places and tried to keep his mind from wandering to more interesting matters like why he wasn't writing.

"Let's try something different," Pandora murmured huskily, sticking her tongue in his ear for good measure. He didn't wipe away the saliva that poured into his ear drum, even when it created distracting glugging and slurping sounds. He longed for Till. She usually knew when he was pretending to be aroused and would wriggle away and slap him on the buttocks. "Quit foolin'," she would say. She was only moderately good at accents and yet constantly attempted them. He guessed her "quit foolin'" was supposed to be American, probably Texan.

Pandora stretched her limbs languorously and rubbed herself against him. Dear God, he thought, I'm losin' it, and choked on a laugh. He tugged at her camiknickers, thrust inside her, gave some token grunts, and listened. She was moaning unconvincingly. Till could moan convincingly. Pandora kept moaning. This pretence will end only in death, he thought despairingly.

Ten minutes later she pretended to come. Honour was satisfied. He imagined his production assistant and came too. Then, he wanted to move back to his side of the bed and go back to sleep, but he knew she valued post-coital intimacy. He provided it, but not too enthusiastically; he had learned the soft way that the author of her sex book thought one orgasm was only an *hors d'oeuvre*.

At last she released him. He rolled onto his back and thought about Till. He wanted to ask her for guidance, for a device to appease Pandora. Till's sexual repertoire was wide, garnered both from her clients and her own experience. Perhaps she could suggest a fetish for him to confess; a fetish which was neither humiliating nor energetic. The only variation he enjoyed was places. He took women where he found them, in studios, cupboards, dressing-rooms, aeroplanes, standing up, from the rear, sitting down. But a wife was different. If you had a perfectly good, excessively expensive, imitation four-poster bed (so romantic, said Pandora signing the cheque), why pretend to be spontaneously overcome by lust in the kitchen? It made no sense.

He was feeling guilty. He was well equipped for guilt. His father was Catholic, his mother Jewish. He felt Catholic guilt about God and sin; Jewish guilt about his mother, his family and his work; about sex, he had the choice.

This morning, he found, he was Jewish. He tried not to hate his wife. She was enjoying herself, reading aloud from the Sunday papers whenever she found references to Pardoes. This could take hours. He should, long ago, have told her that he hated the Sundays because he wrote no new plays to be reviewed in them; that most of his contemporary playwrights were still productive, and when he heard their names he felt murderous with rage.

Lying in Pandora's bed in Pandora's Hampstead house, surrounded by evidence of her care and devotion to his interests – framed playbills, blown-up stills, and, in the downstairs lavatory, yellowing reviews – he wanted to beat his chest and howl. Swamped by remorse after his first wife's suicide, unbalanced by Till's unaccountable rejection, he had decided to try a calm, domestic life, where few hurts were given or received, where – as he imagined – he could write.

He hadn't realised that Pandora's view of married life was a continual feast of togetherness. He had been an only child, a solitary partly by choice, more by circumstance. Living in Dublin, half Jewish at a Catholic school, he was everywhere an outsider. The only thing his parents had in common was outstanding physical attractiveness, and their mutual attraction hadn't lasted. Their marriage was the coldest of cold wars; each continually explained to Ben – they didn't speak to each other – that it was only their nobility, endurance and religious faith that kept the marriage together. It wasn't a good marriage but it was what he knew.

Pardoe marriage was constant companionship, constant prattle.

"Here's a mench of Salome," said Pandora. "Listen: 'charming Salome Pardoe tells me she goes into rehearsal next week for the new Alan Ayckbourn at the National Theatre . . .'"

Ben thought about his elder son. He hadn't expected to love anyone as much as he loved his children: he didn't think himself capable of it, and until they were ten he had seen them only as tumbleweeds in the windy desert of his first marriage. As they grew into adolescence, however, he felt his heart tethered to them by Lilliputian strings, more each year. He loved them more than he ever expressed and he felt, looking back, that he had ignored them monstrously. He had been entirely involved with his first wife and Till.

His younger son he could understand. He was at art school studying design. He would go into television or advertising. His main aim in life was bedding girls, and Ben empathised, merely worrying about Aids. But his elder son – an enigma. He took after his mother's family, was even named after them, Peregrine Bellamy Considine. There had been Bellamys at Agincourt and Blenheim, Waterloo and Sebastopol, Passchendaele and Dunkirk. Now Peregrine Bellamy Considine was in Northern Ireland working for military intelligence.

His father expected, daily, to be informed he was dead; dead without ever having been talked to or understood. He had been a prep-school boy who played for the team, a public-school prefect who believed in traditional values, who took his mother's side against a father he treated first with hostility, now with distant courtesy. For the last two weeks he had been in London staying with his mother's parents. He hadn't even telephoned, though Pandora had rung twice to invite him to lunch, to dinner, to stay.

Now once again he was somewhere in Ulster and Ben knew a part of himself was there. To Ben, the army seemed unimaginably tedious, Ulster intervention madness incarnate. He knew the Irish. But Perry – he never thought of him by his full, ridiculous, alien name – must survive. He must. One day Ben would kiss his son, hug him. The boy had never let himself be touched.

Honey allowed herself two weeks without interruption to analyse her life and make plans for her future. She reflected only briefly that, so far, thirty years had been too short to accomplish this task successfully.

The first week was spent exploring the boundaries of her hurt. Her triumph at the destruction of Steve's film soon ebbed, leaving her exhausted and demoralised. Steve rang up twice, to berate her. He was furious: his rage cascaded over her; she rubbed it into her injuries and hoped they would heal. They didn't.

She woke each morning knowing something terrible was wrong, trying not to remember what it was. The shock of her miscarriage receded and though she often gazed down the garden and tried to feel for her buried baby, the loss of Steve began to dominate her mind again. He still desired her, surely? She had done so much for him, he must miss her, surely? He too must wake up feeling the loss . . .

Conviction that he was delighted to be rid of her throbbed like an ulcer beneath the fantasies, and the void in her life would not be filled. Walking in Holland Park she saw lovers, and thought of Steve; she saw women alone, and imagined them being left by Steve; she saw men contentedly alone and thought of Steve.

Often, when the latest of the late-night television programmes finished, she heard her biological clock ticking in the silence and bit the skin at the side of her nails until her fingers bled; when she woke and saw the mutilations her case seemed hopeless. Despite her brave words to her mother about ignoring her appearance, damaging her body was unimaginable. It was all she had.

At first she had enjoyed walking unnoticed in crowds; not wearing make-up or glamorous clothes, not being Honey Markham. She delighted in how insignificant she could make herself, then became frightened by how insignificant she felt. Being unassuming, she found, was rewarding only when all around her acknowledged her rarity.

There was also the pull of habit. For thirty years her routines had revolved, planet-like, round the star of her body. They had been only briefly disrupted as by the gravitational pull of a passing comet when she made the spontaneous decision to change her life. Now she felt herself falling back into orbit. She started to run again, then to massage, cleanse, tone and nourish her face; the stubble of regrowing hair irritated her and she shaved her underarms and waxed her legs. Finally she rescued the copy of *Vogue* she had kept unopened to reline the cat's bed and leafed through it.

One afternoon, when Honey's two weeks of retreat from human contact was nearly up, she sat listening to Brahms' Fourth Symphony. It reminded her of *Aimez-vous Brahms?*, a film she liked. It also interrupted the silence. When it was over she started *Mucus*. It took her an hour to read two pages; she was determined to let no nuance escape. So far, she found none, but the prose style pleased her. Short words, short sentences.

Finally she put it aside and took a piece of paper and a felt-tip pen. MY LIFE, she wrote, then looked the words up in the dictionary for reassurance. Yes, she had spelt them right. This gave her a confidence which vanished as she caught sight of her mutilated nails with their frames of dried blood. She fetched a pair of black evening gloves and continued to subheadings.

MY LIFE

Whit I have   Whit I want   Whit I can gte

What did she have? Money. Health. Looks for her age. Friends? Till. She put down Pandora, then crossed her out. She put down Jacky and crossed him out. She had no other friends. Steve's friends, none of whom she had liked, had surrounded her; before that, Alexander's. Tom and Maggie dated from that era but you couldn't call them friends exactly, partly because they were a unit, Tom'n' Maggie'n' household. She put down her mother, then crossed her out. Not even willing Honey could class Florence as an emotional asset.

She played the Brahms again, abashed by the miserable total of her assets, but the surging rhythms made her feel worse. They underlined her need. She turned back to the list. *Whit I want*. Steve. A child. *Whit I can gte*. A child.

Simple enough.

Tom Wyatt never hurried in the mornings. Nobody at the office cared when he came in; they probably, if they thought about it at all, preferred to see him as little as possible. In the mornings he pottered between the bedroom and bathroom, and answered the telephone. Calls were seldom for him.

"Hello? Daddy? This is Camilla. Is Mummy there?"

"I'll put you through."

He shaved his upper lip.

"Hello? Daddy? Candida here. Everything OK? Could I speak to Mummy?"

"I'll put you through."

He shaved his right jaw.

"Hello? Hello? Mr Wyatt? Oh dear, is Mrs Wyatt available?"

"I'll put you through."

He shaved his left jaw, rinsed his face, rubbed in hair lotion, wandered back into the bedroom.

"That was Mrs Frith on the phone," said Maggie, breathless from the stairs. Mrs Frith was the treasure who looked after their Suffolk cottage. "She says the tank in the roof burst last night. Our bedroom and the drawing-room are flooded."

"Oh, good," said Tom. He was looking out of the window at the back of the house. He could just see into Honey's garden. Honey was, apparently, weeding by the rear wall. At any rate she was on her knees. Surely one doesn't weed in February, he thought. Her body was slender even in bulky woollen clothes and she rose to her feet with a lithe movement he knew he couldn't emulate.

"You're not listening," said Maggie. "Tom! I said we had a flood at the cottage! A flood!"

"Oh dear," said Tom. "I hope no one was drowned."

"Only our carpets and bedding and curtains and ceilings and furniture."

"Oh dear. Can I help?"

"It's all right. I'm dealing with it."

"Does one weed in February?"

"No. Especially not in the rain. Who is?"

"Honey Markham," said Tom. "She's gone in now." An instinct of self-preservation led him to add Honey's surname, although to him she was not even just Honey; she was She, Her, the Only Woman.

"Honey's been off recently," said Maggie, joining him

in gazing at the deserted garden. "I met her last week and she said she wasn't speaking to anyone for a while. The Steve thing seems to have had a delayed effect. I've been thinking, perhaps another dinner-party, and I'll round up some men for her—"

Tom gulped, gripped by warring emotions. Honey to dinner – superb. Honey as the main course, offered up to the slavering jaws of men free to consume her – atrocious. "I thought you weren't going to ask her for a while. After her conversation last time."

"That's all forgotten," said Maggie generously. She was generous, he told himself, hospitable, self-sacrificing, considerate. Only a man as unworldly as Tom would have been surprised that contemplation of Maggie's virtues should weigh so lightly against his gradually acknowledged desire for Honey.

Maggie was still talking. "I've decided against it. She wants to ask us back first. Decent girl, Honey. She keeps up with us more or less cutlet for cutlet. When I think of all the freeloaders who eat and eat and never ask us back – Madeline, for instance—"

"It's not easy to keep up with us," Tom pointed out. "We do set a cracking pace. If we ate cutlet for cutlet with all our guests we'd die of surfeit. We'd never have an evening's peace . . ."

"Do you want an evening's peace?" Maggie was anxious. "I thought you enjoyed the stimulation of the conversation of lively minds."

Stimulation, to Tom, had other connotations. He gazed at the space where Honey had been.

"Tom? Tom, listen, do you want us to entertain less?"

It was time for a blank lie. If Maggie didn't give dinner-parties they would spend more domestic evenings together with the lurchers, the au pair, and whichever children were currently in residence. He would have to eat and appreciate more of Maggie's food. He would put on weight, develop spots, and his hair would drop out at an accelerated rate. "No," he said firmly. "Could we have Matilda to dinner soon?"

"Matilda Livesey? Of course, if that's what you want." Maggie felt a twinge of suspicion. Twice, Tom had mentioned Matilda. Did he find her sexually interesting? No, not Tom, never Tom. "She's got a lot fatter, Pandora tells me."

"I wanted to talk to her, not weigh her. She's got a lively mind."

"You could call it that. I don't trust Matilda. She has affairs with people's husbands and she *says* things. Pointless offensive things."

"Give me an example."

"Oh, Tom, don't be so – measured! Nearly everything she says is offensive!" Tom went on looking at her expectantly and she dredged her mind. "Once she was eating one of my better efforts – trout, I think, stuffed with salmon mousse and almonds. It was a big party, twelve people, the evening of that terrible day when Camilla was rushed into hospital to have her appendix out in the middle of me recording a programme at Shepherd's Bush. Everyone was being very kind and saying how marvellous it was of me not to cancel the dinner. And I'd made an extra pudding which was particularly complicated, especially the garnish and the decoration – marbling. All things considered it *was* a good effort and people were kindly saying so. Matilda said nothing and I asked her if she agreed, which was stupid I know but I was tired, and she said yes, I *was* marvellous, which couldn't always be easy for the people I lived with, or good for them. As if I'd do anything to hurt you and the children. Would I?"

"Of course not," said Tom, kissing her on a crumpled delicate cheek, thinking of Camilla and Candida who had supposedly grown up and left home and still rang their mother every morning for help, advice, and management.

"You'll take the lurchers for the usual walk? I'm just off to my publishers."

" 'Stimulus'," said Tom. "She meant 'stimulus'. She said 'stimulation' but she meant 'stimulus'." He was waiting for the lurchers to use the dog lavatory. The elder lurcher, far from defecating, appeared to be eating. Tom refused to ascertain the nature of the food. He was trying not to think irritably about Maggie.

" 'Puppy biscuit'," said a female voice behind him. He turned to see a laughing Matilda and a smiling Honey.

" 'Puppy biscuit'?" he asked, then remembered. "Walter Mitty! Excellent story! Was I talking to myself?"

"You were," said Matilda. She was red-faced, wearing a tracksuit, not much fatter than his memory of her, perhaps more solid; certainly older. She had an intelligent face. Whereas Honey – how could a woman her age look so beautiful without make-up, in baggy jeans, trainers and a huge padded cotton top? Her hair was blunt cut to jaw level with shorter pieces at the front, her eyes were clear, the line of her neck still taut, her teeth even in the famous smile. Her skin was faintly tanned, smooth, beaded with sweat; his eye followed it downwards from the neck to an irritating interruption of cotton just before the swell of her breasts. "We've been running," she said.

He glanced at Till in surprise. "I lumber," she said. "Honey runs."

"Not true," said Honey. "Once we get past two miles Till can outpace me easily. She has stamina. Good to see you, Tom. What were you talking to yourself about? And who is Walter Mitty?"

He didn't answer. He was staring at her, enthralled. Behind him, the younger lurcher retreated whimpering from an enraged Jack Russell terrier.

"Walter Mitty is a character in a story by Thurber," said Till. "He lives in his imagination, doesn't he, Tom?"

"What?"

"We'll read it to you," said Till. "If Tom has a copy, which I'm sure he has, we'll pick it up, go back to your flat and read it to you. It's very short. I like reading out loud. How about it, Tom?"

More time with Honey, thought Tom. Till would leave and they'd be alone. "Yes, yes," he said. "Reading aloud, what fun. One of us could take the narrative sections and the other the fantasies. Excellent plan."

"Thank you," said Honey. "Is it a significant story?"

"Significant?" Tom felt even simple words slipping from him.

"Is it important, like *Mucus*? Will it change my life?"

"Probably not," said Till. "It'll help you enjoy the life you have, which is all you can expect from literature."

"*Mucus* changed your life too?" demanded Tom eagerly. "How fascinating!" How much, he thought, they had in common; how sensitive she was.

"It hasn't changed my life yet," she said scrupulously. "I'm only on chapter three. I'm finding it hard going."

"How true that is! Hard going! Yes, indeed! Cruel, senseless, *damaging* going! Don't read any more, Honey, please. It isn't worth your time—"

"Let's not stand here in the rain discussing *Mucus*," said Till, seeing Honey's confusion. "I want a hot shower."

"Is it raining?" said Tom. "Oh yes, of course – the rain!" He raised his face to the rain and felt it trickle down his neck, under his collar. A shower; a shower with Honey. He was taller than she; no risk of her seeing his scalp.

Tom sat on the sofa in Honey's flat, waiting for Till and Honey to shower and change. He clutched a copy of collected Thurber short stories and smiled foolishly. He was exhilarated. He had crossed the Rubicon, sited that morning between Holland Park and Campden Hill

Road. He had previously thought that he need not worry about his preoccupation with Honey because it was essentially trivial; now he felt he couldn't be blamed for his obsession with her because it was overpowering. He pulled his socks smooth, cleared his throat, looked round the flat with proprietorial interest. The flat of the girl he loved. He hadn't been in love since – 1956. Before Maggie, before the Pill and the Beatles and nouvelle cuisine and leisure pursuits; before the loss of innocence, he thought. But Honey was innocent, and God knew he was. "An innocent man," he said. He hoped she would emerge from the shower wrapped in a towel, barefoot. He wanted to see her feet, small and delicate and pink from the shower. At the thought his erection returned and he adjusted the collected Thurber, fortunately a large print edition, in his lap.

"Won't be long," called Honey from the bedroom. She had showered first and was towelling her hair, averting her eyes from Till's nakedness partly out of modesty and partly out of embarrassment. Till's breasts were so big, her body so padded and – used, with stretch marks and broken veins, the kind of body you only saw in Fellini films. Till, on the other hand, studied Honey with aesthetic appreciation. "You are without flaw," she said.

"I'm having serious doubts about my inner thighs," said Honey.

"Don't mention them to Tom, his blood pressure'll soar."

"What do you mean?"

"He's in lust with you."

"Not Tom," said Honey confidently. "I can trust Tom. He's really *good*. He's serious."

"He's seriously interested in your inner thighs."

"Are you teasing?" Honey was confused.

"Only a little. I'm right about Tom, though. Either he lusts for you or he loves you. He stared at you like a rabbit mesmerised by a delectable stoat. Rub some body lotion into my back, would you?"

Honey began this extensive task. "I do hope you're wrong. I want him as a friend and I do *hate* it when men pounce. They go red in the face and their eyes glaze over and you have to be quite rude before they understand. Why did you ask him back?"

"Because we were standing in the rain and he looked so painfully happy; and Lord knows you can put him off, you've had enough practice. Let him have the pleasure of your company a little longer, and enjoy Walter Mitty."

"Just make sure you take him with you when you go. I haven't time for other people's emotions until I've sorted out my own."

Till started to dress. "A February affair, all fog and fantasy. Firelit rooms, art galleries, drives to the frosty country and walks by frozen ponds and the lecherous delights of top tog duvets."

"If you're so keen on the idea, you have him."

"Not at all the same for poor Tom."

Honey didn't think Walter Mitty was funny, she thought it was sad. Tom was abashed by her greater sensitivity, silenced by her presence; he darted wistful glances at her thoroughly covered body. Honey was abstracted and very soon Till was bored. "I must go," she said. Obedient to Honey's glance she added, "Do escort me to the bus, Tom."

"Of course," said Tom mechanically, responding to this call for chivalry, however odd: for why should Matilda want escorting? From what could he protect her?

It was still raining. He erected the umbrella and tried to hold it so Till could shelter. They kept bumping into each other. "Never mind," said Till impatiently. "I don't mind a little rain." She walked apart from him. He felt annoyed by her nannyish tone; he was no longer with Honey; Matilda was walking too fast, and he was breathless. "Wait, wait," he said. Matilda slowed up.

"What time do you have to be at the office?" she asked.

He shrugged. "Never. I'm a mere cipher."

"My next appointment is at two o'clock. It's twelve now. Shall we lunch?"

"Why?" asked Tom with uncharacteristic bluntness. Matilda had a predatory air, and who knew what she meant by lunch?

"We could talk about Honey," offered Till.

"Why should I want to do that?"

"Because you're in love with her. This wine bar isn't bad." Numbly Tom followed her in, shaking his umbrella, furling it.

They sat in a corner. The bar was decorated in brown and dusty pink. The tables round the wall were separated by wooden partitions. The lighting was dim and a cautious glance told Tom there was no one there he knew. He was flustered by Matilda.

"Don't waste time denying it," she said. "Anyone can see you're in love with her. You'd better get your act together if you don't want Maggie to know."

"Does Honey know?"

"I told her. She didn't believe me."

"Was she – opposed to the idea?"

"She wants to keep you as a friend. She hasn't got over Steve yet."

"Are you being tactful?"

"A little."

"Tell me honestly, what are my chances?"

"Of what?"

"Of being Honey's lover."

"The square root of sod all," said Till. "Shall I order for you?"

"Do," said Tom. His shoulders sagged. He felt as if heaven had been revealed to him, then snatched away.

He didn't doubt Till's assessment: she was astute, close to Honey, and, in his judgement, fundamentally kind. He didn't think she would deliberately hurt him.

"It would be a terrible idea anyway," said Till as the waitress retreated. "You'd both be guilty from square one. Besides, Honey doesn't like sex much."

"That's probably because she's so sensitive. She hasn't been . . . properly loved yet."

"And you'll properly love her?" said Till, one eyebrow raised.

Tom was resentful. He had lost his moral superiority by admitting his desire for Honey, and with its loss he realised how important it had been. He now saw himself, and, almost worse, imagined Till to see him, not as high-principled and aloof, but as a balding, inexperienced seducer.

"It's different when you're in love," she said gently. "It doesn't matter how experienced you are, when emotions are involved it's different. I always stammer and blush and bump into things. So does Ben."

That drunken played-out barnyard strutter, thought Tom, why bring him into this? Then a terrible thought struck him. "Has Ben ever had an affair with Honey?"

"No," said Till. Entirely the wrong moment, she felt, to describe the occasion twenty years ago when Honey, Till and Ben had gone to bed together. "Honey's a very faithful person."

"Of course," said Tom. "Honey is all that is good."

Till sighed. The lunch would not be entertaining.

Living alone suited Till in many respects. She enjoyed her own company; she read, she walked, she didn't have to tolerate continual subjection to another's preferences. She could stay up all night, play the same country and western records over and over again, eat only bowls of porridge, leave cups on the floor, do the washing after the late-night horror movie. Her patients gave her plenty to think about, and when she wanted to dream, she dreamt acting.

But a major disadvantage of solitude was that there was no one to point out to her how foolish she was being, no one to check her obsessions or laugh her out of absurdities. She was aware of this; it was partly why she had inveigled Tom Wyatt into lunch. With Honey utterly self-absorbed, the children away, her patients, appropriately, uninterested in her, she went for weeks without anyone asking how she was and listening to the answer.

Her colleagues at the Psychotherapy Centre were amiable, well meaning and, Till considered, deranged. One was still encouraging patients to relive their birth traumas, another conducted therapy sessions with both patients and therapist immersed in a warm bath, the third had abandoned talking altogether and confined his treatment to stroking the soles of his patients' feet. They were not people to whom one would naturally turn for bracing common sense.

Till knew she needed bracing common sense. Since her lunch with Pandora she had spent most of her waking moments thinking about Ben. She was doing it now, as she walked to Bayswater from the wine bar after leaving Tom; searching streets with her eyes, watching cars, waiting for the magic coincidence that was more than coincidence and would restore Ben to her.

Chapter Six

Madeline was fretful. It was her birthday and she hated birthdays. Time was the enemy, and however tirelessly she worked, there was no hope of victory. Occasionally it occurred to her to wonder what she gained by looking younger, but her whole life had been spent capitalising on her beauty and it was too late to learn another strategy. She seldom recognised that her strategy was at fault, preferring to blame other people, stubborn people with false values who didn't recognise her importance. Vernon, for instance. She was younger than he, well preserved, well mannered, charming, cosmopolitan and rich, whereas he was a drink-sodden actor living in squalor. There should have been no doubt which of them was the more important, but he had the presumption to forget her.

She creamed her neck viciously, slapping the skin to increase circulation. Jacky lay watching, propped up on slippery satin pillows. He said nothing because earlier gambits had been shot down in flames. "Honey's been out in the garden again," she said. "Almost every morning she's out there, sometimes with that friend of hers. What's her name?"

"Matilda."

"You said she was an experience. She seemed to me very ordinary and homely. Dull. What's so special about her?"

"Hard to explain," said Jacky. Most of Matilda's early exploits were unsuitable for Madeline's ears. He and Till had worked as a pair when he was cruising for older women; she had acted as straight woman to cover him at hotels and at parties while he roved in search of earlier Madelines. They both enjoyed inventing and embroidering impromptu lies. "She's an original," he said. "She's entirely independent. She makes up her own mind."

"Surely we all do that?" said Madeline.

Jacky refused to agree that Madeline made up her own mind, or indeed that she had a mind at all. Jacky was no intellectual himself but he knew intelligent people and he registered the fact without envy, as he registered money or influence or charm.

When Madeline realised he wasn't going to answer she pressed on with an edge to her voice. "She doesn't have a man, does she?"

"No."

"She isn't moneyed?" Madeline loved this word, which she had picked up from her English daughter-in-law. She used it incessantly, to Jacky's irritation.

"No, she isn't moneyed."

"Oh my," said Madeline.

"She isn't moneyed, but she's brained and hearted."

"Oh," said Madeline, taken aback by his obstinacy and the implication that money wasn't important. "But she isn't at all good to look at. She isn't even an actress any more."

"Ben loves her," said Jacky, reckless.

"Ben? Pandora's husband?" Madeline was furious. She had a hammerlock on most aspects of reality, but about sex she deluded herself, still assuming that if she felt an attraction for someone it would be returned. She often thought about Ben, and she was looking forward to that evening when she was going to dinner at his house. "Now that, if you'll pardon me, I find hard to believe. Unless it was a very long time ago."

"Twenty years ago, but it's still going on."

"I don't believe it."

"Believe it," said Jacky. "I'm going to have my bath."

*

It was two o'clock in the morning and Till lay on her bedroom floor trying to keep up with Jane Fonda's voice. Fonda was strengthening her abdominal muscles. Till was moaning.

There was shouting in the street outside; not unusual. In a pause in the exercise tape Till realised that the noise outside was singing, a drunken baritone rendering of a Harry Belafonte number almost as old as Till's abdominal muscles.

> "Matilda, Matilda—
> Matilda, she take me money
> And run Venezuela!"

Another voice joined in, a rich West Indian bass with a better feel for calypso rhythm.

"Matilda, Matilda—"

"All right, Ben, all right," called Matilda out of the basement window, then scrambled up the stairs to open the front door. A tubby West Indian pensioner supported Ben, who was swaying. "Thanks," said Till, helping Ben inside. "Would you like a drink?" she asked the black man.

"No, I thank you kindly," he said, and wandered away still singing.

"God, you're heavy," said Till trying to manoeuvre Ben down the narrow stairs.

"So're you."

He lay on the sofa, his feet dangling over the end, and it was as if he had never been away. "Are you alone?" he said.

"Yes. Do you want coffee?"

"Not to say want. It might be a good idea. Why are you wearing a tracksuit?"

"Aerobics."

"They're not very effective."

"Did you come here to list my physical defects?"

"If I did it'd be a long visit."

"You're still angry with me?" The last time she'd seen Ben he hadn't been angry, he'd been crying, partly from shock at his wife's suicide, partly because Till had told him their relationship was over; but she had known then that eventually he would be angry.

"No," he said, but he was. He watched her moving round, noting every detail of her ageing, pleased. He drank the coffee, laid his head back, loosened his black tie and closed his eyes.

"What happened to your lover?" he asked.

"Which one?"

"The one you left me for."

"We agreed to part."

"Has he recovered from his injuries?"

"We parted a year ago."

"I hope you gave him a long-service medal. Have you had anyone since?"

"Yes. Just to tide me over. He wanted the relationship to last three weeks, I wanted a year."

"What happened?"

"We compromised."

"Nine months?"

Till laughed. "Spot on. How drunk are you?"

"Fairly. I've been on the wagon for weeks, then Pandora gave a Pardoe party and I couldn't stand it. I behaved badly. Leo was trying to persuade Honey's lodger woman to back a musical version of *Macbeth*."

"Pandora'll never get any money out of her."

"You think that, I think that, the Pardoes don't think. So when Madeline asked me if I thought Leo would be a success as the singing thane, I said, 'a ham's gotta do what a ham's gotta do.'"

"Naughty Ben."

"Smack knees," agreed Ben. "Then, of course, the Pardoes closed ranks round Daddy. I started crawling about the carpet bleating, 'Pardoes good, two legs bad'.

Fortunately Pandora thought I was blind drunk, but I think Circe's husband recognised it."

"Possible. He read a book once."

"Then he lay very still in a darkened room till the fever passed."

"Cheap, Ben."

Ben stretched his arms luxuriously. He could show off for Till, he could make feeble jokes; he could be silent, so he didn't want to be. "More coffee," he said.

"Does Pandora know where you are now?"

"I think she thinks I'm with my current girl. A production assistant."

"Blonde, vivacious, twenty-five?"

"Give or take."

"Take, I expect, knowing you."

"Are you jealous?"

"No."

" 'Matilda told such DREADFUL lies It made one gasp and stretch one's eyes,' " chanted Ben. Till said nothing. It was easier if he assumed she was jealous of his women, though she had repeatedly denied it; that belief prevented him from seeing what she was really jealous of, his work and his wives. Watching him lying on her sofa in her flat she wanted to keep him, she wanted his permanent presence, she wanted him to need her and she knew the only way to ensure it was to keep him uncertain of her feelings and her intentions. She had lost count of the affairs conducted with other men to keep Ben interested. Now, the device wearied her.

When she could have married him, after his first wife died, she had chosen not to because of her children. They disliked him: he disliked them: he disregarded children, thought them a nuisance. A divorce was hard enough on the children without adding to it stepfather Ben. It had been one of the most selfless decisions of her life. She didn't regret it, but she bitterly missed Ben, still,

still. And here he was, as much part of her as the flat, as her children, as her acting.

"Why are you hurting Pandora?"

"She loves me too much. I can't take any more Pardoes. I'm not happy, Till. She's – a nothing."

"She's just Pandora."

"That programme of hers. *Cupid*. She thinks it's wonderful, keeps replaying it on video. You know that bloody song she sings at the end?" He squeaked in imitation. "'I'll be right here playing Cupid/ though chance makes guys and gals look stupid/ We'll put that right with a warm greeting/ For journeys end in lovers' meeting.' She asked me if I liked it. I almost told her, but I'm trying to be kind, so I said, 'Pity they used the Shakespeare line.' Do you know what she said?"

Till shook her head. She only spoilt Ben's punch lines when thoroughly annoyed.

"She said, 'Which line is that?'"

Till laughed.

"And she has that bloody laugh," he said, reminded. "Publicity hand-outs call her chuckle 'infectious'. Like Aids and bubonic plague, I suppose. When she's cross with me her eyes bulge. They're already too close to her nose. When they bulge her face looks like a nouvelle cuisine arrangement of two grapes and a sliver of chicory garnishing a blanquette de veau."

"Don't bitch," said Till. "Drink your coffee. Have you had any trouble from your production assistant?"

"Not yet. No nesting, no clinging. I don't think she's got the Filofax insert for womanly feelings yet."

"Perhaps she doesn't want you."

"Remote possibility. Till . . ."

"Here."

"I can't write."

Till seized this most intimate of admissions, filed it for consolatory recall. "Any idea why?"

"Don't be ridiculous. If I had any idea what was wrong, don't you think I'd change it?"

"You might not be able to."

"And stop being so bloody understanding. Let's go to bed."

"Why?"

"I want to talk to you and my back hurts on this sofa."

"Won't Pandora worry if you're out all night?"

"Since when did you care about Pandora's feelings?"

"She's married to you now."

"Since when did you care about marriage? 'If it isn't working, you're better off out of it.' The gospel according to Matilda."

"I'm older now. So're you. Time is running out. Make the best of what you've got."

Ben groaned. "Set that to music and you could enter it for the Eurovision Song Contest. If I want clichés I can get them at home, but I want to stay with you and hear some new-minted ideas, like how you can wave a wand and turn me into Shakespeare."

"I'm fresh out. No can do."

"I'll settle for Tennessee Williams. C'mon, Till. You know you want me to stay."

Till wouldn't deny it. She lusted after him. It was the way his hair grew on his neck, she thought, the beautiful heaviness of the locky hair and the brown smoothness of his neck. She wanted to stroke his neck, unbutton his shirt . . .

"You're licking your lips, Matilda."

"You flatter yourself."

"I know that look. To my cost."

"To your pleasure."

"And that's God's truth. Do you have a current man?"

"I do," lied Till, her instincts pulling her to the old serviceable deceptions.

"Who is he, then? Do I know him?"

"I'm not telling you. He wants me to be discreet."

Ben laughed till he choked. "He wants *you* to be discreet? How long has he known you?"

"I promised," said Till primly. "And I promised that I wouldn't make love to anyone else, so no chance, Benjamin. I'll talk to you in bed, but that's all."

Benjamin, who had only wanted to talk to Till and had assumed that she would want sex and he would reluctantly accede to her demands, felt the stirrings of arousal. "You're making it up," he said sharply. She shrugged. He was annoyed. "You're not exactly desirable. He must be hard up." She shrugged again. "Nice guide dog, has he?"

"Just as well you're not writing if that's the standard of your material. It's your choice, Ben. You can stay here tonight and talk to me. In the morning, by eight-thirty, you leave. I'll make you breakfast."

"Not that! Anything but that! You still can't cook. You haven't even learnt to make coffee."

"I use coffee bags."

"You would."

"My lover doesn't like them either."

"Fuck your lover."

"It's going to be very very difficult for me, Honey," said Florence. Her eyes were bleary, her mascara smudged from half an hour's steady crying. She huddled pathetically into the least respectable of her mangy fur coats. "Can't you turn the heating up?"

"It's perfectly warm, Mother," said Honey. She controlled her trembling with a massive effort. She was upset but determined, and knew that if she once showed weakness Florence would be at her throat.

"Old age pensioners like me are dying of hypothermia all over London," said Florence. "I haven't been able to pay my gas bill yet. They're threatening to cut me off. I depended on my commission from you. I'm getting on, I don't have much to look forward to, I'm lonely, Lord knows work is hard to find, my rates have gone up, it's not as easy as it was finding men friends to help out, what am I going to do?"

"You haven't managed to save any capital?" Honey knew the answer but had to go through the routine. She still, despite a lifetime's evidence to the contrary, hoped that Florence might acknowledge the claims of reason and justice.

"Capital, capital, you sound like a man. I haven't any sodding money and that's the truth, and no means of earning any. What are you going to do about it?"

"I'll pay you an allowance if you like."

"I don't want your charity. I want my commission. I want you back at work doing what you were designed by nature to do, strut your stuff and smile your smile and rake in the money and pay some of it to me. Where would you be if it wasn't for me? I gave you the start, now here you sit in Campden Hill Road on a trust with enough capital to buy British Telecom outright and your old mother is thrown out to starve in the Earl's Court Road. We had good times, Honey. When you were a little girl I looked after you and taught you and got you work and fed you . . ."

"That's what mothers are supposed to do," said Honey quietly.

"Not my kind of mother."

"I'm not that rich," Honey persisted, "but if you'll talk sensibly about money I'll make a deal. I am never going to work again. Not for the foreseeable future."

"I'll have to talk to the accountant about it, see what you can afford."

"I already spoke to him."

Florence gulped and lit a cigarette from the stub of her current one. "I always handle business for you."

"He's *my* accountant, though, and it's *my* money."

"If you're going to adopt that attitude – What is it, Honey, what terrible thing have I done to you, tell your

106

old mother, I don't deserve this, get me some brandy, you were always so sweet-natured, everyone loves you because you're so biddable, you'll get hard, it'll show in your face and blondes can't afford to look hard, specially not with your looks, I can see them fading now, little lines at the eyes and hardness around the mouth, no wonder Steve left you, he found you too hard and unyielding, it's not as if you have any brain or charm to offer, if you aren't sweet and biddable you have nothing, and get some make-up on, it makes me sick to see you without it, you look faded and yellow and your eyelashes vanish."

"Please don't," said Honey, and sat on her hands so her mother wouldn't see them shake. "We'll talk to the accountant together and decide what you can have."

"I don't want *charity*," shouted Florence. "I don't want you uppity with me. I thought you had proper feelings, Honey, I've been sadly mistaken in you, sadly mistaken. You're unbalanced, that's what it is, having that abortion has turned your brain, not that there was much to turn, lucky for that child you didn't have it . . ."

"Please go away, Mother," said Honey through stiff lips. Florence, horrified, saw she meant it.

"Don't say that, you wouldn't ask your mother to leave, we only have each other, we're alone in the world. Honey?"

Honey fetched a glass of brandy; Florence gulped it. Her teeth, some her own, clattered against the glass. "I'm frightened, can't you see that?" she said aggressively. "You're changing and I don't know what to do." In the face of her mother's helplessness, neither did Honey. She had nerved herself to face a familiar, bullying Florence, but she was not prepared for a genuine capitulation, as this appeared to be. She saw Florence's hands, grubby with dirt encrusted round the peeling scarlet nail varnish, gardener's hands though she never touched even a window-box, old hands gripping the brandy glass, and she almost relented. Then she saw Florence's eyes squinting slyly up through a fringe of much-dyed hair and knew it was a trick.

"I've made up my mind," said Honey. Florence recognised the tone and the expression and knew her cause was lost. Once Honey had set her jaw in that mulish way, she would stick to her purpose until exhaustion set in, and beyond. Florence had seen it and rejoiced in it often enough as the child was growing up. When Honey was confronted with a task that frightened her, that she was convinced was beyond her but that must be carried through, once she gritted her teeth and began to tremble, then Florence had known she would do it. "Do you remember when I taught you to tap-dance?" she said.

Honey remembered. As soon as her first film was finished, the day after her seventh birthday, she had expected to rest, recover, go back to being a child at school. Florence had kept her going through the terrifying weeks of shooting by saying, "Soon be over, soon be over," and the child had faced the cameras counting the days till shooting finished and she could stop being tested and, as she thought, failing, every day. But as soon as the film finished Florence hustled round for more work for her and three months later she found some – if Honey could tap-dance.

She picked Honey up from her small primary school one bright June afternoon. Honey was clutching a piece of paper, a certificate for the best handwriting in her form. Florence glanced at it perfunctorily. "That's not important now. You've got an audition tomorrow morning, and tonight you learn a tap-dance routine." She hustled her onto the tube, through the rush-hour crowds who jostled and pushed, with Florence gripping the child's wrist in case they were separated. Honey lagged behind trying to read the advertising posters. She was a dreamy, reflective child when Florence allowed her to be. They stopped at a dance shop and Honey was fitted with white tap shoes. "We'll have to rough those up before the audition. They look too new," said Florence as they reached home, a room in a street off the Earl's Court Road given over entirely to cheap hotels. It was on the first floor, a slice of the drawing-room of the original house, with a large window whose light was blocked by a sign which Florence, when she remembered, nagged the Greek owner to remove. "Self-catering facilities in all rooms," the sign said.

Honey tried to put on the shoes, wrestling in vain with the stiff buttons, while Florence boiled a kettle on the self-catering facility, a gas-ring so grease-encrusted that each time it was used a smell of rancid fat permeated the room. "What's tap-dancing?" said Honey, gingerly walking in the heavy shoes.

"Drink your tea then I'll show you. Wind up the gramophone, look alive."

They had a record of Fred Astaire singing "Top Hat". Florence wound and demonstrated and wound and shouted and Honey, slowly, painfully, began to acquire some simple tap steps. She was well co-ordinated and, later, a good dancer, but at seven she was still very unpolished; Florence's hysteria frightened her; with each scream Honey was more wooden, more left-footed, and soon completely exhausted. She dreaded making a complete fool of herself at the audition, and she dreaded getting the part, because then she would have to work on another film.

After three hours Florence called a break, opened a tin of sweetened condensed milk, a recognised treat, and they sat side by side on the bed eating it with spoons. "I can't do it," said Honey. "Mum, I can't do it."

"You have to," said Florence. "Otherwise we'll starve." She had found that simple threats worked. "We'll have no food."

"Not even condensed milk and tomato soup?"

"Not even that. I owe the bank lots and lots of money

and there aren't any jobs for me. You *have* to work, Honey, there's a good girl. Do this for Mummy. You've almost learnt the steps."

"I haven't," said Honey, "and I'm getting worse, not better. Are you sure we'd starve? I have school lunches."

"What about me?"

"I could bring my seconds back in a handkerchief. Morag's father doesn't work, and they don't starve." Morag was her best friend, a small canny Scots girl, daughter of a trade union activist. "She says we live in a thing called the wafer state and that means the state gives you money if you don't have any. Haven't you heard about it? Morag says it happened after the war."

"The wafer state isn't for us," said Florence, as usual making no attempt to unravel Honey's ramblings. "The wafer state's only for Scots people and the working class. We're better than that, Honey. We're real people who have to earn our living. Unless I can find another uncle for you."

This threat was enough to convince Honey. She hated the uncles. The hotel room was bleak but at least partly her own place. When they lived in men's flats or houses she felt like an unwanted piece of furniture, like a folding bed, who should be packed into a small space and kept in a cupboard. She finished her condensed milk, wiped her mouth, and set her jaw.

She learnt the steps and performed them well enough to get the part. After that Florence moved her to the stage school because there at least she would learn some dance, even though there were fees to be found, usually two terms in arrears. Honey made no friends after that; she worked too consistently.

"Yes, I remember the tap-dancing," said Honey, for whom it was one of the worst memories of a harrowing childhood. "Why?"

"Because I worked very hard to teach you those steps. We worked nearly all night and I gave you all I had.

It was tiring and boring but I went ahead and did it for you. Remember that, Honey, when we start talking money."

Honey stared at her mother in amazement. Clearly, Florence saw the incident as reflecting well on herself. There was no reconciling two such opposing points of view, though Honey made a massive effort to see it Florence's way; perhaps she had been an unusually timid and incompetent child.

"We'll see the accountant tomorrow," said Florence quite cheerfully. "Pass the brandy bottle, there's a good girl."

"My time with Madeline is running out," said Jacky. "Do you think this mascara is too much?" He was studying himself in Honey's dressing-room mirrors. Her face appeared behind him, serious in consideration of the important issue.

"You're using the evening lighting," she pointed out. "Here." She flipped a switch and the lights round the mirrors changed to a much bluer daytime glow. "Depends how macho you want to look," she said. "It's very effective but it makes a definite statement."

"Do you think it'll annoy her son, the international banker who lives in Weybridge?"

"I'd need to know more about his sex preferences to answer that."

"Sex is what happens with your equally rich wife to prevent her from leaving with her money and the presentable children. Homosexuals are degenerate Aids carriers with Marxist views. Sex education should not be taught in schools; the family unit is all-important."

"You'll annoy him. Do you want to?"

"Probably. Madeline's getting on my nerves."

"Impossible, you don't have any. What you mean is, you're getting the itch to move on."

"Could be," acknowledged Jacky, experimenting with

111

eyeliner. "There's no future in it and I have to work very hard."

"Do you want some coffee?"

"I'll make it." Jacky made coffee and Honey watched him in companionable silence. Unusually for him, he showed signs of wanting to confide in her rather than sing for his coffee by listening; he had popped down for a chat while Madeline was at the hairdresser and Honey was glad enough to see him. After Florence's departure she felt sick and shaken, and Jacky's burble was a soothing bath in which to recover. "Madeline's grandchildren call her Aunt Madeline," he said. "Rather strong, don't you think? I don't like her son. He's forty-five and looks older and Madeline is very torn because she's possessive about him but doesn't like them being seen together in public because she thinks he makes her look older, though between you, me and the mascara, what could?"

"Why don't you like the son?"

"He's bigoted, smug and stupid. I know I live on bigoted, smug and stupid people but when they're women I don't mind, because they're so vulnerable and I can spread a little happiness."

"And gain a little cash."

"That too. The son's mind is like a conveyor belt, churning relentlessly after money; he doesn't spend it. His wife is worse. She's English and she looks down on Madeline because she's American and she sets her lips in a tight line when anything offends her ideas of what is smart, and she wouldn't help someone dying in the gutter unless they went to the right school."

"Don't tell me you're developing a social conscience in your old age?"

Jacky shuddered, curling his feet under him in the armchair, wrapping his hands round the coffee mug, instinctively shifting from one graceful pose to another. "Don't say old age, don't mention the passing years."

"You could still pass for thirty."

"That's not good enough. I'm forty-three next birthday and I need to find a rich wife."

"Really no hope of Madeline?"

"No. And she won't let me meet any of her rich friends. I'm always off duty when there are unattached women who she dreads picking me up and carrying me off in their bearer bonds. She likes to show me off; I have to arrive at the end of parties so everyone can see what she has to come home to, but I don't get to talk to any of them long enough to get a toe-hold. Also – I'm worried about Aids."

"Your test was negative, you said?"

"Yes, but it's going to cut down my cruising. The lights are going out all over San Francisco, Honey, and they won't be lit again in my lifetime. I don't like the prospect. I'm beginning to feel the chill winds of eighties' morality, and I need a good solid meal-ticket for protection. So I'll have to junk Madeline, but I'd prefer her to junk me. You know how I hate hurting people. So I thought if I could pick a fight with her son I'd be out on my ear and everyone would be happy. I could wear an earring, of course. That would incense him."

"Where would you live?"

"I've still got that room in Westbourne Grove, the studio flat. I could play poker for a while. I have a standing invitation to a game in Hong Kong."

"Do you still cheat?"

Jacky shuddered again. "Don't say that either. Sometimes I help the deal along a little, but cheating at cards – no gentleman would do that, and you know I'm the perfect gentleman. Thanks for the coffee and the company, Honey. Sometimes I get tired of never saying what I think and feel. That's the trouble with my line of work. I lie so much I never believe what I say."

"You can believe me," said Honey.

"I do," said Jacky. "You are the nicest, kindest, straightest human being I've ever had the pleasure of meeting."

"What about Till?"

"She's the kindest crookedest human being. Seriously, Honey, you have a rare gift. Being with you is as easy as being alone, and much more pleasant."

"Do you think I'd be a good mother?" asked Honey. Florence's words were needling her.

"The best. Are you having a baby?"

"Not at the moment, but I want one. Can you keep a secret, Jacky?"

"No," said Jacky. "Not as a general rule. Who don't you want me to tell?"

"Madeline and the media."

"I can manage that."

"What do you think about sperm banks?"

"Very little. It's not a subject that has intruded on my life so far. I once tried to be a sperm donor in California, I thought it would be more lucrative than blood, but it turned out to be less and you have to keep turning up every week and wanking into a dish and the stimulating material they offer you is heterosexual. So I decided against it. If I need petty cash, poker is less damaging to the susceptibilities. I like to think there's romance in life."

Honey was only briefly distracted by this uncharacteristic statement from someone whom, if she had known the words, she would have regarded as the supreme sexual pragmatist. Her interest in sperm banks was much greater than her interest in Jacky's value system. "I want a baby."

"Quite right too," approved Jacky. "Most women do, I find. One of the reasons I always choose post-menopausal lovers. And you're considering sperm banks? What's wrong with the traditional method?"

"If I can't have Steve's child I don't want anybody's."

114

"But you would be having somebody's, you just wouldn't know who he was."

"That's what I want." Once she had started to talk it all spilled out, now she was set free to explain what she had been brooding over and incubating for weeks. "I don't want to love anyone else. I don't want a man, I can't deal with them, I've been thinking about myself and what's the matter with me and I just don't think I know how to cope with relationships. I pick one person and cling to them and suck the life out of them by clinging, that's what I learnt and it's too late to change, I can't bear to be alone and so I hang on. I have to learn to be alone before I have another man but it's getting too late to have a baby, my berlogical clock is ticking and ticking and the alarm will soon go off and there I'll be, without a child or ever the chance of one. I want to go on, Jacky, I don't want to just die when I die, I want there to be people who remember me as a mother and grandmother and maybe even great-grandchildren who'll watch my films and know it was me and they have my blood."

"Of course you do," said Jacky.

"Do you really understand?" Honey was touched and delighted. She always feared, when she put forward an idea or a plan, that whoever she told about it would point out some obvious, central flaw which any normal, intelligent person would have thought of before.

"I understand completely," said Jacky. He hadn't been listening. He was wondering if he could persuade Madeline that his birthday was imminent and that she should buy him some luggage. His last set of Louis Vuitton had gone to a gambler in settlement of a debt. He couldn't leave Madeline with dignity until he had some suitcases to pack his clothes in, and although he thought Louis Vuitton luggage vulgar unless you were Louis Vuitton, as of course the only initials one displays are one's own, at least they impressed hotel staff. Honey was still talking.

115

". . . and in this country it'll be too difficult, because it's all controlled by doctors and they seem to want you to be married or at least present a man who wants to be a father. I've tried two places. But America's always different and that's where I'm going."

"Absolutely right," said Jacky, his large and beautiful eyes fixed on hers with simulated attention.

"You think so?" Honey felt the enterprise flowering under his encouragement. "You don't find anything – disgusting – in the idea?"

"Not in the least. I don't see how any sensitive person could," said Jacky, uncertain whether she was referring to America or sperm banks or perhaps some other element of her scheme she had mentioned while he was thinking about luggage.

"Oh, Jacky!" She kissed and hugged him. He didn't mind, even though she was a younger woman and he usually shrank from their touch, because she was so beautiful and unsexual. He kissed her back and she sat on his lap being cuddled. "You'll make a wonderful mother," he said genuinely. If he hadn't had his own mother he could imagine wanting Honey. She was so delicate, so vulnerable; a delight for a son to dress, escort and protect. Honey was crying gently. "I hope so," she said. "I'd do my absolute best. I'd read all the books and love my child, absolutely love it, and never make it act."

"Did you hate the acting?"

"Yes."

"But you were so good at it."

"I don't care. It was awful, a nightmare, and I'd never put any child of mine through it. I'll send them to proper schools and get them coaching if they fall behind. They might even go to university. Can you imagine that, a child of mine?"

"Do you plan to have more than one?" Jacky shifted slightly. Her weight was creasing his trousers.

"Yes. I want two because I don't think it's fair being an only child."

"I enjoyed it," said Jacky. "You can have such a lovely relationship, just a mother and son." Honey felt but did not say that perhaps Jacky was not a good example of the arrangement. She sensed his unease and got up. He waited till her back was turned to stand up and smooth out his trousers. "I'll have to go upstairs," he said. "You are kind to listen to my grumblings."

"And you to mine. Don't you ever get tired of listening to women?"

"Only when they're Madeline. When I love them like I love you – that's a different matter, not professional; listening from the heart."

"And keep it secret about the sperm banks, please."

"When are you going?"

"Next week." She imagined the plane ticket, now waiting for her at Thomas Cook's in the High Street; she imagined the trip, the search and the discovery that she was sure would result. She also thought about the magazine clipping she was using as a bookmark in *Mucus*, describing how a woman in America went to a genius sperm bank, a single woman who now had (so she said) a brilliant little boy. But the woman had been university-educated herself, so presumably, Honey thought, she must be very bright. Anyway, the idea of genius sperm appealed. Till had once explained that children were a mixture of their parents' genes and she imagined a child halfway between her brain power and genius being at least normally intelligent.

Jacky took their coffee mugs, washed them, dried them and wiped the draining-board.

It was early evening, already dark, and Till was walking home through the drizzle, which she didn't notice. She felt exuberant, omnipotent. It was the day after Ben's appearance. He was back, and even if he never saw her again, which she promised herself she would try to persuade him was the right course of action, at least he had shown interest; he still, in his peculiar way, loved her. Or needed her. There was still a bond between them. She treasured the bond and thought about his writing. Why had he stopped? What could help him to start again? It was an excellent problem; partly professional, with an extra spice of personal involvement. Till felt happy. She was talking to herself, attracting curious glances. She crossed the road, thinking about her last patient that day, a woman whose childhood was absolutely the worst she had ever heard described, yet who refused to cherish it as an accomplishment, unlike other patients who had to be constantly reassured that their parents had been iniquitous. At last there was some improvement, definite improvement in the patient. Perhaps her work was worthwhile after all, perhaps she was producing results. Then practicality reminded her that the therapist who stroked patients' feet also claimed results and her optimism was dashed, but only briefly.

She turned off Ladbroke Grove down a side street to the local shop. Ahead of her was a small knot of people gathered around a recumbent figure. She usually enjoyed street incidents but tonight she wanted to get home and sort out her clothes. She'd told Ben she had a lover; if he reappeared and she was to make her fiction convincing she would at least have to spruce herself up, be a woman who had a lover rather than a woman who had been wearing the same battered skirt for the last month. She might even go out and buy some new clothes; certainly she should get a rinse for her hair to mix in the streaks of grey, perhaps make an appointment with a decent hairdresser for a fashionable cut, insofar as that was possible given the limitations of her hair.

"Leave me alone!" a familiar voice shouted. "I'm perfectly all right, leave me alone!"

It was Vernon Cole. She went to see what was

happening. He was lying face down on the pavement with his arm down a grating, groping ineffectually for something. Astride him stood a very short woman in her sixties, dressed in the incongruous clothing of a bag lady, setting about her with a broken umbrella. "Will you all mind your own business for the love of God and leave the master alone, before I set the police on you?" Beside her stood, hackles up, a balding and mangy mongrel, mostly black with the usual mongrel yellow-white patch over one eye. He growled threateningly. Fumes of whisky ascended from where Vernon lay.

"He's drunk," muttered an outraged middle-aged woman, one of those whose lives are fuelled by outrage. "Disgusting. Making an exhibition of himself in the street."

Vernon looked up from his labours. "Madam, I assure you that I never, ever, make a *free* exhibition of myself. I am merely trying to recover some property."

"And lucky you are to watch it, and honoured you are," began the Irishwoman with the umbrella, "for isn't he the greatest actor you'll ever see . . ."

"It's that chap from *The Jewel in the Crown*," said another woman.

"Sure and he was never asked to that series which was a shame and a disgrace," said the Irishwoman.

"It doesn't matter, Biddy," said Vernon. "Ignore these people and have a look. Can you see it?"

The mongrel chose that moment to attack the outraged woman, who withdrew muttering that she would have the police on them for owning a savage dog. "Hello, Vernon," said Till. "Can I help?"

"Probably," said Vernon. "Good to see you, Matilda. Can you disperse the crowd? They're in my light. I need to see down the grating, and they appear to be convinced that I am ill or drunk, which is not the case." He sounded sober.

"What've you lost?" asked a young, be-suited man.

"I dropped something down this grating," said Vernon, "and I am trying to recover it. 'That is all ye know on earth and all ye need to know,'" he intoned in his rich, booming stage voice. "Please go away, all of you, or I shall recite to you from the works of John Keats the Romantic poet."

"I like a bit of romance, myself," said the woman who had wrongly identified him as being in *The Jewel in the Crown*. "Were you in *Brief Encounter*?"

"I am only Trevor Howard on Tuesdays," said Vernon.

Fortunately at that moment the screech of tyres and the crunch of metal and glass signalled that an accident had taken place fifty yards up Ladbroke Grove. Several of the group appeared to feel that this was more promising even than Vernon's one-man show, and when loud voices were raised in altercation the knot of people wavered and broke, hastening towards not only an accident but also a fight. When they had gone Till squatted beside Vernon. "Shall I try?" she said.

"Do." He heaved himself up, assisted by the Irishwoman. "You're looking for my rug. Foolish accident. I dropped a bottle of whisky and trying to prevent it from breaking I dislodged my rug; it's easily my best and we start shooting next week."

Till peered into the grating; no sign of the wig. She slipped her hand through a broken bar and felt for it, resolutely blocking her mind to the other objects she touched in this endeavour, almost asphyxiated by the fumes of whisky emanating from the nearby, shattered bottle. At last she found the wig and fished it out. "It'll have to go to the cleaners," she said. "It smells awful." All three of them gazed at the smelly mat of hair, and the dog made an ineffectual lunge at it, evidently identifying it as a small animal.

"My dear, come and have a drink and a wash," said Vernon. "You too, Biddy. Thanks for your help." Three of them and dog went up to Vernon's flat, which was even grubbier than Till had remembered it. "I'll have to change," said Vernon. The front of his suit was sodden and stained from the wet pavement, which almost concealed its accretion of food and drink stains. "You two help yourselves."

He vanished and Till was left alone with the Irish-woman. "I'm Biddy Keefe," she said, "Sir Vernon's maid. I've just been cleaning which is why the flat looks better. Sure and himself is a difficult man to keep straight but we work on it, don't we, Othello?"

The mongrel looked up lovingly and collapsed across Biddy's feet in a paroxysm of foolish affection. "I'm Matilda Livesey," said Till. "I'm glad to meet you, Sir Vernon's mentioned you to me. Why do you call your dog Othello?"

"Sir Vernon called him, maybe on account of his jealous temper. He's a very affectionate dog and good company. Not that I live alone mind you. Men are so important and if you live alone you go queer, so I keep Conor though sure and he's a trial; the dog has more sense." Biddy was producing an assortment of drinks from odd cupboards and the refrigerator while Till washed at the sink. "Take your choice. I'll be having the gin if himself asks me. Mostly he doesn't ask me so I make do with the leftovers and he doesn't notice or if he notices he doesn't care so no harm done."

"Orange juice," said Till, helping herself.

"Orange juice when you're offered the hard stuff. It's easy to see you've never seen the whites of hardship's eye. God bless you I hope you never do, though you're no chicken so the shadows will be closing in tomorrow or the next day, for sure."

"I hope not," said Till, watching amused as the woman poured gin into a saucer for the dog.

"We can all hope, can we not, but it's pissing in the wind as Conor would say. He's a vulgar man but better than nothing and the remains of a fine tenor."

"Do you live near here?"

"Two streets up, in the council block."

"I live in that road too."

"You'll live in the gentrified houses with all the Yuppies and their little black cars that park outside our block so we can't get to the rubbish bins."

Biddy was very small and thin but her eyes were bright and alert and her rag-bag of clothes had been chosen with an eye for bright colours, topped off by a red hat with a purple feather stuck in its brim. She enthusiastically supped the gin and urged Till into the living-room. "Do you have a full life? Would you say you're fulfilled? I wouldn't exactly say that about myself but it's a question I learned to ask at the women's group I attend on the Tuesdays. I wasn't so eager for the inspection of my genitals. Not that I object to genitals but at my time of life no part of my body can bear much inspection, but the girl who runs the group has a way with her, and she said to me, 'Biddy,' she said, 'if it'll discomfort you inspecting the inner labia then surely you don't have to for the most powerful sexual organ is the mind.'"

"I'm fulfilled," said Till.

"That's grand. How many young ones have you?"

"Two. In the late teens, a boy and a girl. Not so young."

"They're always young to their mother, God bless them. I have only the one an important man in America and he sends money but isn't the whisky a terrible price for Conor?"

Vernon reappeared in a clean suit wearing his second-best wig. He looked remarkably healthy and Till said so. "Thank you, thank you. I've been drying out recently because as I told you, next week I start work in Hollywood. A cameo role in an American series adapted from a novel almost as long as the Bible and much duller. I saw Leo Pardoe last night and he doesn't look well at all, I'm afraid, and he's younger than I am."

"You were at Pandora and Ben's last night," said Till, jumping at the chance to mention Ben's name. "Was it fun?"

"Eventful. Benjamin was on form, insulting everybody. They'd asked that ghastly Madeline woman and she eyes me up and down like a prize pig at a fair. She has designs on me but I gave her short shrift."

"Don't you feel sorry for her?"

"Not in the least. If women are going to behave like men they must expect to be rejected now and then. God knows I've been rejected often enough."

Biddy brought him a weak whisky. "Don't complain at this now, sir. We've to keep your eyes and head clear for next week." She gazed at him, the dog gazed at her, each with the same adoring expression. It was a domestic scene. Till felt excluded, and, briefly, lonely. Ben's arrival had disturbed her equilibrium and the pattern of her life; she felt absurdly deprived because he wasn't there with her, because he would never be there with her.

"I must go home," she said, imagining Ben's telephone call ringing in her empty flat.

Chapter Seven

Honey never wrote letters.

Late for work, Till grabbed her post from the pigeonhole in the hall of the flats and scuttled down the front steps, riffling through the bills for real letters and through the real letters for Ben's writing. She didn't find it. A week had passed and no message from Ben. What did you expect, she told herself, not expecting herself to listen. It was only halfway to work that she recovered from the disappointment sufficiently to look again, and recognise Honey's careful childlike hand. "dearest Till, I haev gone to the USA by miself. I will be bcak next weke, all news than, love Sarah (Honey)."

To America? By herself? To the best of Till's knowledge, Honey had never hitherto gone further by herself than Bond Street. Good girl, she thought opening her other letter.

It was from Amanda's headmistress. "Dear Mrs Livesey, I have been trying to reach you on the telephone but have received no reply, although Amanda tells me you are in London. Perhaps you have been busy recently with social engagements." The headmistress didn't approve of Till, much preferred her ex-husband. "In the normal course of events I would have approached Colonel Livesey but as you probably know he is currently in the South Atlantic.

"Unfortunately Amanda has been discovered smoking; to compound the offence, she chose to smoke in my study. Smoking is a very serious offence and as Amanda has been cautioned on two previous occasions I have no alternative but to ask that you come to see me as a matter of urgency to discuss her future here and the options open to us."

Honey chose her clothes for the trip very carefully. She wanted to seem self-assured, efficient, happy; independent enough to be a single parent, loving and sociable enough to be a good one. She took only as many clothes as she could pack as hand baggage; she was only staying a few days. Her return ticket was open. In the travel agent's a week ago, not booking a return flight had given her a sensation of freedom, but now in the taxi on the way to Heathrow as she checked her ticket for the hundredth time it added to her pervasive anxiety. Could she check into hotels by herself? Would she be able to cope with the clinics? What if she had entirely misunderstood the article and Americans, like the English, didn't give single women sperm? What if the article was simply inaccurate, as magazines so often were?

She sorted through her travelling handbag. Passport, ticket, money – dollars, pounds – the address, obtained from American directory enquiries, of the Significant Seminal Resource, the genius sperm bank near San Francisco, and a small dictionary, in case she had to fill in forms, always an ordeal. She also carried *Mucus*, which she was now halfway through.

The first set-back came earlier than even she had expected. At check-in she was told that her flight was delayed for five hours. All round her passengers complained and some bustled off to transfer to other flights. Instead of trying herself she accepted the check-in clerk's offer of a room at a nearby hotel to rest and wait, and followed the cowed group who had also chosen this option to the airport hotel.

Once inside the room which was panelled in plastic wood and dominated by a huge television, she lay on the bed looking through the net curtains into a landscaped

125

inner courtyard with drooping tub trees, gripped by an enervating sensation of anticlimax. Now she wouldn't be in New York until evening; she faced four hours, at least, in this room which reminded her of every hotel she'd ever stayed in with Steve. She expected him to open the door and start complaining about the inefficiency of airlines, the inadequacy of the hotel. The disruption of her arrangements so early was a bad omen, a sign that the purpose of her trip was obscurely cursed. She tried to sleep but failed; daytime television didn't keep her attention and the video channel was showing a disaster movie. As one aeroplane ploughed into another she wondered if this too was an omen. The device provided for coffee-making was broken and when she had packed and repacked her case several times she was left without resource.

She had a voucher for a free meal. She felt food would choke her, but she wandered downstairs to look at the restaurant. She passed a massive room decorated in fake wood and darkness, which announced itself as the Sir Walter Raleigh Bar. "Pop in and enjoy the atmosphere of a real English pub," the sign offered. Inside four Japanese were being served by a Spanish barman.

The restaurant was at the far side of the foyer which was decorated in red and black with vast tubular overhead lights and imitation leather chairs. Half empty, it was blocked by a large sign. "Please wait to be seated," it instructed. A queue of restive would-be diners was waiting and was not being seated. She puzzled her way through the menu displayed by the door. The cheapest item, "Wright Brothers' Hamburger With All The Trimmings", cost six pounds. Even though it was free to her Honey hesitated to charge the airline for food she would not eat.

Back in the foyer dazed travellers read and re-read the boards displaying information about airline departures. It was a limbo for people irritated by a breakdown in arrangements. A wave of loneliness overcame her and she escaped back to her room, started work on *Mucus*. One chapter and three hours later she returned to the foyer and asked the man on duty at the reception desk for news of her flight. She could have occupied more time reading the boards but she needed human contact. The man – the youth – bore a label, "Mark Palgrave, Asst. Manager". He was only just eighteen, if that. He had rashly decapitated his pimples with a close shave and his pale green eyes glinted a panic which receded when he realised how simple were Honey's demands, how genuine her gratitude.

She was dispirited by the information that the bus for her flight didn't leave for another hour. Back in her room, she watched the telephone. The temptation to ring Steve was strong; eventually she succumbed to it and listened to his answering machine for five minutes. Then she rang his sound recordist's wife.

Steve and the rest of the crew were in Las Vegas, staying at the Golden Nugget. Another omen, she thought. A clear indication that she was meant to see Steve on this trip. Las Vegas. That wasn't far from San Francisco; she could easily stop over and see him. Surely his anger would have subsided by now, surely he would be glad to see her, so far from home. There was always something appealing about meeting people one knew far from home. She resolutely ignored the fact that last time she had spoken to Steve he had been cold, determined, indifferent to her. She was convinced with the utter certainty of fantasy that it was ordained that she should see him now. She went back downstairs to the pimply Assistant Manager. He produced an airline map of America. Yes indeed, it would be easy to fly to Las Vegas for a day or two, to the Golden Nugget. "I have to meet a friend there," she said, to voice it into reality.

"A very exciting place, Las Vegas," said the Assistant Manager. "I've always wanted to go there." In his case, thought Honey, always must have been a very short time.

"Me too," said Honey, who had never previously given the place a thought. Suddenly it seemed attractive, bizarre. "What do you know about it?"

"Only what everyone knows. It's the place to gamble; casinos are open all night; Frank Sinatra appears there; you get cheap food if you gamble."

"Cheap food?"

"That's what I've heard."

"How generous."

"I expect they claw it back on the gambling profits. Nobody in the hotel business gives something for nothing," he said with the air of one who knew. He was delighted to have found a girl who was not only beautiful but also, though sophisticated in appearance, evidently even more naive than he.

Honey was imagining a city of philanthropists dedicated to the enjoyment of visitors, to making people happy. She was losing touch with reality at an accelerated rate, the dislocation increased by the limbo-like hotel and the inability to proceed with her journey. She had lost all sense of herself as a person with a past, future, and friends; she imagined herself arriving at this marvellously philanthropic place to be greeted by a delighted Steve who would welcome her back, then she needn't even go to the sperm banks.

"Why smoke in the headmistress's study?" said Till, turning onto the M40 and heading for London. Amanda, who was feeling frightened, disoriented and guilty, covered it with aggression.

"Why not?" She hunched up her long legs and propped her feet on the glove shelf, which was in imminent danger of collapse, silently daring her mother to object.

"Because you're more likely to get caught."

"Do you think I *wanted* to get thrown out before my A-levels?"

"Yes," said Till.

"Since you're so clever, can you tell me why?"

"No," said Till.

"You're a bloody awful mother," said Amanda bitterly. "I expected sympathy."

"I can't imagine why." Till was angry with her, not for the trifling misdemeanour, but for disrupting her plans. With Amanda staying with her in the flat there was little chance of making any progress with Ben.

"You know you don't care about me smoking. You smoke yourself."

"I'd prefer you not to. It's expensive, unhealthy and unattractive. But I'm annoyed with you for getting into such a silly row just when you need to work for your A-levels."

"I only have to get two grade Es."

"I think it's stupid, that's all. Counter-productive."

"You just don't want me at home."

The truth in this annoyed Till beyond restraint. "That's rubbish! You know I only want the best for you!"

"*That*'s rubbish. You don't like me very much, and you certainly don't want me around. Don't think I want to be with you any more than you want me. I'd much prefer to stay with Daddy but as he's bossing the penguins around at present there isn't much choice, is there, and I'm certainly not staying with step-ma Claire without Daddy."

"I thought you always accused me of interfering and being possessive?"

"You used to be but I think it was a pretence and we're now seeing the real you, self-absorbed and indifferent."

"I'm never indifferent to you, Amanda. You are half my immortality."

"That's what I mean, self-absorbed."

There was silence. Till overtook a veteran Morris Minor,

129

one of the few cars on the motorway that could not go faster than hers.

"You've had your hair cut," she said as neutrally as she could manage. Amanda's hair was now shoulder-length with spikes in front, rather like Honey's. It was a style which demanded bones, and Amanda's face gave no visual evidence of these; it was round, pink and smooth. "I like it."

"Do you?" Amanda twirled a strand round her finger and tugged at it sharply. "I wasn't sure."

"Tomorrow we'll look for a tutorial college."

"Do you think Daddy will be very angry?"

Till did. Charles, always conventional, grew more so with time and Claire's influence. "At first," she said. "He'll get over it. Remember we date from a time when getting thrown out from school was a terrible thing."

"Really?" Amanda gazed open-mouthed at this unimaginable dark age. "I haven't been entirely thrown out. They'll let me back to take the exams."

"It'll probably be a pleasant change for you in London."

"All the best people have been chucked this term. It's all Miss Turnbull's fault, she's got no imagination and she wears Crimplene suits."

"Did the Crimplene suits cause you to smoke?"

"You know what I mean. Only a pervert would become a headmistress. Anyway, can you imagine how dull, staying in schools all your life? You lose any grip on the real world. It stands to reason."

"What is the real world?"

"Is it being a shrink that makes you ask such half-wit questions?"

A red Ferrari passed them, doing at least a hundred. Till gazed enviously after it. She loved driving fast and, recently, had had no opportunity to do so.

Amanda pulled at other strands of her hair in an apparent attempt to scalp herself. Till began to feel some sympathy for her. She had behaved like the adolescent she was and as a consequence had been ejected from an institution supposedly designed for adolescents into what she called the real world. "We could go to a film tonight."

"OK. What?"

"*Top Gun?*"

"Yuk."

"*Room with a View?*"

"Seen it."

"*Hannah and her Sisters?*"

"Seen it."

"We could stay at home and watch television. You could make spaghetti bolognese. Yours is much better than mine."

"I must admit, it is rather." She was beginning to perk up. She knew her mother well enough to expect no recriminations, no punishments, and few lectures. She had wanted to be with her mother recently, she had wanted to be happy. She didn't know how to achieve that but there was a solidity, a comforting quality to being with Till, who usually did what she wanted to. At her father's house people were constantly trying to please each other and as a consequence most activities were an uneasy compromise that no one enjoyed.

Honey reached JFK at five in the evening, too late for her connection to San Francisco, which she did not now want. She heaved the straps of her two bags as confidently as she could onto her shoulders and strode through the terminal as if she knew her destination. At least there had been no trouble going through immigration; for the last hour of the flight she had worried over her visa. She had looked up "multiple" and "indefinite" time and again but she was still not sure if she had understood them correctly. The immigration officer had hardly glanced at her, stamped the passport, stamped the form (the result of two hours' intense application after lunch) and wished her a pleasant stay in the US. She had smiled in relief and he had smiled back. "All right!" he said admiringly.

"All right," replied Honey. She repeated the words to herself like a talisman as she strode purposefully through the crowds.

The girl behind the airline desk looked very like the girl behind the airline desk in England, but glossier, as if a setting coat of transparent nail varnish had been brushed over her, skin, hair, clothes and all. "Las Vegas, no problem. How do you wish to pay for your ticket?"

"You accept credit cards?"

"Any major credit card."

"Is this a major card?" Honey passed across her American Express gold card.

"Sure is," said the girl, processing the paper work with flying fingers, punching the VDU, reading messages from the background of flickering green. "We have a direct flight eight thirty a.m."

"That'll do fine. Where can I get a taxi into the city?"

"Right through there." The girl pointed. Honey walked in that direction but was soon bewildered by the signs. She asked a woman in the paramilitary uniform of a security guard, "Are the taxis this way?"

The woman looked at her. She had a pasty face pitted with remains of acne scars. She was chewing gum. She didn't reply. Honey asked again.

"Why don't you ask someone?" said the woman with a strong nasal accent like Barbra Streisand's. Honey moved away, snubbed. New Yorkers were famous for not being helpful, Till had told her; there was a joke Honey could only half remember about an English person asking the way in New York. She wanted to be with Till who, even if she didn't know what to do, guessed purposefully and was unabashed by being wrong.

Her nerve gave way and she asked a man. He would

132

help. He did, taking her to the cab rank, asking her where she was staying and if she wanted a native New Yorker to show her the sights. She brushed him off gently, glad to be able to do something familiar. Then the cab driver wanted to know their destination. Honey went blank. She had often stayed in New York, with Florence, with Steve. "St Regis," she said, pulling a name out of the past.

The drive into the city was like the drive into any big city, but more so; more bridges, apartment buildings, scrap-metal yards, neighbourhoods. Honey felt panic rise. So many people and none of them cared about her. She didn't have one single telephone number in case things went wrong. She should have contacts, she knew, but she had left that to Steve.

The St Regis restored her confidence. It was the kind of place she knew, quiet, courteous, welcoming because she had money. I'm rich, she thought as she showered and changed. She remembered reading in *The Times* that being rich was having enough money to do what you wanted; she understood the truth of the observation, safe in her room at the St Regis. She also felt grateful to Florence. Although her mother had incessantly pointed out that, alone, Honey would never have made a career, up to now she had seen the career as exhausting and painful, a blight in her childhood, a constant anxiety later. But without the career there would have been no money, and only money could give her the power to travel alone in this expensive, ruthless country, and to find Steve.

It was two o'clock in the morning. Till and Amanda had watched television through the *Epilogue*, then Amanda prowled through the flat cracking her knuckles and looking for something to read. Eventually she found a volume of plays. Till read articles in professional journals until her brain would grasp no more statistics.

133

Amanda was reading and cracking her knuckles. To stop her, Till asked, "What's the book?"

"It's a play. *The Eye of Childhood*."

"Oh. That's by Ben Considine."

"I know. It's bloody good. I didn't know he was a proper writer."

"He was a friend of mine," said Till.

Amanda snorted. "I remember. Always turning up. I wonder Daddy didn't divorce you earlier."

"That isn't why we divorced."

"I'm not interested," said Amanda. "I'm never going to get divorced. I'm going to stay married for ever."

"Good." Till was hurt. Her divorce – not the parting from Charles which had been a successful move, but the fact of a broken marriage – still made her feel a failure, an unfamiliar and unpleasant sensation.

"What's Ben's latest play, then?"

"He's only written two. Nothing for ten years apart from screenplays and soap opera scripts."

"Why?"

"I don't know."

"Probably ran out of material," said Amanda wisely. "I did that with my poetry."

"I didn't know you wrote poetry."

"When I was younger. I stopped when I realised it was the same poem over and over again. This play's auto-biographical, isn't it? About his childhood?"

"Yes."

"What was his second play about?"

"His first wife, his marriage."

"There you are then. Those are the only two things he's ever felt anything about."

"He's married again now, to Pandora Pardoe."

"It can't matter to him." Delicious words, thought Till, then paused as she realised the corollary: that she herself hadn't, and didn't, mean anything to Ben either. And he still hadn't rung. In fact nobody had rung for three days,

134

not even her most importunate patient, and Amanda's school had been trying to reach her without success; the exchange she was on was notoriously prone to gremlins. Perhaps there really was a fault in her telephone. Tomorrow she would check, and call the engineers.

"Today I have lunch with an author," said Tom proudly.

"Good," said Maggie. "Avoid fish. I'm doing fish for dinner."

"An author," said Tom again.

"Anyone I know?"

"A new author. A novelist. I've started reading manuscripts again."

"Really? I thought you were too important for that. Don't be later than six, will you? I won't have time to walk the dogs."

"Why can't Inge walk the dogs?" Inge was the new au pair.

"She's having a *crise*. I gave her two days off to sort out her boyfriend."

"I've changed my policy at work," said Tom, watching Maggie strip sheets off the bed. "Why are you doing that? Shall I help?"

"I'm doing that because the daily woman has flu and it's laundry day. Don't bother to help, you're hopeless at bed-making." She cracked a linen sheet out of its folds and floated it onto the bed.

"Couldn't Clarissa do that?" Clarissa was staying for a few days while her husband was in Tokyo on business.

"She's hopeless at bed-making too. Tell me about your new policy at work."

"My new policy is that I do some."

"What?"

"Work."

"Oh, good," said Maggie not understanding. "That'll be nice for you."

"It isn't," said Tom. He wanted her to listen, to

understand. "It isn't because there's no work for me to do. They've excluded me. So I'm reading manuscripts."

Maggie only knew publishing from the author's point of view, but she knew a great deal about employees. "Won't that annoy the people who should be reading them?" she said smoothing the pillows.

"I haven't noticed," said Tom. "Why should it?"

"Oh, Tom. If they're ambitious and they enjoy the work – which they must because heaven knows the pay is vile – then if you butt in it'll be disastrous. Couldn't you just get on with the PR?"

"I'm not even in the Public Relations Department."

"But that's what they said you'd do, public relations at a senior level. I remember the agreement."

"I remember the agreement too, but apparently there isn't anyone who combines sufficient seniority with sufficient impotence for me to be allowed to relate to them publicly."

"What do you mean, impotence?"

"Lack of power."

"Can we talk about this some other time? I'm in a frantic rush to do the aspic before I go to the Bush."

"Of course," said Tom. He felt the obligation to share his preoccupations with her; he couldn't discuss Honey, so he must give Maggie the chance to discuss his work. Now he felt guiltily pleased that, as she wouldn't take it, he could inwardly accuse her of insufficient devotion to his interests. At the same time he was too scrupulous to be unaware of his manipulation. He well knew he had chosen an impossible moment.

Left alone in the bedroom with a neatly made bed, he gravitated inevitably to the window. If he couldn't see Honey, looking at her garden was much, much better than nothing. He saw her spirit there drifting through the narrow length of green under the leafless trees. In his imagination she never wore modern clothes, she wore long, clinging, shimmering thirties dresses and delicate satin slippers. Even in imagination he was courteous: she was never naked in the garden. In the shower, of course . . .

"What exchange is that?"

"243."

"I'll put you through to the engineers." Till held the telephone between shoulder and ear, checking through her appointment list, putting her notes in order.

"Engineers." Till explained that her telephone wasn't ringing for incoming calls. The man was polite, probably fresh from a customer relations course. Shorn of reassurance, his words were discouraging. Till learnt that the lines in her area were overloaded, that it might take days to trace the fault, that too many Notting Hill subscribers wanted a telephone but that the courageous men from Telecom would be right onto it. She replaced the receiver, blew visible dust from her desk. The cleaners at the Psychotherapy Centre were ineffectual. They always turned up but only went through the motions of cleaning. In her more pessimistic moments Till felt this appropriate to the work of the Centre.

Her office was a small square room entirely lined with books, with a couch against one wall in case a patient wanted to lie on it. Her desk was aslant one of the window corners so she could look up from her paperwork and watch the street. The Centre was in a Bayswater square of high stucco houses; several were hotels, others divided and subdivided into service apartments. Few families lived there; the population was largely transient, many were Arabs. The garden in the centre of the square was neglected and usually empty. Too few of the people qualified to use it stayed long enough to bother with a key.

Till had worked there for fifteen years and only two of the original residents were still to be seen coming and going. Lately, with another precipitous rise in property prices, some of the houses were being converted into luxury flàts. Three builder's skips were dotted about the square.

Sometimes Till reflected that she could have been in Harley Street, could have charged fixed fees and made a proper career in psychiatry instead of dabbling, as she effectively did, working on the fringe of medicine with patients who came to her through word-of-mouth re-commendation, or, rarely, walked in off the street knowing they were unhappy and wanting someone to tell them why as cheaply as possible. She had decided to join the Centre as a compromise, still hoping for an acting career.

Vernon had chosen her for the part in *Captain Bridge* after seeing her in a student production at Oxford; then she had assumed because she was divinely gifted, now she supposed because it was good publicity for the film and she was cheap. During filming and a year later when she was well reviewed she had fantasised about acting, expecting an instant career. Only her father's pressure had made her finish her medical training. By then she was married with two small children, used to a full-time nanny; she would have done anything rather than lapse into domesticity. Work at the Centre was a compromise: flexible, so that she was ready for the perfect part; not full-time, so she could at least pretend to be an army wife occasionally.

The temporary arrangement had lasted fifteen years and she did not envisage changing it now. She had only five minutes before her next patient, the actor. He had arrived already, she'd watched him up the steps, but she wanted the five minutes to herself to savour the good news: her telephone was definitely out of order so she had been waiting for Ben's call believing he wasn't interested enough to ring whereas in fact he could have been – probably had been – calling every hour.

She flipped through her notes on the actor, hoping but

not expecting to find a new approach. Otherwise, it was time to tell him they were making no progress and he should consider ending the treatment. That would be ethical, and a relief, though it would mean less money just at a time when she needed more. Amanda's tutorial college fees were her responsibility, she felt. Charles had Claire and the house to keep. Perhaps ethical considerations could wait.

But as the door opened to admit the actor, eager once more to rehearse his childhood, she knew that even money would not induce her to listen.

Tom's new author lived in southern Ireland and his name was F. Y. Purves. The novel had been the rounds. The manuscript was tattered and coffee stained; the front page, retyped and fresh, made the rest look tattier. The book itself was short, elegantly written, and most peculiar. It was set in the South of France, probably pre-war, and some of the characters – the more balanced and intelligent ones – were animals. It had touches of Coward wit and Weldon savagery, but the overall flavour was Purves. Tom had written asking if he/she was ever in London, and the typewritten reply had been prompt but uninformative as to age, sex, and background. F. Y. Purves was often in London, could come to lunch at any time if given a week's notice, and had provided a contact address in Cadogan Square. The lunch had been arranged and now Tom sat in the most expensive restaurant he knew near Covent Garden awaiting his mystery guest.

He was very excited. Next to the pleasure of reading a worthwhile manuscript by a new author was the pleasure of meeting the author and giving his opinion. He had prepared telling phrases and ordered two Martinis, the chosen drink of the novel's hero, a ferret. He kept smoothing his hair as he glanced through the manuscript to savour his favourite passages, grateful to the author for providing a stimulus almost strong enough to divert his mind from Honey.

F. Y. Purves turned out to be an Anglo-Irishwoman in her seventies. She was tall; her figure widened from a normal torso to gargantuan hips. She reached the table where he was waiting, lurching unabashed between other tables, brushing against them and clattering plates and cutlery as she came. Her hair was firmly set in blue waves; around her neck a fox fur sported bright pebbly eyes almost as bright as her own.

"I hope you're prepared to buy me lots of food," said the woman. "Call me Fay. A family nickname from the nursery. Because of my size. Nurseries are so like the army, don't you think? My family have a simple sense of humour and I was always on the large side."

She was shouting. "I'm delighted to meet you," said Tom, enunciating much more clearly than usual to accommodate his guest's deafness.

"I'm not at all deaf," she boomed. "I took to shouting out hunting."

"You still hunt?"

"Not as much as I'd like to. I ride at sixteen stone and the expense of mounting me is terrible. You're anti-blood sports, I expect, though how a publisher can adopt that position I'll never understand."

"Why a publisher particularly?"

"Given the savagery of his own profession. To the poor authors, and the readers come to that. Good, a Martini. Thoughtful of you."

"Your hero's drink," said Tom.

"Is it now. Which novel are we discussing?"

"Have you written more than one?"

"I've two others with publishers at the moment. I've plenty of time on my hands, you understand."

Tom was disconcerted and disappointed and his urbanity failed him in the face of this hulking woman who required none of the sensitive nurturing he was eager to give. "Shall we order?" she said. "We can talk business later. Is three courses all right with you?"

"Naturally," said Tom, shifting in his chair at the prospect of yet more food. Recently he had developed indigestion; he believed since October, when Maggie had started work on her latest cook book – pâtés. Tom could not imagine any meat or combination of meats which he had not tasted in a pâtéd form. Annoyed with F. Y. Purves, Maggie and the world, he ordered steamed fish, then conscience smote him and he rescinded the order, hoping that Maggie's fish was not pâtéd.

Fay seemed happy enough to sit in silence presumably contemplating the mountains of food she had chosen, sipping her second Martini and looking round with her pebbly eyes which he suspected observed a great deal too much for comfort. "About your novel—"

"I've remembered which one we're talking about now. The one with the animals. That's the best of the present batch even if I say so myself."

"I'm very impressed with it," said Tom, reluctantly following his prepared path. "Your style . . ."

"Ah, don't worry with the flattery," she interrupted. "In the words of Yeats, 'for God's sake, how much?'"

"How much?" Tom felt as if a vampire were draining his blood, weakening his will. This was too bad. She seemed to have no sense of appropriate behaviour. Where was the gratitude, the readiness to discuss her book, to be impressed by the arcane knowledge of publishing that he possessed?

"What exactly is your position in the firm?"

"My position?" With shaking hands, he straightened knives and forks. "Is this the first of your novels to be accepted for publication?"

"Oh dear no. I've had two literary careers already. D'you want me to tell the tale?"

"Please do," said Tom. He felt tired, disjointed, and old. He tried to listen but only caught fragments of her

141

long and, to judge from the response of nearby eaters, lively story. Eyre and Spottiswoode, Gollancz and Collins came into it; soon she started asking questions that revealed she knew more about publishing, even current publishing, than he did.

"So what it boils down to is that you like my book but you're not in a position to make me an offer, is that it?"

That was it, shorn of self-delusion. He couldn't be sure of having enough influence in the firm, despite his high-sounding title and considerable salary, to guarantee that they would publish one novel. He hadn't intended the discussion to reach that point at all. He had imagined himself encouraging her, making telling analytical points, suggesting that she found an agent to protect her interests. He even had a short list of names and addresses to produce in response to her request for guidance. After that, he planned to start the process of manipulation within the firm that would culminate in the decision to publish.

She talked on, loudly, about publishers she had known, about her grandson who was doing well in Penguin, though he wasn't going to stay there long because it was so important to move around, not to get stuck in a rut. People were watching them, including, two tables away, a senior editor in Tom's own firm. Panic seized him. I'm losing my grip, he thought. I haven't given the matter sufficient consideration. I'm making a fool of myself. Till was right I am Walter Mitty, I'm losing touch with reality. His indigestion gnawed away and he felt absurdly on the brink of tears. I must not cry, he thought. What will she think of me? What will I think of me?

"You've eaten nothing at all," said Fay. "You don't look well. Here, waiter, get us water. And another bottle of wine for me. You don't mind, sure, Tom? It's on expenses after all." He waved an assenting hand, casting about wildly for something to say that would pre-empt the whimper that trembled on his lips. Why couldn't she have been unworldly, impressionable, responsive, he thought looking at this battleship of a woman who was providing the last nail in the coffin of his confidence. I'd never even have been employed if my father hadn't owned the firm, he thought. I can't do anything. I'm perfectly useless. I have walked all my life on the stilts of birth and education.

"Did you hear anything I said? Tom?" The woman was tapping the back of his hand which lay shaking on the table.

"I'm sorry," he said. "I'm sorry."

"Ah, don't be," she said cheerfully. "I expect it's a bad day for you. Don't we all get them from time to time? Will you be wanting anything from the sweet trolley?"

Tom shook his head.

"I'll just have a taste of everything," she said.

Chapter Eight

In Las Vegas it was sixty-one degrees and clear. The sun was bright. As the plane circled Honey looked down over desert. She was prepared to be delighted; for people who wanted to please her, give her cheap food, seemed concerned about the niceness of her day.

The taxi driver was the first disappointment. "You wanna see the Strip?"

It was a question expecting the answer no. "Well . . ."

"Good. The traffic's terrible and it ain't much to look at in the daytime, nor nighttime come to that."

"What's the Golden Nugget like?"

"Ain't bad. You gotta reservation?"

"Yes." She had called from New York.

"Just asking. They've got some kinda convention, cops or security guards, sumpin' like that."

"At least I'll be safe."

He whistled between his teeth. "You from Australia?"

"England."

"Close enough. All your English cops straight?"

"Most of them. As far as I know." Policemen of any nationality were always nice to Honey.

"Is that the truth?"

A little dashed, Honey checked her money and credit cards for comfort. Soon she rallied. "Have you lived in Vegas long?"

"Twenty years."

"Do you like it?"

"Nope."

"Why?"

"Hate gambling, hate the sun."

"Is there much sun?"

"You'd better believe it."

Honey sat back and looked around her. They were passing through a desolate suburbia of dusty wooden houses which gave way to sudden palaces set in a wilderness of car parks with neon lights framing huge signs advertising names she didn't recognise. It was like a film set waiting for the crews to move in. So few people walked the streets that she could count them. When her taxi stopped at a traffic light a pick-up truck paused beside them piled high with discarded bar stools. Beside the lights a billboard announced "35% of Nevadans chose cremation last year". The wait lasted long enough for her to read it.

She felt an inner chill. "Have you always been a taxi driver?"

"Nope. I was a croupier for fifteen years. Did well, as a matter of fact. I was in charge of a shift. Couldn't stand it, though. Being watched all the time. Trust, talk about trust. The casinos hire guys to watch the croupiers. They lie on their stomachs above the ceilings just watching to see if we're ripping them off."

"And were you?"

"Not if we valued our health."

"I suppose the people who come here to gamble enjoy themselves."

"I guess. Better to stay home and chuck dollars into the garbage disposal, I reckon. How d'you suppose these guys get so rich? Not from letting the tourists win, that's for sure. Gambling's a mug's game. You a gambler?"

"No."

"Why'd you come?"

"To meet a friend."

"Sure he's still a friend?"

"What do you mean?" Honey was startled. How did the taxi driver know about her?

"That's another gamble, human relationships. I avoid 'em. Here's the Golden Nugget, lady."

Honey overtipped him, shouldered her bags, went inside, noting with astonishment that the pavement in front of the Golden Nugget was covered with white carpet. The hotel was enormous, glittering; most surfaces were lined with white plastic imitating marble. The receptionist was predictably friendly. When Honey had her key she asked about Steve. Yes, agreed the receptionist, he had a room there, but he was away right now, would be back the next day; no, it wasn't hotel policy to release guests' room numbers, but Honey could leave a message and Steve would get it, for sure. No problem.

Honey moved away, sat down in a squashy white mock leather chair, and thought. There was a problem. Steve might very well not reply to her message. If he won't reply then he doesn't want to see you and what are you doing here? said reality. Once he sees me he'll realise how much he missed me, said fantasy. I'll get in touch with Kevin, the sound recordist. He'll ring me back, tell me Steve's room number. Then I'll knock on his door and his face will light up when he sees me and we'll go to bed and he'll hold me and we'll make a baby.

Baby, she thought wandering through the overgrown plants in their white marblised beds towards the lift. Her baby was at home in Campden Hill. She wanted to be there too. Twenty-four hours to fill in this alien place full of fat women in tight polyester trousers clutching Styrofoam cups full of tokens, their fingers black from feeding the one-arm bandits in a rhythmical sequence like prisoners performing a futile but compulsory task. She walked along the row of green baize tables, each surrounded by a knot of people watching the cards flipped over by the croupiers. She looked up. The ceiling seemed opaque. Was it true what the taxi driver said, that men lay on their stomachs looking down at her looking up? Would they suspect her if she looked up?

She joined a lift already full of burly men, very likely policemen though they were wearing gaudy clothes, resort clothes which fitted them like sausage skins. I want to go home, she thought, then despised herself for weakness. The room was comfortable enough, air-conditioned to goosebump level, with windows that didn't open, overlooking a pool, fountains and palm trees foreshortened by the view from the twelfth floor. In the bathroom were free gifts. Shampoo, conditioner, bubblebath, soap, all wrapped in green packets emblazoned with the name of the hotel in gold.

On the bedside table, between the two huge beds, were menus for room service, instructions on using the many facilities of the hotel, and a short guide to the rules of blackjack and roulette. She started to read them. It was still early afternoon local time though her inner clock registered midnight and disorientation; she wanted to sleep. She refused to sleep. If she went to bed now she'd wake up in the middle of the night and she shrank from solitary exploration of late-night Vegas.

I'll just rest, she decided; took off her shoes, snuggled under the cover and closed her eyes.

"They haven't mended the phone yet," said Amanda, not getting up when Till came in. She lay on the sofa. On the floor around her were two cereal bowls, three coffee cups with cigarette butts in the saucers, and piles of books. Mahler thundered from the record player and the television, mute, flickered in the corner.

"How do you know?"

"I asked the operator to ring back and nothing happened. You said it'd be fixed by this afternoon."

"I said it might be. I was being optimistic. Who do you expect to ring?"

"Friends," said Amanda airily.

"Ring them."

"No way." She watched her mother as she picked up

147

the cups and bowls and took them into the kitchen to wash. "Aren't you going to say anything about the mess?" she said uncertainly. "I meant to clear up . . ."

"What's to say? Have you had a good day?"

"Hellish. Nothing to do. The telephone isn't working."

"I know," said Till. "It'll be mended in a day or two. Any luck with tutorial colleges?"

"I didn't look."

"We can visit some tomorrow. I have two hours free in the morning. Did you unpack?"

"I'll do it tomorrow. What's for supper?"

"Decide, then go and do the shopping."

"Why can't you?"

"Because I've been working and I'm going to have a bath. The money's in my coat."

Amanda could only cook spaghetti and risotto so supper was risotto. After they'd finished Till took the plates to wash up. Amanda watched her. "Daddy's coming back next week."

"Yes."

"Will you speak to him first?"

"If you want."

"I'm miserable," said Amanda grandly.

"I'd noticed."

"My whole life is waiting. Waiting for the phone, for exams, till I go to Oxford."

"Whose phone call are you expecting?" said Till again.

"Nobody special. What are we doing this evening?"

"You do what you like. I'm going to watch television."

"God, you're so middle-aged."

"Stop being so rude to me," said Till mildly.

"It's like a prison in this flat, it's so small. We're on top of each other all the time."

"Go for a walk."

"It's freezing outside. They said on the news that the wind was straight from Siberia."

"You can borrow my long anorak."

"That's hideous."

"But warm."

"Are you trying to irritate me?" said Amanda accusingly.

"I'm waiting for you to grow up."

"Pompous old cow."

"Dry up the glasses, would you?"

Tom walked the lurchers after dinner. There were no lights in Honey's flat and the curtains weren't drawn. Despite the bitter cold he stood outside for several minutes while the lurchers obediently waited, rhythmically smacking his coat with their heavy tails. There had been no lights in Honey's flat the night before either. She must have gone away. Unless there had been an accident. She might have slipped, hit her head, injured herself. Behind the door of his own house opened and young people came spilling out, three of them his daughters, all his dinner guests. They engulfed him in a chattering flood. Why do they talk so loudly, he thought. Why do they suppose anyone would want to hear them?

"We're going over to see Fergus, Daddy," said Clarissa. She was his eldest, supposedly his favourite, though since her marriage he occasionally found himself disliking her.

"Oh? Where does Fergus live?"

"In Fulham. He's just bought a house and we're going to warm it for him. Are you all right?"

"Perfectly."

"Why are you standing here?"

"Why are you going to see Fergus?"

"I told you, he's . . ."

"Never mind," he said moving away. She followed.

"Daddy?"

"Goodnight, Clarissa." He walked purposefully up a cul-de-sac until his children and their friends were out of

149

sight. Then he retraced his steps and looked once more at Honey's blank windows. Madeline's door opened and before he could retreat Jacky was beside him.

"Evening, Hamzavi," he said briskly.

"Hi, Tom," said Jacky. He was wearing black leather trousers which fitted in places Tom usually tried to forget; under the street lamps his eyes gleamed exotically in full make-up; his face was framed by the high collar of a black leather flying jacket. Tom's instinct was to end the encounter as quickly as possible but Honey took priority.

"Any idea where Honey is?" he asked.

"Which way are you walking?" said Jacky.

"Towards Hyde Park."

"I'll go with you. Do you like the cozzy?"

"The cozzy?"

"Utterly late Elvis, don't you think?" Jacky was skipping along, sketching tap steps as he went, swinging round lampposts. "It's the help's night off *chez* Cabot Goldberg," he said in an explanatory tone. "I'd be cruising if I wasn't such a coward. Women are tiring, but who wants to waste away, and one can't exactly ask for a blood test, can one?"

"I have no idea what you're talking about," said Tom crossly. They were attracting attention.

"Never mind, Thomas, you're not my type."

"Where's Honey?"

Jacky pouted. "Couldn't you pay the *least* attention to me? Just for once?"

"What do you want me to say?" said Tom gruffly.

"Ask me where I'm going."

"Where are you going, Hamzavi?"

"To the Leather Lust and Rampant Rubber Ball, Wyatt."

"Oh," said Tom. They stopped for traffic at the foot of Kensington Church Street. "Is that in aid of a charity?"

"All benefits to the outcasts of society: the perverts,

the lonely, the incongruous and inappropriate and suddenly adventurous . . ."

"You're making fun of me." Tom was frustrated and aggressive. "I didn't invite your company."

"But you want to know about Honey, is that right? Can it be that she has cracked the cement of your propriety? Will we see you in the divorce courts pleading irresistible impulse and mortgaging your future to alimony?"

"Been drinking, have you?" said Tom, checking each passer-by, dreading a familiar face.

"No." Jacky pouted at his reflection in a shop window. "This is a reaction from months of undiluted Madeline."

"You're embarrassing me."

"Ultimate sin in the English book of uncommon prayer. The eighth and most deadly transgression. Kill someone and it's a bad show; embarrass them and you'll be left alone with a revolver. Tell you what, Wyatt, let's leave the dogs with the revolver and let's you and me go to the Porchester Hall."

"Why the Porchester Hall?"

"To the Leather Lust and Rampant Rubber Ball."

"WHERE THE HELL IS HONEY?" Tom shouted so loudly that heads turned.

Jacky whimpered affectedly. "Passion has painted a delicate flush on your elegantly modelled cheekbones, Thomas. Honey is in the United States. She'll be back next week."

"I'm going back home. Goodnight," said Tom.

"Goodnight," said Jacky. "Give us a kiss?"

It was half past one and Till was nearly asleep when the bell rang.

"I'll get it," Amanda called scrambling up the stairs. Ben, thought Till, grabbing her least tattered kimono, pulling at her flattened hair.

"Oh, God," said Ben, "you're not alone." He clattered

down the stairs, filling the flat with his height and his assertiveness, brandishing a bottle of whisky which he gave to Till. "I've brought you a present," he said, shrugging off his coat and handing it to Amanda who dropped it on the floor. She was undressed for bed in a nightshirt which just covered her bottom. She gripped the hem with clumsy fists and tugged it downwards. Her legs were pressed tightly together. Evidently she had only just realised how nearly naked she was.

Ben watched her with appraising interest. "Why don't you fetch a dressing-gown, Amanda, if you're going to join us?" said Till moving between them. Amanda hesitated. It was her instinct to refuse any of Till's instructions, but she was blushing with self-consciousness. "And put Ben's coat on the banisters as you go."

Ben turned away. "Here's some whisky, Till."

"I don't drink it."

"I know. I do," he said fetching a glass, watching Amanda's youthful flesh taking the stairs two at a time.

"That's my daughter Amanda. You remember her."

"She's grown up."

"Physically, yes. It happens. You can't stay, Ben."

"I wasn't intending to. Why aren't you answering the phone?"

Briefly, Till considered the advantages of lying; she could say she didn't want to speak to him, that she'd been leaving all calls unanswered. That would raise her several notches in Ben's regard. But it was a cheap trick and a risky one. Amanda might well mention the non-functioning phone. She explained.

"It's bloody inconvenient," he said. "I wanted to speak to you. Pandora's changed the dates of our skiing trip. The technicians up in Manchester are on strike so no *Cupid* recordings, and she says she wants a rest and a change now, so we're going tomorrow."

"Does she know you saw me?"

"No. She's after the BBC blonde. Were you waiting for my call?"

"I'm waiting for several calls."

"Don't try to shit a shitter." He reached out a hand and pulled gently at her hair. "You must do something with it, Matilda. Courageous indifference to your appearance is one thing, middle age another. I have missed you."

"And you won't miss me middle-aged?"

"I don't know."

"You're a looks snob."

"Show me a man who isn't."

"Mummy," called Amanda from her upstairs bedroom. "Mummy."

Till was angry; not at Amanda, but at the circumstances that had combined Ben's serious attentions with the obtrusive presence of Amanda who needed her and who had the right to demand first priority. She went upstairs to find Amanda huddled in her bed, shoulders reproachfully hunched. "How long will he be staying?" she asked.

"Not long. Why?"

"I don't like him and I don't want him here at this time of night disturbing us."

"I don't mind and it's as much my flat as yours."

"What about my feelings?" said Amanda working herself up into a little sand-devil of self-pity. "You're my mother, after all."

"What has that to do with it?"

"I don't like . . . I don't want . . ." Amanda was crying. Behind the self-dramatising was a real and bleak emotion, which Till didn't want to confront.

"He'll be going soon."

"Matilda," called Ben.

Till stopped halfway down the stairs, torn by an intensity of emotion unfamiliar since her parting with

153

Ben and the divorce. She had reached a sort of peace. Now she had to feel, to want what she couldn't get, to do what she should rather than what she wanted. When she was younger her emotions had driven her; she had tried to restrain herself, with no success. Then, she had attributed the failure to weakness of will; now, she wasn't convinced that strength of will was anything more than a self-congratulatory description for the capacity to control weak impulses. Certainly, now, she could control herself better, weigh options more realistically. She could also imagine other people's feelings more powerfully and often that prevented her from acting in her own interest.

"Till, I have to go. I'm collecting Pandora."

"Bit late for her." Pandora slept and ate to a regular time-table and regarded anyone who didn't as morally lax.

"It's because of the changed arrangements for going away. She has to clear work. She's reading scripts with Salome."

"What kind of scripts?" Till was jealous.

"She's looking for parts in a sit-com and Salome has a good nose for that kind of thing so they read the scripts the agent sends."

Till could see them sitting in Salome's presumably luxurious house surrounded by heaps of potential parts, all of which Pandora would squeak and giggle through. "It's no use looking down your nose, Matilda. If you pitch your tent in Siberia it's not fair to complain of the cold. You could have been an actress but you chose not to."

"Stop reading my mind. If you're not staying, why did you bring the whisky?"

"For the next time. How long is the girl here?"

"Indefinitely."

"Oh, God. Can't you send her to Charlie?"

"No."

154

When he'd gone, she took the whisky, put it in a cupboard. It was insurance.

Recently, Honey had slept very deeply and lurched, confused, out of her dreams. This time she thought she was in a refrigerator. She was icy cold, it was dark, there was a steady background hum. Then the shapes of the hard-edged windows, the outsize television, the bedside lamps, emerged from the background of grey. It was the middle of the night in Las Vegas. She groaned. Exactly what she had meant to avoid. She had slept for hours wearing make-up. She could feel her clogged pores gasping for air; she was gasping for air herself. There was plenty of conditioning but no air.

She put the lights on, inspected the windows again; they were still hermetically sealed. She adjusted the conditioning system to warm and ran the bath. Two-thirty a.m. The wrong time.

She cleaned her face and neck, lay in the bath looking at her finely shaped thighs, well-defined knees, tapered calves and narrow ankles and feet. They did not reassure her. She inspected her inner thighs to see if the crêpiness had spread. There was just a trace.

Downstairs there were people gambling. Two tables of blackjack, two poker games, active roulette wheels and the persistent clatter of the fruit machines. Honey took a stool at the bar next to an old man wearing a cowboy hat. Behind the counter, the barman read a large textbook, his finger creeping across the page. When he noticed Honey he whipped the book out of sight.

Nearly an hour later, Honey let Beau buy her a second orange juice.

She wasn't sure about Beau though he seemed sure about himself. He was in his twenties, blond, with a body-builder's head set into his broad shoulders like granite, a square chin, more than the average number of square white teeth. He was very good-looking and he had been talking to her for some time. She always had trouble sitting alone in a public place, and the most reliable defence against men trying to pick her up, she had found, was to choose a harmless companion early on.

She chose Beau, first because he was handsome and she felt sorry for handsome people, and second because he was a type familiar to her from years making films: he was the boastful electrician. Of all film technicians, electricians were in her experience the vainest. Either they told funny stories or they performed feats of physical skill like smoking while walking about on their hands. Beau was not in reality an electrician though he was certainly boastful. She had listened to his account of his birth in Birmingham, England (illegitimate son of a duke), his army training (in both the SAS and the Marines), his move to America (as bodyguard to a very prominent member of the US goverment). He was now describing his time as a stunt-man in Hollywood.

"They really paid you half a million dollars for three days' work?"

"It was dangerous, very dangerous. No one else was fool enough to take it on, but it was easy for me after the Marines."

His lying didn't worry her; men nearly always lied to impress her, though seldom as blatantly and naively as Beau. It was the aura of disconnection and malfunction that was disturbing. His eyes didn't smile when his lips did and his hands frequently jerked in uncontrollable irregular spasms.

"What did you have to do for the film?" she asked.

"Too complicated to explain."

"I know a bit about it."

"You wouldn't believe what a man has to do in the Marines. We had to bite the heads off live rabbits and drink their blood."

"Why?"

"Survival training. And we learnt more about killing than you want to hear. That was our graduation exercise. We had to kill a man and get away with it."

"Kill a man?"

"Or a woman. I chose a man. Only a pervert kills women. Easier to get away with, mutilate the bodies, make out it's a sex murder, see. Cut up the body."

"Oh, no!" She shrank away from him, revolted. The old man in the cowboy hat on her other side was still nursing a beer, staring into the glass. He would be little help in an emergency. She began to look about her, discreetly, for other possibilities.

"It sounds bad," he said, his accent reverting to pure Birmingham as it had done before when he felt his audience losing sympathy, "but it's a hard world out there and us Marines had to be ready to keep the peace, ready to fight."

"Which film did you work on?"

"That's enough about me. Tell me about you," said Beau once more attempting an American intonation, smiling his open piano-key smile. "Why are you here alone? It isn't safe in Vegas for a woman alone. Had any trouble yet?"

"Trouble?"

"You're being watched by that guy over there." He nodded his head towards a very big man in his forties with a heavily scarred face who was sitting at an outlying bar table, staring in their direction. "He's got his eye on you."

"Maybe he works for the hotel, as security."

"No way. He could be a sex-murderer, a pervert who can only get it up with a corpse. I don't want to frighten you but America's full of those, something in the water."

"In the water?"

"Yeah. Too much fluoride. If a person ingests too much fluoride it sends them crazy. It's a medical fact. I've got clippings here to prove it." He slapped crumpled

157

newspaper clippings on the bar between them. Honey knew she could not read them. "I haven't got my glasses with me," she said.

"That's what they say, about the fluoride and the murders. Fifteen girls murdered in Nevada in the last month alone by guys who were perfectly normal, like you or me, then they drank the water and it drove them to terrible sadistic barbaric cruelty. That's why I never drink water in the States because I really respect women. My mother brought me up to take care of women. See here, this poor girl. Her breasts were sliced right off like carving a chicken."

"Let's not talk about it any more," said Honey. She glanced from Beau to the scarred man. Both were staring at her.

"Excuse me, I've got to go to the little boys' room. Mind you're here when I get back," said Beau.

Honey beckoned to the barman. "What's the book you're reading?"

"Math," he said.

"Math?" She smiled encouragingly and secured his attention.

"I never finished high school. Did you finish high school?" He was about twenty, dark, with thin lips and irregular teeth. He appealed to Honey more than Beau.

"We don't have high school in England. I never passed examinations."

"Right. Over here we have high school, then college. I wanna go to college, but first I have to graduate high school. I'm learning by mail."

"Good for you."

"It's hard though. I work days in a car rental office, nights here. I gotta save, see? For college."

"That's really good," said Honey admiringly. "Would you do me a favour?"

"Depends what," he said cautiously.

"I want to know the room number of that man over

158

there. Is he staying in the hotel?" She indicated the scarred man.

"Yeah. He's with the convention group. Sorry, lady, we're not authorised to release room numbers . . ."

"I know," said Honey. She put her hand over his and smiled into his eyes, a full-dress Honey smile. He gulped. "I'd be really, really grateful," she said, "if you could get it for me quickly."

When Beau returned the barman had retreated to his book. "My real name is Martin," said Beau. "You can guess why they call me Beau." Honey shook her head. "You know Beau Bridges?"

"Yes. He's very nice. I met him . . ."

"Know why he's called Beau? Because he's beautiful, that's why. I try to keep myself beautiful, work out with the weights, run every day like they taught me in the SAS to keep myself combat-ready at all times so I can protect pretty ladies like you, just like my mother would have wanted. What's the number of your room?"

"The number of my room?"

"Yeah, see, that man over there, when you leave the bar he'll get your number from the barman," said Beau very quietly. "Then he'll follow you upstairs and he'll knock on the door and then he'll come in and . . ."

"I'm sure that's not going to happen," said Honey. "He's just an ordinary man who likes the look of me."

"Pleased with yourself, aren't you? Think men like you? Girls like me too."

"I'm sure they do."

"I miss England. Good old England. Was it cold when you left?"

"Freezing."

"I was back for Christmas this year, a real family Christmas. I took presents for my nieces and nephews. The boys like transformers, you know, those toys that change from a truck to a robot and back again. We had Christmas puddings and mince pies and we went to church at midnight." His eyes were glistening with synthetic emotion.

"Time for me to go to bed," said Honey, manufacturing a yawn. "It's been really nice talking to you, but it's nearly four o'clock and I'm leaving on an early plane."

"Sure you don't want to give me your room number? I could protect you."

"I'm sure that won't be necessary," said Honey. "Thanks for the drink." She smiled impartially at Beau and at the barman, and left.

On the way up in the lift she wondered how long it would be before Beau asked the barman for her room number, how long the barman would make him wait before he agreed, and how long after that the scarred man would drag himself from bed or bath to open his door to Beau. It was a simple enough device but all hers in conception and execution. She was modestly pleased.

Her room, when she returned to it, had changed from a tomb-like threat to a convenience. Her confidence flowed and with it her grip on reality. No point, she knew, in waiting to see Steve, no point in deluding herself. She would take a seat on an early plane to San Francisco and, with any luck, would be at the Significant Seminal Resource before lunch.

Mrs Deirdre Glucklich was a pleasant woman in her fifties with a neat figure in a severe navy blue suit and a cream silk blouse fastened at the neck with a brooch too large to be a real sapphire. The Significant Seminal Resource was in a small office building near a shopping mall in Marin County; Mrs Glucklich's room contained an abundance of plants, a desk with a leather blotter and a small wooden name-plaque, some chairs, a cork noticeboard displaying snapshots of well-turned-out, handsome babies and toddlers. She was an enthusiast. "Our founder is a visionary. His belief in improving the genetic pool shows itself in implementation. As you see around you the Significant Seminal Resource is dedicated to the production of a new generation of healthy intellectuals." All Honey could see was a manifest dedication to the cultivation of house-plants.

"We are in ardent pursuit of the *mens sana in corpore sano*."

Even had Honey been familiar with the tag she would hardly have recognised Mrs Glucklich's rendition. She listened with close attention, hoping soon to understand a word here and there. "All our donors are men of distinction in their own fields. We accept sperm by invitation only. None of your students and no-hopers giving sperm for the price of a meal. We welcome overseas interest, especially from Britain, once the cradle of democracy and scientific advance. We understand that the tragedy of infertility strikes equally at couples the world over."

She paused for breath while Honey noted that she must represent herself as a tragically infertile couple. Her first husband would do well enough: the likelihood that the Significant Seminal Resource would ever find out that he was long buried seemed remote. "The task is not an easy one. Naturally enough all our candidates are important, busy men, and the commitment to donation is onerous. There are technical problems in addition. I mean, you can have a leader in his field who's prepared to come in once or twice a week for six months to accommodate us. You can have this fantastic person but then his sperm doesn't freeze well. What do you do? Regretfully we have to refuse. We have to be able to assure our couples of maximum quality in the sperm we provide. Top achievers don't always produce top sperm."

Honey nodded. "What do we have to do?"

"Your husband isn't with you on this trip?"

"I'm afraid not. He was otherwise engaged," said Honey, with a mental apology to long-decayed Alexander under his respectable tombstone in a Sussex village churchyard.

"I'll explain the procedure. We have application forms for you to complete with details of your educational background and your intelligence. Have you ever taken an intelligence test, Mrs Markham?"

"I'm actually Mrs Alexander Pincus. Markham is my stage name. I'm an actress."

"Talent in artistic matters is certainly a bonus, but our founder has never believed in co-opting eminent artists as donors; the mental balance is so often perilous, I fear. Here's a copy of our questionnaire." Honey took it, wondering whether from the point of view of the Significant Seminal Resource it was better to be illiterate or blind. Fortunately Mrs Glucklich didn't wait for her to read it. "You submit the application together with other forms notarised in accordance with our procedure and a form completed by your medical practitioner." Till can do that, thought Honey, relieved to have understood something. "Your application is reviewed by our Board and if it is approved, then you have access to our Bank."

"And where does one – do I – have to—"

"Are you inquiring about insertion of the sperm? We will provide you with very full instructions and a container for the material to be preserved in dry ice. A refundable deposit of 500 dollars is required for the container. Unfortunately our insurance will not permit us to ship the material overseas, but you are very welcome to take delivery of it at any point in the continental United States and then insert it in an ambiance of your choice. Many of our couples like to make a little ceremony of the occasion. Soft lights, romantic music, often classical music because our recipients are very, very cultured people, and who knows how early are the significant influences on the unborn child?"

"How do you insert it?"

"We provide all the necessary equipment and you will be very fully briefed. Let me show you our donor catalogue."

Another wad of information was thrust into Honey's hands. "You will notice we distinguish the donors by colour coding. For example you might choose donor Crimson 3, this donor is an accomplished chief scientist with two doctorates from major universities. He has English ancestry, distinguished good looks and a friendly, outgoing personality. Tell me about your husband, Mrs Parcus."

"Pincus. He's a surgeon. He's tall, kind, and clever."

"It looks like a good match. Crimson 3 is over six feet and his tested IQ is 165: very very high. The information he provided doesn't include kindness but I think we can assume that. It takes a very kind man to accommodate us weekly for no financial considerations. We pay expenses, of course. I wish this kind of service had been available to me when I commenced married life. My husband brought a very unhappy genetic heredity to our marriage bed. Several close relatives never even made college. Alas my own children have intelligence levels below the average of the population and one of them is developing arthritis in his mid-twenties. This kind of tragedy could so easily be averted if only people would take more care over reproducing themselves. What was your father, Mrs Pincus?"

According to Florence, Honey's father was a gondolier who had shared Florence's bed in a station hotel in Rome. Once Honey had taxed her mother with inconsistency: surely gondoliers were Venetian? "Even gondoliers travel on trains," Florence had replied. For present purposes, Tom Wyatt would be an appropriate father, Honey thought; she described the Wyatt family, much to Mrs Glucklich's satisfaction. "What a pleasure it is to hear about such a united, happy family. Five brothers and sisters and the means to maintain them.

Truly fortunate for you, Mrs Pincus. You must be grateful for such an ideal start in life: material prosperity and cultural resources. Tell me about your marriage. Where is your home?'' Honey launched on an account of the long-past time with Alexander Pincus, careful not to make her tone too elegiac. As she talked it became clear to her that she didn't want to go back to being the precious toy of a man whose life was already arranged and decided. It had stunted her; if it was still going on she would be even more stunted, perhaps irreparably so. Now, in her tentative moves towards independence, she was finding that there were things she could do or feel that were better, however insignificant they might appear to others, than a smooth and orderly existence as a component. Myself alone, she thought.

She left the Seminal Resource with a folder full of material and Mrs Glucklich's effusive good wishes. In a coffee shop in a nearby shopping mall she ordered a hamburger to buy time and read with the food cooling in front of her. The longest and most complicated form was the one that donors had to complete. Most of the diseases or conditions listed there were a jumble of letters to her. Retinoblastoma, mucopolysaccharidoses, psychiatric treatment – she just managed to read that, and wondered if it was a disease – pyloric stenosis, depression, chromosomal translocation, learning disability. She knew what that was, and she had it. Presumably if a donor or his family (parents, grandparents, sibling or child) – had suffered from too many of them, he would be excluded.

She pushed the folder aside and sipped coffee. She could probably manage to be accepted by the Significant Seminal Resource with Till's help and consistent deception, but she didn't want to. It was a male place. Rules, order, exclusion, sharp edges and judgement. Behind Mrs Glucklich's pleasant manner was a visionary and idealist director who knew what was best for mankind and would bend mankind to his will, using womankind as the medium. Every well-organised inch of the place spoke with familiar voices. Do this, Honey. Listen to me, Honey, I know more than you do. Stop being so hysterical, Honey. You're so unworldly. Obey me and like it, Honey. Smile, Honey. Male directors and producers and writers and editors and reporters and photographers and masturbating audiences with Florence as their go-between. Honey couldn't articulate it precisely but she felt it acutely. Take this sperm, Honey, checked by men, screened by men, guaranteed genetically pure by men, and breed us supermen. She didn't want supermen. She wanted a child to love her, a child to love.

If she told the truth, the Resource and Mrs Glucklich as their representative would feel that she herself should not have been born. Florence, her gondolier, their casual mating, were opposed to everything the Resource stood for. Yet she was glad she had been born: for no reason she could defend, just the vigorous sense of minute-to-minute enjoyment that she felt most keenly now when by all logic she should feel she had nothing. Her career was gone and soon her beauty would be a matter of patches and reconstruction and making do; she lacked a man; but she felt alive.

Why? she thought, concentrating so hard her forehead wrinkled and she pressed her head between her palms. Why was she glad? Her answer was fragmentary and unsatisfactory. Because she had come from England by herself on a quest of her own choosing; because she had booked her tickets and chosen hotels and made appointments. She had nearly made a catastrophic mistake in deciding to approach Steve, but had withdrawn in time, by her own decision. She had come to San Francisco and hired a car and found her way about without Steve to direct her, as he had all through their long stay last year. For those tiny reasons she felt better than she ever had.

Better, she thought, starting the hired car and setting

off back to her hotel, much better. She remembered a long-ago conversation with Till when Honey asked if Till's patients ever got perfectly well. Most didn't, said Till. Wasn't that depressing? said Honey. Remember, said Till, for most people "perfectly well" is out of reach but "better" is still magnificent. Driving confidently through the well-clipped lawns and clean white houses, excluded as she was from the stable marriages and the nets of family relationships so valued by Mrs Glucklich, probably the least educated person in Marin County, Honey felt magnificent.

Back in the hotel she sat at her window high above the bay, looked out through the fog to the Golden Gate Bridge, listened to a country and western station because it reminded her of Till. She flipped through the Yellow Pages. "Sperm Banks": there was one entry, the Feminist Women's Health Co-operative in an industrial suburb. What a splendid country, thought Honey, to have sperm banks freely available in the Yellow Pages. She knew from the Americans she had met that they represented an enormous range of types and attitudes. Where there was a Mrs Glucklich who didn't suit her there would be someone, somewhere, who would; San Francisco, home of oddities, was surely the place. She sang along to the chorus of the country and western classic pulsing from the radio: "It doesn't matter where you've played before, California's a brand new game." She dialled the sperm bank, made an appointment for the afternoon. Then she decided to go downstairs for lunch. Lunch, alone in a hotel restaurant, against her mother's conviction that a girl alone in a public place loses face, people will think you can't get a man, terrible things will happen to you. Terrible things nearly had, in Las Vegas, but she had circumvented them. Beau had helped her, unintentionally, far more than a kind man could have done, simply by being an easy adversary. Till had once said that, too. Always accept unexpected gifts gratefully. You never

166

know whether you'll enjoy expected ones. Thank you, Beau, thought Honey, imagining him somewhere in neon Vegas changing from a robot to a truck and back again.

"Sure we can help," said Ms Fishkind.

"Even if I don't have a husband or a live-in partner?"

"No problem." Ms Fishkind tilted her chair back as far as it would go, which, in her tiny, crowded office was not far, and smiled broadly. Like Mrs Glucklich, she was welcoming and courteous, but there the resemblance ended. She was younger, very dark, with thick black hair in a shaggy cut, no make-up, jeans and a sweater which had probably been woven at high altitude by a Peruvian Workers' Collective. She radiated warmth. Five minutes after entering the office Honey had described her situation honestly because she expected it to be tolerantly received. It was. Ms Fishkind ("call me Betsy") gave the impression that she heard much stranger stories daily.

Their conversation was often interrupted by telephone calls. Now and then assistants popped their heads round the door. They could enter no further because Honey's chair was wedged between door and filing cabinet. Behind Ms Fishkind were photographs of her son from birth to three: eating in his high chair, tottering through gardens, held on laps. "What kind of forms would I have to fill in?"

"About your medical experiences, your fertility. Like this." She hooked a drawer open with the toe of her boot, pulled out a form, passed it across.

Honey looked at it, looked up. "I read very slowly," she said daringly. The words bounced round the room and back to her in accusation, but Ms Fishkind's expression didn't change. "Take your time," she said, answering the telephone. While she talked into the receiver Honey puzzled out the form. She could read it much more quickly than anything at the Seminal Resource, but not because the words were much simpler. When she had grasped it she returned to the heading, which mystified her. MEDICAL HERSTORY. It definitely said MEDICAL HERSTORY.

"Mmm hmmm," said Ms Fishkind into the phone. "Would you care to share with me the nature of your fertility problem . . ? I understand, yes. We would try to help . . ."

Honey clicked. A feminist organisation, of course – not "History" but "Herstory". She found it appealing, and, as far as her own life was concerned, far more accurate.

"I can manage this," she said when the call ended.

"Sure you can. Let me explain our procedure . . ."

Honey listened and understood. The phone rang again. "Excuse me." Honey watched while Ms Fishkind talked. This time it was a potential donor, who sounded, from the responses Honey could hear, anxious and embarrassed. "You would be required to donate semen on our premises . . . in complete privacy . . . you would stimulate yourself into a receptacle we would provide for you . . . may I enquire as to your ethnic origin? Filipino, that's wonderful. . . we have several Filipino mothers who would be very grateful for your contribution . . . strict confidence, of course, entirely your own choice . . . look forward to your visit."

"You don't mind that I can't read very well?" said Honey.

"Not at all. Your baby won't mind."

"Are you sure?" said Honey, knowing as she spoke that it was a foolish question.

"I can't think of one good reason why she should."

"She?"

"Or he. Love 'em, feed 'em, listen to 'em, they're happy as clams. I'll give you all our materials to take away and read at your leisure. Come back when you've figured out what you need to know and we'll sign you

168

up for one of our programmes, if that's what you want. Look forward to it."

By dinnertime Honey had worked through all the material. It was easy enough to understand. She bought a postcard of the Golden Gate Bridge and, waiting for her clam chowder, addressed it to Till. "Staying a weke or too. Wish yu were hear." What else could she write to convey a fraction of the joy she felt? She wrinkled her forehead again. Words, what it would be to have words. Perhaps her child would have words and could interpret for her like an English-born child of a Pakistani immigrant. A line came back to her from a film she acted in – a typical Honey part she'd played, a girl who listened and smiled and looked beautiful – the script had been in verse. She counted the quantities of the line on her fingers. Till had explained, coaching her with the dialogue, about quantities: how you hadn't to alter them, how they were part of the music of the sense. Her new version fitted and she wrote it with great care. "Oh brave new wirld, that has Ms Fishkind in it."

Chapter Nine

Till's phantom lover was more effective than several of her previous real ones in forcing her to improve her appearance. She emphatically did not want Ben to find out that she had lied. It was such a transparent, vulnerable lie; it would have given him so much information she did not want him to have about her insecurities and her interest. So during his absence skiing her hair was tinted from decaying mouse to bright brown, cut and blowdried so it swept back from her face. It did not, in her view, make her look much better, but it did signal that she was trying. "You look like Margaret Thatcher," said Amanda derisively. "Why do you bother, at your age?"

"I'm glad you like it."

"I didn't say that."

"Sorry. I'm going deaf. It must be my age," said Till, and went clothes shopping.

She also made an effort to go out in case Ben cross-examined Amanda about her movements. In two weeks she saw *The Cid*, *Les Liaisons Dangereuses*, *The House of Bernarda Alba*, and Domingo singing *Otello*. These gave her such a dark view of the human condition that she went to *Crocodile Dundee*.

Amanda, left alone, read Honey's postcard for the hundredth time; it had been lying by the telephone for days and she spent much of her time by the telephone, but Jonathan still hadn't rung. ("Are you sure you're not waiting for a special call?" Till repeatedly asked. "Of course not. Shut up, Mummy.") Reluctantly, Amanda was beginning to believe that he wasn't going to. She knew he knew the number; she'd left messages with all her friends at school who saw him often.

He wasn't going to ring. But he'd danced with her at the sixth-form party, all evening, then behind the Sports Hall, on the grass, they'd made love, so that meant he must care about her. Possibly. He had been quite drunk. But he'd definitely cared enough to make love to her and surely that meant something. There was no one to discuss it with. She was afraid to mention it to her friends; she had heard them talking about Jonathan before, saying he would lay anything that moved. She had laughed at the time because he meant nothing to her, he was just another Eton boy with a smooth line of talk, beautiful clothes and a father who owned half Scotland.

The experience had been fantastic. Well, quite fantastic. Well, actually, painful, embarrassing and over before she wholly knew it was happening. They were lying on frozen grass under the windows of the Sports Hall coffee shop (what if a member of staff had patrolled past?) and he had lifted her skirt and then – but it was supposed to be significant, it was a turning point, she was a woman now. Sort of a woman. Harry would be good to talk to except that he didn't rate Jonathan who had been in his house at school and whom he referred to, when he bothered, as that vain little squit. Harry wouldn't have anything encouraging to say and she would be embarrassed mentioning it.

Why was everything so EMBARRASSING? There was always her mother, of course, but she'd be shocked. No, she wouldn't. She should be shocked but she wasn't a proper mother and she'd certainly say something crushing and what she would call realistic which meant cynical, pessimistic and hopeless, and without the hope that Jonathan would ring her, Amanda thought, she had nothing.

Till didn't care about her anyway. She'd been out nearly every night, not that Amanda wanted her to stay

171

in of course because she was so boring, but it was the least a mother could do. She kept saying, ask your friends round, but most of her friends were at school and if she wasn't alone when Jonathan rang she couldn't talk about – it. Matilda didn't want her there, it was clear, even though she did her best to be helpful and had done the washing-up every day. Almost every day. At least three times, without being asked, and what did it matter if her room was a mess anyway, not that Matilda seemed to care. Then she said such heartless things, for instance only that morning when Amanda had protested about Till going out again and Till said, "Never mind, adolescence is a self-limiting affliction." Silly old woman. Thinking she was still a real person who had boyfriends like that wretched Ben Considine who kept ringing up since he got back from St Moritz, married as he was, and using the telephone line that Jonathan would have been on if only Matilda had some sense of maternal duty.

The doorbell rang. "Oh shit," said Amanda, after the first delirious conviction that Jonathan would be waiting outside subsided. It was bloody Ben Considine, fancying himself on the doorstep in expensive clothes though not as expensive as Jonathan's. She intended to keep Ben out but before she knew how it was done he was inside, sipping his own whisky. She didn't like him but she had to admit he had charm. Very few seventeen-year-old girls could be alone with a Ben Considine intent to please and remain unimpressed. Amanda wasn't one of them. When he left Amanda believed he'd been interested in her. She'd even told him almost everything about Jonathan. He suggested that she enjoy herself, go to parties, seem successful and happy (he seemed to think she could); when Jonathan heard this he would be more likely to ring her, not less. Could be. Ben said she had good legs, she was pretty, she was clever. Of course all of that was true; perceptive of him to notice. He hadn't mentioned her breasts. Perhaps you couldn't expect him actually to say "breasts" but he could have said "figure" or "body". If he'd said "You have a good body" that would have included breasts. As it was, perhaps a criticism was implied.

Amanda had told Ben how impressed she was with his plays. That was another blot on her memory of the conversation. He hadn't seemed to value her opinion. Didn't he know she'd got into Oxford? After he'd gone the flat seemed much bigger and she felt exhilarated and discontented. She took her clothes off and examined her breasts in the mirror. Nothing wrong. Not too big, not too small, firm. She tried putting a pencil under them. It fell on the left side but it remained on the right despite judicious wriggling until she lifted her arm. Was the right breast droopier than the left? Was that why Ben hadn't valued her judgement? Was that why Jonathan wasn't ringing?

She leaned to one side and took a handful of the flesh thus squeezed together. Yuck. She must lose weight. This thought took her to the refrigerator where she ate a quarter of a pound of cheese with Hellman's mayonnaise while she planned her diet.

Honey needn't have stayed in San Francisco for a month. The full preparation programme at the Feminist Women's Health Co-operative only took three weeks, and Ms Fishkind was, in any case, quite willing to arrange an accelerated course just for her. But she was happy in California and, besides, it was a practical move. When she did produce a child, people would be curious about its father, and then she could hint that she had met a man in San Francisco who was too important or too married to name.

It took her a very short time to accustom herself to the idea that the father of her child would be a Caucasian male in his mid-twenties whose frozen sperm would be kept in a little plastic phial packed in dry ice until she inserted it with a syringe in an ambiance of her choice. The process

173

reminded her of film-making: technical and laborious in production, with a powerful aesthetic and emotional result. The readings she took of her basal metabolic temperature interested her; she liked the idea that her body was ticking over every month waiting to be fertilised and producing a little peak of heat as a signal at the best times.

It is difficult to feel like a stranger in San Francisco, consumed as it is by self-importance; alone among American cities, what matters there is not who you were or where you came from, but merely the fact of your presence. Honey had moved from the downtown hotel to a cheaper but pleasant motel in Palto Alto. "Your stay here," Ms Fishkind said, "is an opportunity for growth." She was keen on growth. I'm growing, I'm growing, Honey thought, choosing her own motel, adapting the room to her needs by buying a cassette recorder and tapes to listen to and lengths of silk to cover the walls. She fastened the silk to the walls with what she discovered the Americans called "thumb-tacks". The room was on the ground floor at the back of the motel overlooking the pool which, at this time of year, was out of use. It still contained water and floating leaves. Every morning the leaves were scooped off by the muscled black man who did the garden work. Honey sat often at the writing-desk by the window, which slid open (she liked that) to let in air. She finished *Mucus*, puzzled. What had Tom meant by saying his life was changed by it? It seemed so like one kind of horror film. Perhaps he didn't go to horror films. Perhaps there was a virtue in the writing she didn't recognise. Perhaps her child would, in years to come, be able to tell her. Or Till could tell her now. She knew it would be useless to ask Ms Fishkind, who discussed books only in terms of what they said. Even Honey knew that it was equally if not more important to address yourself to how they said it.

One Saturday morning Honey drove into the Centre to help. Saturday was always busy: Ms Fishkind's efficient assistant, Ella, was sick; two voluntary helpers were away. Hovering on the outskirts, observant, peripheral, Honey had quickly picked up the dynamics of the Centre. Only Ms Fishkind and Ella worked effectively. The rest, volunteers, were merely officious. The only other salaried employee was a youth plagued with virulent acne and so obese that he could not perform the function for which he was hired: to carry heavy boxes up the narrow wooden stairs to the first floor. He could just fit up the stairs himself; carrying boxes, he became repeatedly wedged and had to be extricated with much pulling and shoving by the wiry Ms Fishkind.

At first, Honey had wondered why Ms Fishkind went on employing him. Then, as she got to know her better, she realised that Ms Fishkind was tirelessly generous, that she put people first; that the youth, probably friendless and in need of the friendly acceptance of the Centre, was an object of charity. The better she knew Ms Fishkind the more she reminded her of Till, an American Till without irony and self-deprecation; more direct, much less complicated, much sunnier, but still a person who would work until she dropped to protect other people from the undeserved consequence of their vulnerabilities.

Honey enjoyed helping Ms Fishkind. She had never felt able to help Till. If she had, she thought, she would perhaps have loved her even more.

As Honey had suspected, that Saturday the Centre was in chaos. The new volunteer answering the telephone hadn't yet cracked the workings of the switchboard. The obese youth was wedged on the turn of the stairs with Ms Fishkind tugging from above. Two first-time donors waited in the reception area, apparently on the point of bolting.

"Sarah!" called Ms Fishkind with relief. "Can you attend to these gentlemen? Make them comfortable in the Generosity Rooms. Sterile containers in the cabinet. I'll process the paperwork later."

Vital paperwork, thought Honey. One of the donors was black, one Chinese. She fetched dishes and smiled at the black.

"Hi. I'm Sarah. Glad to meet you."

"You sure are beautiful," said the black. "Hi. I'm Abraham. You can call me Fingers."

"Follow me, Fingers." The Generosity Room was actually a generosity cubicle with a couch, a chair, a washbasin and just enough room for one person to stand. Honey perched on the couch to let Fingers stand inside the closed door. "This is a really kind thing you're doing," she said. "I suppose this is your first visit? Right. We'll leave you in complete privacy. You'll find stimulating material in this literature." She pointed to a stack of magazines in the corner. "When you've made your donation into this dish, come on out into the reception area and Ms Fishkind will complete the paperwork."

"How much?" said Fingers.

"Quantity doesn't matter," said Honey, thinking he meant sperm and wondering if he had a regulating mechanism. Sometimes, as now, she felt her sexual inexperience keenly.

He laughed, showing very white, sharp teeth. "I've no problems in that area – your little dish will be brimmin' over. I meant dollars."

"Twenty-five dollars," said Honey, edging past him to the door.

"No way you'll stay and help me out? It'd be faster than the literature."

Above them, Honey could hear the youth dislodged with a final crash. She was unworried by Fingers' advances; he was so obviously strutting to cover his nervousness. "You're on your own," she said and reached up to pat his face. "I've got to work."

At five-thirty, Ms Fishkind and Honey were alone in the office. "You're great at this kind of work, Honey," said

176

Ms Fishkind attending to the answering machine, covering the typewriter, feeding the plants. "Pity you have to leave, otherwise I'd ask you to consider helping out on a financial basis. Ella's leaving soon."

"Do you mean it?"

"Sure I mean it." When asked this Ms Fishkind always looked puzzled; perhaps, thought Honey taken aback at the idea, she only ever said things she meant. "You're terrific with the clients and you're so smart."

"Smart?"

"Yeah."

"I'm stupid," said Honey.

"No way. You're the quickest learner I ever saw. Maybe there's someplace like us in Great Britain? You could work there."

"There probably is but I wouldn't have the nerve. England is – England is – failure, for me."

"So move," said Ms Fishkind. "Come to the US of A. Come work with me. But first, come over to supper tonight."

She lived in a small frame-house in an area Honey didn't know, in a street of houses just like hers with small fenced back yards and a tidy, low-income, striving air. They sat in the kitchen. Ms Fishkind's lover, Kathleen, was tall, raw-boned and monosyllabic. She and Ms Fishkind often exchanged open, loving smiles and stroked each other. Outside it was raining and their four-year-old son was watching the rain.

Kathleen served food; Honey recognised none of it. It was vegetarian and not unpleasant: bean sprouts and alfalfa and puréed pulses, unsalted. The household drank no tea or coffee or alcohol or carbonated soft drinks. The kitchen was papered with the child's drawings. The conversation was malice-free. Honey could not imagine a comparable English evening so lacking in bitchery. She expected to enjoy it but it had a kind of blandness, like the food, which soon palled. She began, for the first time since coming to San Francisco, to feel homesick. She sipped her drinking yoghurt and imagined she was in a gigantic American playpen, filled with approval and devoid of sharp knives.

"She has to go out sometimes," said Ben crossly. His voice was tinny on the telephone line. He had rung Till at her office, waiting for the ten-minute gap between patients, knowing her routine.

"She doesn't, at the moment, except to go to her tutorial college, and we can't even rely on that."

"Let's risk it. I need to see you."

"Need?"

"Want, would like to, whatever."

"Occupy yourself with the BBC blonde."

"I do, but not for the same purposes. Couldn't we meet somewhere else? Where do you meet your lover?"

"At his place."

"What about his wife?"

Till hesitated, luxuriating in the pleasures of fiction. She could invent a wife, she could widow her phantom lover, make him bisexual and send his current lover abroad or commit him to an Aids clinic . . . "She spends most of her time at their house in the country," she said. "She's a sad woman. She hasn't been the same since their younger son died. She ran him over in their garage. It was a terrible accident, and instead of bringing them closer together it—"

"Left him with sole use of the London flat. Excellent," interrupted Ben. "Do you have a key?"

"No," said Till, biting her tongue to prevent herself continuing with a description of her lover's phobic reaction to keys since his elder child choked to death on one.

"Ask for a key, or isn't he that interested in you?"

"I wouldn't use his place to meet you, anyhow."

"Why?"

"It wouldn't be fair." It would also be a great deal too much like work to find a real flat for a phantom lover.

"I want to *talk* to you," said Ben angrily.

"Take me out to lunch."

"Someone might see us. Pandora's worried enough already about my unexplained absences."

"And your unexplained drop in sexual activity in the home?"

"No. I'm keeping that up."

"Oh, good."

"Sex isn't my problem."

"Don't boast."

"Just stating a fact. Can't write, can rut. Nobody does it better."

"Few talk about it so much. What are you feeling insecure about, Benjamin?"

"Do you know what I'm doing as we speak?"

"Staring at a blank piece of paper in your study?"

"Worse than that."

"What can be worse than blank paper?"

"My Pardoe-commissioned rewrite of the musical adaptation of *Macbeth*."

"I hope there's a nice production number for the witches."

"Stop laughing, Till. It isn't funny."

"Of course it is. I suggest a Busby Berkeley number, full chorus of girls in stockings dancing down steps, each carrying one of the ingredients for the spell. Eye of newt and toe of frog – you'd have to make them large enough to be visible – finger of birth-strangled babe, liver of blaspheming Jew – they might even get you on racism there, perhaps it should become liver of Conservative Cabinet Minister . . ."

"Do you know how many plays Shakespeare wrote?" pursued Ben.

"In the high thirties, wasn't it?"

"And do you know why he managed to write so much?"

"Talent, I suppose. Couldn't we abandon the Socratic method here?"

"No. Because he wasn't married to a Pardoe. Men are different from women—"

"Yes, they talk more balls," said Till. "I have a patient any minute, Ben."

"Who is more important than me."

"At the moment. Goodbye." She replaced the receiver, still smiling. Talking to Ben made her feel alive. Deliberately, she looked no further than that.

Tom Wyatt was walking home to pass the time, through Hyde Park. It was a clear late February day: no cloud, bright but not warm sunlight, frost underfoot. It was a very cold winter but Tom enjoyed the sparkle of frost on the grass, the chill of the air in his lungs, because very soon he would be safe inside the well-insulated, centrally heated house. His pace slowed as he walked up Campden Hill Road, past Honey's. Still no sign of her; nothing for a month. She must still be in America.

Madeline was there, however. She was getting out of a taxi and he raised his hat to her, intending to walk on, but she wanted to talk and he had to stop; one couldn't walk away from a female acquaintance. They worked through the weather, her health, London property prices and the stock market. He was driven to ask after Jacky; her already drum-tight face seemed to tighten further. "Jacky has gone to Kenya," she said, and folded her lips together with stapling determination.

Three weeks after she arrived, Honey drove into San Francisco to buy another book. Part of the drive was along an archetypically American street. On each side were fast-food restaurants sporting gigantic plastic representations of the plastic food for sale within: a huge hamburger dripping mucoid mayonnaise, a fish, a giant steak platter. There were cut-price furniture stores and

7-Elevens and traffic lights strung across the street like Christmas decorations left over from twelfth night. She was fond of her car, the sub-compact with a stick-shift that the car-rental clerk had anxiously questioned her about. "Sure you can handle a stick-shift, now?" What a country, where changing gear was an accomplishment.

It was a rare day, with blue sky. She parked the car at Fisherman's Wharf, spent an hour in a coffee shop watching the tourists on the sidewalk outside, then ambled through the slow-moving crowds till she found a bookstore. The proprietor was a relic of Haight-Ashbury in the late sixties. He wore tattered jeans, a Janis Joplin T-shirt, long hair and love beads, and he was not in the least surprised by her request. "I want a book about life," she said.

"You got an author in mind?" His eyes were dreamy with hash and his face gaunt, but he got up from his chair briskly enough.

"A philosopher."

"Plenty of those. John Lennon?"

"Not exactly. Someone more traditional."

"You know the Bible at all?" he said, running his hand along the shelf. "Descartes? Machiavelli? Karl Marx?"

"What would you recommend?"

"I don't read a whole lot any more. I'm into meditation, making contact with the philosopher within."

"I don't have much within," said Honey. "And I don't read very well, either."

"You visually impaired?"

"What?"

"Can you see?"

"Oh, yes. I just can't read quickly."

"You Pisces?"

"No, Cancer."

"I knew it was a water sign. Deep and still. Endurance and strength."

"That doesn't sound like me."

"And humility. Here's the book for you."

Honey turned it over in her hands, flicked through the pages. "Who was Mark Arelus?"

"Marcus Aurelius. He was a Roman Emperor and a great guy. The advantage as far as you're concerned, most of his *Meditations* are short so you can take 'em one at a time."

"Is it a famous book? Will people in England have heard of it?"

"Sure."

"And is it respectable? If I quote from it, will people laugh at me?"

"Why should they?"

"England's different from America. Everyone – everyone's read the same books. The people who've been to university, I mean. They all – most of them – say the same things, and if you say something different, or quote something out of fashion, then they look at each other and smile pityingly at you."

"That's really weird." He was apparently in no hurry to make a sale, to go back to his chair, to pursue other customers or do anything except lean against the shelves and talk to her.

"Did you go to university?" she asked.

"Mm-hmm."

"Where?"

"Near Boston. A school called Harvard."

Honey laughed. "That's an English thing to say. Understatement. Everyone's heard of Harvard, even me."

"Why *even* you?"

"Because I'm ignorant."

"No, you're not. I'll bet you know all about something. Everyone has an area of specialisation."

"And that's an American thing to say. Encouraging and hopeful. How much do I owe you for the book?"

Chapter Ten

"I'd have died if Jonathan hadn't rung," said Amanda, bringing another pile of clothes down the stairs and scattering them over every available surface.

"I'd probably have killed you," said Till, obligingly swinging her feet to the floor so there was more space on the sofa.

"Ha ha. What should I wear, Mummy?"

"Three days in Scotland?"

"At a *castle* in Scotland. With *very rich people*."

"Three sets of day clothes including something to walk in. Two evening kits."

Amanda was torn. Her recent assumption that Till knew nothing warred with her childhood conviction that Till knew everything. "What kind of evening stuff?"

"Whatever you look prettiest in."

"What kind of day stuff?"

"Avoid bright colours. Everything in Scotland is shades of peat. How are you getting up there?"

"I was wondering about the car." Amanda moved from foot to foot, well aware of how little credit she had with her mother.

"The drive will take hours," said Till, thinking of how much clear time she could have with Ben. "Why don't you go up with Jonathan?"

"He flies."

"Sure his parents will be there?"

"Of course they will."

"Sure they know he's asked you?"

"He'll tell them."

"You're going tomorrow. That's less than a day's warning. Are you sure it's wise to go?"

"*Wise?*"

"How reliable is Jonathan?"

"Don't interfere."

"I don't want you to get hurt. He doesn't ring for a month, then he invites you to stay three hundred miles away without making any provision for you to get there. Does he drink?"

"A little."

"Snort a little coke now and then?"

"Why do you ask?"

"Because he sounds a lot like boys I used to know when I was your age."

"In Queen Victoria's reign. I suppose you avoided boys like that when you were my age?"

"No," said Till. "I ate them for breakfast, and that's what I suggest you do. If he wants to see you, he can see you in London."

"He asked me to stay with his *family*." Amanda threw down the skirt she was holding. "You're spoiling it." She turned away so Till could not see her tears. "What do you want me to do, miss my chance? He's easily the most attractive man I've ever met. He's just such a *hunk*."

"He'd still be a hunk in London."

"Are you forbidding me to go?"

"I think you're too old to forbid," said Till, determined that she shouldn't go for her own sake, longing for her to go so that there would be time for Ben. "I'd be sorry if you went, though. I'll miss you this weekend."

"Why?"

"I like your company. I hoped we'd go to the theatre."

"What to see?"

"Your choice." Till looked woebegone, realised she was overdoing it, toned it down to suppressed regret. Amanda, young but no fool, was suspicious.

"Why so keen on my company now?"

"Reasons," said Till enigmatically.

"Anything to do with the man you've been seeing?"

"What man?"

"Come off it, Mummy. I don't believe you've been trailing out on cold wet nights to acquaint yourself with the latest in London theatre."

"I have," said Till. "I'm just feeling a little low, that's all."

"And you want me to cheer you up?"

"Not if it's going to ruin your love life."

Amanda looked at her mother, slumped, middle-aged, almost pathetic. She felt sorry for her, protective and superior. Till would see how unselfish she was. And perhaps – not that Till was right about Jonathan, but after all he wasn't very reliable. He was too exciting to be reliable, and it would be appalling to turn up if his parents weren't expecting her—

It wasn't until Honey arrived in England that she fully realised how anxious it made her. At the airport, she had forgotten not to be Honey Markham. She felt confident and happy and the reflection of her feeling in her manner drew attention: she was a Personality again. People looked at her, whispered, nudged each other as she passed. The family ahead of her in the passport control queue asked for her autograph; the man who stopped her in Customs said, "Welcome to England, Miss Markham. Been making a film in the States? I wish you would. I really enjoyed *The Daughters of Captain Bridge*. They showed it on telly at Christmas, you know. Whatever happened to the other girl?"

"Which one?"

"Not Pandora. My wife watches her every Saturday on that show. I meant the little one."

"Flea. I'm afraid she was killed in a car accident ten years ago."

"Shame. She was so pretty."

"And Matilda is a psychiatrist."

"Matilda?"

"The girl who played the eldest sister."

"Ah, well," said the man indifferently. He was plump, balding, ginger-haired with fingers like hirsute skinless sausages. "She wasn't so pretty, was she? But you look just the same."

"Thank you," said Honey, knowing that a woman in her late thirties was supposed to be flattered by the information that she still looked eighteen, feeling herself sucked back into relying only on her looks. Had she exercised enough in America? Had the sun – what there was of it – damaged her skin? "I think psychiatrists do very useful work," she said, determined not to appear to agree with his value-judgements.

"Mad, most of them," said the Customs man, pleased to talk to her, letting the passengers scuttle past unsupervised.

"But it's more useful to be a psychiatrist than to be pretty."

He laughed, unattractive himself, secure behind the assumption that any man could judge any woman as flesh with the approval of everyone who listened. "Very few men would agree with you there."

Honey, recruited to the women's cause by instinct, partly informed by Till and Ms Fishkind, might have left the starting gate decades behind Gloria Steinem and Germaine Greer but was determined to finish the course. "Very few people agreed when whoever it was said that the earth went round the sun. Galilee, wasn't it?"

"What?" The man began to be annoyed. Honey was supposed to smile and thank, not argue.

"The man they put to death for saying the earth went round the sun. I think his name was Galilee. He was right and they were wrong, all of them, so just because most people think something doesn't make it true."

"Thank you, Miss Markham. Move along, please,

I have work to do. You sound like a woman's libber."

"And everyone knows that women's libbers are either dykes or too plain to get a man, right?" said Honey, and smiled. Lust and annoyance writhed in his face. "Thank you," she said, swinging her bag over her shoulder.

"Galileo," said the Customs man. "If you're going to argue, at least get your facts right." You stupid bitch, his voice implied.

"But the earth still moves," said Honey. "Have a nice day."

Once in the arrivals section of the airport, she had to lean against a pillar, she was shaking so much from the encounter. She was proud of herself even though she'd mistaken Galileo's name, but she was also deeply upset. She had been so rude, by the Customs man's standards, and she wasn't used to it. "Treat with respect the power you have to form an opinion," she said to herself. It was her favourite of Marcus Aurelius' observations so far; she had reached the end of Book Three. Only twenty-five pages in a week's steady work, but she had understood every word. Perhaps he wasn't a real philosopher, if she could understand him? That's what Florence would say. Back in England, thoughts of Florence were not easily dismissed. But surely Marcus Aurelius knew more than Florence? Not only had he been an Emperor but his *Meditations* were still being read nearly two thousand years after his death, in translation and in another country. Florence could hardly expect the same immortality. Florence's immortality would be in her child and her child's children.

Meanwhile Honey had to get a taxi. A little recovered, she made her way through the terminal. She began to feel it had been a mistake not to bring back sperm with her. In America it had seemed a good plan to wait a few months, to chart her temperature so she was sure of the best time for conception, to prepare herself for pregnancy. But now at Heathrow she had become Honey in England, vulnerable, ignorant. Passers-by were staring at her. She must get back to the flat, ring up Till. What would Till say about the sperm banks? Ms Fishkind and Marcus Aurelius insisted that it didn't matter what other people thought, that she must make her own decisions. She agreed with the principle, had reservations about her own case. She was so likely to be wrong, and if she was wrong then her child would suffer. Perhaps she would be a selfish mother like Florence and her child would hate her.

"Children tend to hate their parents anyway, on and off," said Till the next day. "Amanda hates me at present." She was driving Honey down to Southampton to put flowers on Flea's grave. It was the tenth anniversary of Flea's death. Honey had gone each year so far, though she had never mentioned it to Till, who she knew had a brisk attitude to bodies, graves and ceremonial remembrance. Today, however, Till had got rid of Amanda for Sunday lunch at her father's; Ben was incommunicado inside Pandora's proprietorial stockade, and driving Honey's BMW down the M3 was a treat.

So far, Honey hadn't paused for breath. Till was fully briefed on sperm banks, Ms Fishkind, Americans and Marcus Aurelius. What she had chiefly heard, what delighted her, was the happiness in Honey's voice.

"So you don't think it's too cruel to have a child without a father?"

"Absolutely not, if you won't feel guilty. Would you tell it the truth?"

"Don't you think one should always tell a child the truth?"

"Not if a fantasy is more sustaining and it'll never find out. What most people mean by telling the truth is giving their own interpretation, usually the grimmest possible interpretation, of whatever happened. This is a beautiful car, Honey."

"I couldn't tell Florence, then. She'd surely tell the child."

"Make up an American lover. I would."

"That was my plan, but I'm not good at inventing."

"Borrow my phantom lover," said Till laughing, and explained about Ben and her lies. Honey was worried.

"That's terrible about the child being run over."

"It wasn't run over. It doesn't exist. I invented it."

"But you just invented it to run it over."

"That's what fiction means."

"I'll make up a happy lover of my own, thanks."

"Excellent. Is this the turn-off for the cemetery?"

Till parked in the deserted lot – it was lunch-time – and when she turned the engine off and opened the car door, the only sound was the whine of wind in the yew trees. The cemetery was high on a hill overlooking Southampton; below it, allotments ran seedily down the slope to a new housing estate. In the distance, stray beams of sunlight glinted off the oil refinery storage tanks behind the funnels of two huge liners.

"Can you remember where the grave is?" she said, opening the back door to remove armfuls of white roses.

"Along here." Honey led the way through rows of tombstones, most of them recent and ugly, white marble or black marble flecked with colour. "It has something nice written on it. I like to think it's true about Flea. Whenever I think of her I think of the tombstone as well." She stopped in front of a particularly large slab of black marble with letters in gold, almost unreadable apart from the two words emblazoned at the top: PERPETUAL FELICITY. The rest of the stone, Till puzzled out, said "In memory of Jadwiga Bednarowska, 1938–76". Honey was occupied disentangling the roses from their wrappings. "Honey, this isn't Flea's grave."

"Yes, it is," said Honey. "That's her name, see? Felicity. Felicity who lives for ever, that's what perpetual means. I looked it up."

"Don't you remember the funeral?" It had been a nightmare of photographers; just before her death Flea was engaged to a duke's eldest son; the combination of his smart friends and her show-business colleagues had made the funeral news. A minor member of the Royal Family had even attended. Flea's shabby parents were shouldered aside, graves were trampled, because the photographers had been misdirected to the wrong church for the actual service and so had come on to the interment. Vernon had slipped into the grave and had to be helped out by the officiating priest and Till while the undertaker's men grimly clutched the coffin. "I'm sure the grave was at the end of a row," said Till. "I remember thinking what a beautiful view she had over Southampton Water."

"Whose grave is this, then?" said Honey, bewildered.

"Someone called Jadwiga Bednarowska, presumably a Pole."

"I couldn't make out that bit, only the year of death, 1976. Why does it say Felicity?"

"That's a word as well as a name. It means 'happiness', 'eternal happiness'."

"Oh," said Honey blankly. "I've been bringing roses to the wrong grave, all these years." She divided the roses into two bunches, left one bunch on Jadwiga's grave. "We'd better look for Flea's, then."

Doggedly, she followed Till until they found the grave. "Felicity Cousins, 1958–76". "This is it," said Till.

"I'm such a fool," said Honey strewing the roses, "I know nothing."

Till sat on the low wall, swinging her legs over the steep drop. "Sarah Markham, you are beautiful, healthy, intelligent, sensitive and rich. You own a BMW. If you want sympathy from me you've come to the wrong place. Come and look at the view. Lucky Flea, rolled round in earth's diurnal course with a view of Southampton Water."

"That isn't Southampton Water, surely. Isn't that the docks?" Honey joined her on the wall. Her legs were much shorter than Till's; she couldn't touch the sloping ground beneath her and the drop made her nervous.

"How come you know so much about Southampton?"

"Alexander used to sail. We stayed with some of his friends near here for Cowes Week. Do you believe in life after death?"

"Only in the memory of friends who bring roses."

"To the wrong grave." Honey drew her legs up and clasped her hands around her knees. "It could have been either of us dead."

There was a pause, then she said consideringly, "I'm not really beautiful, you know."

"What do you mean?"

"I'm just very pretty. I have an ordinary face, perfectly regular. If I do myself up differently people can't recognise me."

"Useful for films."

"Not if you don't play character parts. The best kind of film face is like Meryl Streep's, peculiar but fascinating. But I looked very like Flea, for instance."

"She was lovely too."

"That's exactly my point."

"What are you getting at, Honey?"

Honey didn't answer. After a while, Till asked, "Who else have you told about sperm banks?"

"Only Jacky, and he promised . . ."

"*Jacky?*"

"Don't you trust him?"

"Not where his own advantage is concerned."

Honey shook her head. "What use could it be to him?"

"Next time he goes on one of his gambling sprees and loses everything he has and gives markers for what he doesn't have, your secret might seem a marketable commodity – something to sell—"

"I know what 'marketable commodity' means," said Honey petulantly. She still wasn't convinced. "He'd only get the odd thousand, if that."

191

"The odd thousand can seem oddly attractive when odd people hold your marker."

"Seriously?"

"Very seriously."

Honey began to gnaw at the skin round her nails. "What should I do?"

"I can probably fix him. I don't think the statute of limitations has run out on his ex-wife's jewels."

"What?"

"Never mind."

"Do you mean *blackmail*?"

"Only between friends."

"Would you speak to him for me?" Honey seized Till's arm; Till could feel it bruising. Gently, she loosened Honey's grip.

"I'll speak to him. We don't want to go plunging in looking keen. It'll put up the value he sets on your secret. Softly softly catchee Hamzavi."

"Is that where the telly title came from?"

"I think so. Softly, softly, catchee monkey."

"I never knew that."

What Honey didn't know, thought Till, would fill the British Library. Sometimes, Honey irritated her; her innocence invited betrayal. Briefly, she sympathised with Steve.

"What are you thinking?" Honey sensed her disapproval. "I don't like it when you don't – approve of me."

"Don't cling, it never helps."

"I know," said Honey blinking back tears. "I'm working on it. Ms Fishkind said—"

Till was alone in her flat. Amanda had decided to stay the night with Charles and Claire; Honey was having supper with Florence. Till had stayed in the bath for two hours reading a book on cosmology, skipping most of the mathematics. Her skin was softened and wrinkled but her mind was restored. The strain of Amanda's presence came fully home to her only when it was briefly removed.

She was drying her toes, reflecting that they looked like a pink variety of reconstituted prune, when the phone rang. Ben didn't identify himself; he assumed she would recognise his voice, which of course she did. "Old man Pardoe has been rushed to hospital," he said.

"Is he seriously ill?"

"I don't think so, but Pandora's at his bedside. The doctors say he'll have to rest for weeks."

"Does this mean you'll have to rewrite *Macbeth* so that the hero is recumbent throughout? That'll tax your technical skill—"

"Shut up and listen, Livesey. Are you still being faithful to your ridiculous lover?"

"Yes. A woman's word is her bond."

"Not in my experience, and in this case a woman's word is a pain in the ass. It means I'll have to see my blonde first."

"A ram's gotta do what a ram's gotta do. Tell her I support the BBC all the way and I don't begrudge a penny of my licence fee."

"Have you paid it?"

"Oh, I think so."

"I'll get to you by midnight."

"Make sure you shower first."

"She and I usually shower together."

"Make sure you shower after you and she shower. I have my pride."

"I didn't know your pride was invested in hygiene."

"Will you be spending the night?"

"Yes. Pandora's going to kip over with Salome. She lives near the hospital."

"Which hospital is he in?"

"Who cares? See you later."

After she had washed and dried her hair, tidied the flat, put make-up on and ironed her nicest Victorian nightdress, Till laughed at herself. She took care not to laugh within sight of a mirror because laughing made her lines worse. She was behaving foolishly, like a girl without a girl's assets and hopes. There could be no future for her with Ben; she couldn't afford him. At present he lived on Pandora. If he divorced her she would be vindictive, and a Pardoe vindictive was an effective Pardoe. Ben would be lucky to work again unless he managed to write a decent play, and in Till's view this was unlikely, because he had lost his nerve. That made him more attractive to her; more vulnerable, more human; but he lacked the resources to cope with impecunious failure. He would merely sulk and drink.

He arrived before midnight. "Let's go to bed," he said on the doorstep, handing her an azalea.

"Where did you get that?"

"I pinched it from Zara."

"Who?"

"The BBC blonde. Her name is Zara. Her flat is already grossly over-planted and she didn't see me out because she was sleeping the sleep of a Yuppie due to catch the early-morning shuttle to Glasgow. And I thought you'd like an azalea."

"Bed, then."

Till was already in her nightdress and she lay stretched across the bed under the warmth of the duvet watching him undress. His movements were deft; like most men who often undress in strange bedrooms he didn't waste time looking for places to hang his clothes but folded them neatly on a chair, hung his jacket on the back, shucked off his boxer shorts and put them close at hand. He had done that ever since he was chased naked through the streets by an angry and unexpected husband.

"Why boxer shorts?"

"Chosen by Pandora."

"I liked you in those little French slips with seams."

"No one wears them any more."

"My lover does."

"Ever since his other child was suffocated by boxer shorts, don't tell me."

"Don't laugh at human misery. It was a dreadful thing for his wife to kill her own child."

"I'm laughing at your capacity for invention."

Till felt herself on crumbling ground. Better not to insist on the truth of her lies, since Ben was intuitive and he knew her too well. He probably still believed there was a lover and it was best not to push her luck over the garage tragedy. He was lying beside her, twining toes. She rubbed her foot against his leg, feeling the muscles and the familiar shape of bone, the well-defined ankle. "Zara wears Opium," she said burying her face in his hair.

"For me, Zara is opium. Forgetfulness."

Till groaned. "This is me, Matilda. Remember? You don't have to give me that old line. Burying your tragic soul in fitful pleasure. Is she good in bed?"

"Not as good as you."

"Who is?"

"Very few," he said slipping his arm under her shoulders and hugging her. "No amateurs."

"You classify me as an amateur?"

"Absolutely. The last great amateur. The sixties live in the person of Matilda."

"I'm retired."

"What about your lover?"

"He's a pensioner's lover. Undemanding, hesitant, gentle."

"I love you, Matilda."

"What?"

"You heard."

"You never say that."

"I just did. I have missed you painfully."

"You know I love you, Benjamin."

"I hoped so. Until you went buggering off with that Marine. What did you see in him?"

"He was reliable. I always knew where I was."

"On your back." Simultaneously, they turned their heads to kiss. Ben's nose collided with Till's brow-bone and they both wailed in pain, then settled down again. "Couldn't we get rid of one of these pillows? You know I hate them," said Ben.

"Chuck as many as you want." They lay in silence, listening to the noises in the street outside. Further down Ladbroke Grove a gang of youths were yelling and kicking cans. There was the tinkle of broken glass, probably from a headlight.

"Where's your car parked?" she asked.

"Closer than that. It's insured, anyway." He held her more tightly. "Why are you wearing yards of calico?"

"In case I inflame you with the touch of my body."

"You've inflamed me, you've inflamed me. The calico isn't working. Shall we take it off?"

"Can't we just talk and sleep? Tell me how you knew Amanda wouldn't be here tonight."

He chuckled. "I made a deal with her, that she'd stay over with Charlie to leave me the night with you."

"I thought she didn't like you."

"I've worked hard with her, twice. She likes me."

"And did you also engineer Leo Pardoe's illness?"

"That was luck."

"Not for him," said Till.

"Your sympathies are as broad as your luscious hips."

"Your lines are as weary as my tits."

"Funny how potent cheap lines are."

"Noel Coward wrote more plays than you."

"And he got more parts than you."

"You've taken my nightdress off."

"You'll have to pull it over your head."

"As the contortionist said to the bishop."

"Hush," said Ben kissing her neck. "It's past the time for talking."

"No, Benjamin – absolutely not – no, Benjamin—"

"Swisser swatter," whispered Benjamin.

Chapter Eleven

"What does 'swisser swatter' mean?" said Pandora. She and Till were waiting for Honey in a restaurant in Covent Garden.

"Why?" fenced Till.

"Because – look – " Pandora produced from her bag a folded sheet of Ben's grey paper. The first half was covered with the draft of a scene from *Macbeth, the Musical*. Till was disappointed to see that Ben had not taken her advice on the witches. Instead of Busby Berkeley he was apparently inclining towards Bob Fosse. When it broke off he had repeatedly typed "swisser swatter Benjamin's a fool swisser swatter Benjamin's a fool".

Till calculated. Eventually, Pandora would find a Pardoe to interpret for her. Might as well explain. "I don't remember it very clearly," she said. She had been searching libraries for the past two days, since the night with Ben, to check her recollection. "It's a quotation from Aubrey's *Brief Lives*."

"Aubrey who? What else has he written? Do you know him?"

"His last name was Aubrey and he lived three hundred years ago and wrote a collection of biographies. This comes from the biography of Walter Raleigh, a well-known seducer."

"Like Ben."

"If the condom fits—"

"Matilda!"

"Sorry. The words come from an anecdote about a

particular woman who was fending him off in the garden. He pressed her up against a tree, lifted her skirts and stroked her. She kept saying, 'No, Sir Walter, sweet Sir Walter, no, Sir Walter, sweet Sir Walter'. As she got more excited her words disintegrated into 'swisser swatter'. It may be nothing to do with that, of course,'' she added disingenuously.

"How did Aubrey know what she said?"

"I don't think he did know. It was just a good story."

"I don't see what's good about it," said Pandora grumpily. "I think it's a grubby little story. Was he married?"

"Not then, I think. He married a woman the Queen disapproved of, later."

"Why did the Queen disapprove of her?"

"It wasn't her choice. She wanted to keep him for herself."

"Hmm," said Pandora suspiciously. "Why have you bought new clothes?"

"I couldn't find any old ones in the shops," said Till.

"What do you think Ben meant by writing that again and again? I'm really worried, Till."

"Why do you think Honey's so late? It isn't like her."

"I asked her to come at one-thirty. I wanted to talk to you first. Help me, Matilda."

Pandora seemed worried. Her skin was sallow and drawn; her dyed hair looked dispirited. "I want you to promise me this is in confidence!"

"I promise," said Till, draining her glass of wine and signalling for another: they were each paying their own bill.

"He's seeing another woman."

"Another woman as well as whom?" said Till, alarmed. If Pandora had guessed that the BBC blonde was not alone on Ben's horizon, Till would be in difficulties.

"Another woman as well as me," said Pandora impatiently. "I told you he'd been faithful and I thought he had, but in the last month he's been sloping off so often, and being so nice to me, that I'm sure he's seeing someone else. It's because he's depressed."

"Pandora, I've tried to explain that Ben always *has* other women. He doesn't *see* them, however. He doesn't have the faintest interest in them."

"If he doesn't have the faintest interest in them why is he writing quotations from sex books again and again?"

"Perhaps he's planning to use the episode in *Macbeth, the Musical*."

"I don't believe it. 'Swisser swatter Benjamin's a fool'. How could that fit into *Macbeth*?"

"Literary licence?"

"I think it's guilt. He's saying he's a fool for having sex with other women. Couldn't that be it?"

"It could," said Till, who preferred to think it a compliment to her.

"He sounds less suicidal, though, doesn't he?"

"Much less. How's Leo?"

"Not too bad. He has to stay in hospital another week. How did you know he was ill?"

You stupid cow, Till berated herself, stupid amateurish slow-witted over-confident cow. Now get out of that. "My latest lover," she said. "The man I bought the new clothes for."

"How did he know? We've kept it out of the papers."

"He's a journalist. You know they always get tip-offs from the hospitals."

"Have you seen Ben lately?" Pandora was on the trail. Till chose her words carefully.

"I told you last time we lunched that I hadn't seen Ben since your marriage." She was sitting with her back to the door and she heard the sudden hush then babble of voices that heralded the arrival of a public figure. "Here's Honey," she guessed.

Pandora was disconcerted. "How do you know?"

"Hello, both," said Honey. She and Pandora kissed

in the ritual cheek-fanning gesture. "Love your suit, Pandora. Very French."

"Love yours. I'm not sure . . ."

"Just a little thing I picked up in San Francisco."

"Sure beats Aids," said Till pulling out a chair for her. "I'm just telling Pandora about my lover." She caught Honey's hand under the table and squeezed it warningly to prevent her from blurting out inconvenient truths about Ben or the phantom lover.

Honey's mental processes were not as quick as Till's but her physical composure was superb; years of film work enabled her to sit and smile and look as if her hand was resting casually on her lap instead of being painfully twisted. She raised her eyebrows slightly. "How much have you told Pandora?"

Till babbled on, inventing, embroidering her inventions. All would be well if she could stop Pandora asking her a direct, unavoidable question; if she did, Till wouldn't lie. But Pandora soon tired of the subject of Till's lover and seemed reluctant to return to the subject of Ben while Honey was there.

"Seen Jacky Hamzavi lately?" said Honey, pursuing her own interests once they had ordered.

"I haven't *seen* him," said Pandora with the self-importance of one first with the news, "but guess what?"

"He's left Madeline?" tried Honey.

Pandora was disappointed. Honey was right. "Much more than that. He left with one of her BEST FRIENDS!"

"I didn't know she had any," said Honey without malice.

"One of her least worst enemies, perhaps," suggested Till.

Pandora was unstoppable. "He met her at a party and the next thing Madeline knew, they were off on a photographic safari in Kenya."

"With Jacky as part of the carry-on baggage," said Till.

"Then only last week I saw Madeline at drinks with my

parents, and she told me – delighted about it – that Jacky had been in a terrible accident in a Range Rover that overturned. He was nearly killed. He had a fractured skull, a broken leg, a broken arm. She seemed to think it served him right."

"Where is he now?" said Honey.

"In a hospital in Nairobi."

"Far from Fleet Street," said Till reassuringly.

"But I expect he's short of money?" Honey wrinkled her forehead anxiously.

"What?" said Pandora. "What has Fleet Street to do with it?"

"And poor Jacky," said Honey. "Do you suppose his face is intact?"

"So long as his pelvis survives he'll be employable," said Till. "We must get in touch with him, mustn't we, Honey?"

"I don't understand what you're both talking about," said Pandora, balked.

"It's quite long and complicated," said Honey. "I'll explain if you like." She launched into a dull and fictitious account of what she had said to Jacky and what Jacky had said to her and what they were both wearing at the time. Soon Pandora interrupted with a description of Salome's success at the National Theatre and Honey's secret was safe.

Towards the end of their lunch Honey went to the loo. Immediately Pandora leaned forward and hissed, "What *should* I do, Till? About Ben?"

"I don't see what you can do. Why do you object to him screwing around?"

"It's humiliating."

"I don't see why."

"You're being obstructive," said Pandora. Of course Till was, and she hesitated. Pandora was more serious about this than she had ever seen her about anything except her family. Pandora sensed her advantage and pressed it. "I don't want to be happy, Till, it isn't that. Remember what Dostoevsky said, 'with love, one can live without happiness'. That's how I feel. If I can only keep him, I'll look after him."

Till hadn't known Dostoevsky's views on love and happiness and was astounded that Pandora did. With one of her occasional shrewdnesses, Pandora correctly identified her reaction. "It's all right," she said, "I haven't taken to literature. I saw it in *Cosmopolitan*, but I think it's really true. I love him – absolutely."

"I don't think he'll ever leave you," said Till.

"Why?"

Matilda hesitated again. It would be too hurtful to give the main reason: money.

"Because of the money?" said Pandora. "I think you're right, though he could find someone rich, of course, though maybe not with so much influence in media circles. But I don't want to keep him chained to my bank account, that would be humiliating too. I want to understand him better, I want to know what he's unhappy about and change it. Sometimes I think he hates me. He looks at me as if he hates me."

"It's not just the money," said Till. "I'm sure he'll want to make a success of his marriage. He was very damaged by Jane, you know, by all the chaos and fighting and futility. He never loved me as much as he loved her; I was more useful, that was all, more comforting."

"And would you be more comforting now?" Pandora was staring. Till felt she was only inches away from asking the question Till didn't want to answer.

"I don't know," she said. "Perhaps he finds marriage too difficult. Lots of people do. I do. But he wants to have a good marriage, I bet. That was his intention . . ." She tailed off, remorseful at the cheap point she was about to score.

"That was his intention when he asked you to marry him?" said Pandora. "I know all about that."

"Oh." Till would have liked to hear the version Ben

had told Pandora but knew better than to ask. Treating Pandora justly was one thing, volunteering as a punchbag quite another.

"And he worries about Peregrine."

"Does he?"

"Very much. They still don't talk, you know, and Ben's very Jewish. Being cut off from his own son—"

Till recoiled from a discussion about which Pandora was better informed than she. Pandora was the wife with the rights, the sitting tenant. If she also had information Matilda was completely excluded, and she felt very territorial about Ben. Ben was hers.

"I wouldn't know," she said dismissively.

"I was thinking of religion. Do you think religion would help? Ben cares more about it than he ever lets on. I was considering conversion."

"To Judaism?"

"Or Catholicism. Either. Do you think it matters?"

"Depends whether you want to cook or pray," said Till flippantly.

Usually, Till had a good conceit of herself; too much so for many people's taste; but the encounter with Pandora had unsettled her. She had been thoroughly reminded where Ben belonged, where his future lay, and how unhelpful it would be for both of them if he continued to see her. She wanted to go back to the Psychotherapy Centre and treat individuals more insecure than she until her equilibrium was restored, but Honey insisted on giving her a lift in her taxi. "What shall we do about Jacky?"

With an effort, Till pulled herself away from thoughts of Ben. "He's safe in a hospital in Nairobi. If he broke his leg badly he's probably in traction."

"They have telephones in Africa." Honey was trembling. "We must stop him talking. We must—"

"You're over-reacting. He's probably forgotten all about it—"

"It's just a – thing to talk about – to you, but . . ."

"Topic of conversation."

"All right, topic of conversation. Who cares about the words? You know what I mean, don't – look down on me—"

"Patronise me."

"It's MY LIFE," said Honey. "It could ruin all my plans. I'm not going to bring up a sperm-bank baby. Think how it would be teased."

"All right," said Till. "What do you want me to do?"

"I want you to ensure that Jacky never tells my secret to anyone, and I want it done quickly."

"It will cost money," said Till.

"How much?"

"Around two thousand."

"No problem. What are you going to do?"

"Fetch him back to England, look after him to make sure he's not short of cash, and explain to him the advantages of his silence."

Back at the Psychotherapy Centre, there were several messages on Till's desk, transcribed verbatim by the receptionist/secretary, one of Till's ex-patients who had broken down under the emotional strain of being a court reporter at the Old Bailey.

"This is Benjamin Considine, is Matilda there? Bloody hell, doesn't she ever go to work? I'll call later."

"Oh, hello, could I speak to Dr Livesey? Oh, gosh, sorry. Yes, please. Tell her Amanda rang and will be staying with Daddy and Claire another night because we're decorating the spare room and I'm doing the wallpaper. Thanks a lot."

"This is Martin Bullard. I had an appointment with Dr Livesey for five o'clock. I will not be attending for treatment as I have found the Lord as my Saviour and He has shown me the Way. Kindly ask Dr Livesey to send my account up to date."

"Hello, Julie, is that you? Harry Livesey here. Is Mummy in? Wouldn't you know it. Be an angel and give her a message. Tell her I'm coming up to London tomorrow and ask her to meet me at Paddington. The train gets in at ten twenty. If she doesn't turn up I'll find my own way home. How're things with you? . . . (the rest of the conversation isn't relevant, Dr Livesey)."

Till tore up the messages, watched them flutter into the wastepaper basket. Harry tomorrow, good. No patient at five o'clock, not bad; but he'd turn up again, unless he kept a firmer grip on Christianity than he had on jogging, Scientology or the Open University. She hoped he did. The chances of her treatment curing him were slim.

She dreaded the evening. No Amanda and no definite arrangement with Ben, so she'd sit edgily waiting for the phone, doing her hair, not settling down to anything. If she went out, to the theatre or a concert, she would spend the performance imagining Ben's call ringing in her empty flat or him standing excluded on the doorstep. She could ring an ex-lover and meet for dinner; but then so much time would be spent catching up on developments in each life there'd be no conversation.

The same applied to women friends, most of whom she hadn't seen for months, whose intervening lives would certainly contain triumph and disaster which they insisted on recounting; which, usually, she would have wanted to listen to, but not tonight.

She got up and moved round the room aimlessly, feeling trapped. Fifty minutes of listening to the four-o'clock patient: an almost unbearable prospect. But, watching the eager arrival of her favourite patient as she ran up the steps of the Psychotherapy Centre, not quite. A far more potentially profitable fifty minutes than waiting for Ben.

" 'That men of a certain type should behave as they do is inevitable. To wish it otherwise were to wish the fig-tree

205

would not yield its juice,'" said Honey, effectively to herself; Florence wasn't listening, she was screaming abuse and throwing handfuls of letters about the flat. The reflection should have been calming but it merely emphasised Honey's inferiority to Marcus Aurelius, because she did indeed wish that the fig-tree, in this case Florence, would yield a different juice or depart and yield juice elsewhere.

"Bloody fan mail. Don't think I'm going to deal with it any more. If you won't get off your backside and work you can hire your own secretary. I've got my own career to think of."

"What about Michele?" said Honey. Michele was the typist who came in three times a week to the office in Earl's Court from which Florence organised Honey's career.

"Michele *kaputt*, gone. Office *kaputt*, gone. No more Honey Markham, that's what you said, no more career. Fat chance I'd keep Michele."

"But the accountant arranged for me to pay Michele and the rent of the office. He gave you the first quarter's cheque in advance."

"I needed the money." Florence avoided Honey's eye and plucked nervously at her scarves; one of her many heavy bracelets became entangled in the scarves and some minutes of undignified wrestling followed while Honey groped for comfort from Marcus Aurelius. "'Leave another's wrongdoing where it lies,'" she concluded finally.

"Why do you keep quoting the Bible?" said Florence impatiently, yanking the last bracelet free with a tearing sound.

"It isn't the Bible, it's—"

"Don't tell me what it is. I do think people who insist on telling me things are the most ghastly bores. A few weeks in America and you've turned into one of them, full of uplift and platitudes."

"I thought—" began Honey.

"Don't think, it doesn't suit you. You're not equipped for it."

"Yes I am—"

"Shut up and listen. Your head is as empty as my bank account—"

"I won't discuss money," said Honey. "We've settled that."

"Oh, have we? Have we? You may think you have, going off to America and finding a new lover and ignoring your mother. The ingratitude of the young. Sharper than a serpent's tooth it is to have a thankless child as you'd have known for yourself if you hadn't aborted your bastard—"

"NO! NO!" shouted Honey, drowning her mother's raucous, booming stage voice. She seized a stack of letters from Florence's hand with enough force to startle her mother into silence. "I won't listen. You've said the same things about a million times and each time they hurt me and I won't stand still to be hurt any more. Leave these letters and I'll hire a secretary myself. I WONT BE HURT!"

"Brave words," muttered Florence, disconcerted. "I'm sure we'd all like not to be hurt—"

"NO!"

Mother and daughter faced each other. Honey was trembling. Florence saw she had her mulish expression; there was nothing to be gained by pushing her. Florence laughed unconvincingly and sat down, collecting the letters scattered on the floor within reach. "All right, Honey, all right, pet. All over now. Give us a smile, come on. Just a family tiff."

Some family, thought Honey. Mother, daughter and cat cowering under the desk evidently eager to escape. She thought of Marcus Aurelius, she thought of Ms Fishkind, she thought of the baby she wanted and Jacky Hamzavi in a hospital bed in Africa ticking away like a time-bomb to demolish her plans. She took a deep breath, relaxed her neck muscles, steadied her voice. "I'll get you a drink," she said.

Till had finished the bottle of white wine Ben had left in the fridge. It was nearly off-licence closing time and it suddenly seemed vitally important to buy more before she was left with a wineless flat. When she reached the street outside she realised it was a warm evening; the steps of neighbouring houses, the open windows had their complement of women gossiping in Mediterranean languages, children and dogs playing. She leaned against one of the pillars at the foot of her steps, closed her eyes and thought of nothing. Gradually she realised a canine tongue was lapping her ankles. "Sure and leave the doctor alone, Othello," said a familiar, Irish voice. "Good evening, doctor, how's yourself? Enjoying the evening air is it, or have you drink taken?"

Till focussed on the tiny, dishevelled figure of – of – Vernon's cleaning woman. "Hello, Biddy," she said forcing her tongue round the words. "Both, I think."

"Isn't that grand, and I was just hoping for a friendly face. Himself is still in Hollywood, and haven't they taken Conor into St Charles and sent me away to wait for news. I'm all alone with a paper of fish and chips. Walk on home with me, there's a sufficiency for three."

"Three?"

"You, me and Othello. He's partial to the batter. Come along now if you're coming. Sure and the police round here are so racist if a black dog like Othello stands around the streets isn't he picked up on Sus."

Why not, thought Till and fell in with Biddy in her slow progress along the pavement. She was leading Othello on a string and the dog stopped every few paces to Hoover up scraps of decaying food. "Shall I get something for us to drink?"

"Consider yourself in the matter," said Biddy. "I've beer at home and a drop or two to strengthen up the tea.

I'll not be taking too much on account of waiting for the news from the hospital."

"How serious is it?"

"Not easy to tell. Isn't Conor prone to turns and dizzy spells, and tonight in the Elgin he fell to the floor and the ambulance men took him. At the hospital they made serious faces but who's to know? Not that he was breathing so well."

"What did his breathing sound like?" pursued Till, thinking that a professional approach might sober her up.

"I wouldn't say it sounded like anything much on account of he wasn't doing any when they wheeled him away into the hospital."

"Oh dear," said Till following her up the smelly, concrete staircase. Biddy's flat was on the second floor of a five-story council block some hundred yards from Till's. The front door was bright blue and peeling, the lock flimsy, the walls patterned with graffiti. The boxy living-room was an extravaganza of pink: curtains, net curtains, home-made lampshades, a telephone doll with a cream telephone nestling in its pink skirts, cushions piled on the fifties sofa, not unlike Till's own, but pink. It was not an orderly room nor a clean one but it was consistent and welcoming. In a corner there was a foot-high plaster statue of the Virgin Mary in blue and white robes pink-washed by flickering night-lights in red holders. "Sit yourself down," said Biddy. "Is it beer or tea?"

Till gazed at the statue. The nuns at the convent where she had spent her schooldays had had a special devotion to the Virgin. Sisters of this statue had haunted her childhood and adolescence: she had learned to bow her head in a jerky automatic movement to the statues as she passed; in retreat she had prayed to them, gathered flowers for the votary vases. As an adolescent, she had resented the dreamlike self-absorbed smile of the

Madonna. It seemed to represent a conscious serenity she never hoped or expected to achieve, the smile of a woman who had given birth to the Saviour and hadn't needed to descend to sex to do it. Now, in Biddy Keefe's flat, the Virgin seemed like an acquaintance so long-standing that, suddenly, she was a friend, and her small smile and outstretched hands spoke of resignation and endurance.

"Beer or tea?" said Biddy again.

"Tea please." Till was beginning to think more clearly. "I'm so sorry about Conor," she said. "Is there anything I can do?"

"Ah no," said Biddy. "It's the company I'm wanting. Are you a big eater as a general rule?"

"I'm not very hungry now."

"Better to eat. We'll divide the food between us. Is it a warm plate you prefer?"

Till sat on the sofa. Othello sat up in the kitchen doorway watching the division of the spoils. As soon as the plate was put down for him he gulped it clean, staggered to a pile of pink cushions next to the radiator, scratched feebly to rearrange them and collapsed with a grateful grunt. The flat smelt distinctly of dog, with overtones of beer and fried potatoes.

"Are you feeling low yourself this evening?" said Biddy, delivering the food and starting on her own plate. "We could turn on the telly but isn't it entirely Aids this week, and I'd be lucky to live to die of it at my age. The master's back tomorrow, thank God. He gives me an interest. How's your love life?"

"Not so good," said Till. "That's why I've been drinking."

"And isn't it the grand excuse. Conor's past an excuse: he drinks because it's day and because it's night. I'm sorry for your trouble, would you give me the details?"

Till, light-headed, began to explain.

"Ah, now, it sounds as if you're used to more than one

man at a time and when it's only the one left and he's another's then the chill strikes you. Myself, I've always stuck to one at a time. Mind you at four foot ten and me legs beef to the heel like a Mullingar heifer I've not been spoilt for choice. But isn't it the strange thing, for the older person like myself it's not the sex it's hard to find but the romance."

"Alison Lurie said that too." Till was finding Biddy's train of thought hard to follow and hoped to start a hare of her own choosing.

"She wouldn't have known the heart of it unless she lived with Conor. Who might she be, a friend of yours?"

"A novelist."

"I've never had any great respect for writers, sure, and who can't make things up?"

"Particularly the Irish. My mother was Irish."

"Whose mother wasn't? Gentry, was she?"

"I suppose so. I still have a cottage in Ireland, near Youghal. I go there every summer."

"I never go back there except for the funerals. It's a dying country with the young leaving and the unemployment and priests telling the women what to do. It's the memories, just the memories take me back. When I was a young girl by the sea and I'd lick the salt off my arms for the taste," said Biddy.

"You can still do that."

"It's not the same when the wrinkles hinder your tongue."

"I know what you mean," said Till. "I miss being young. Not all the time, only now and then. Last week, for instance, I was watching television and it was tennis – Yannick Noah – he's a very good-looking tennis player. I thought, I'll never again be young enough to attract a man like that, just for a night, just for fun."

"Isn't it 'pull' the expression? You want to 'pull' Yannick Noah?"

"That's it."

"You're not past that, surely to God, a good strong girl like you."

"I am. Right now I couldn't pull a lavatory chain."

"You're a great girl entirely. Tea now, with a drop of whisky through it?"

"Why not?"

"Think of this," said Biddy pouring out two cups and a saucer of tea, splashing in three dollops of whisky, serving Othello first in his corner, "you were young at the right time for a woman. Myself I wasn't emancipated till I was your age and the chances narrowed down to Conor, bless him. The girls who are young now isn't it the condoms and the questions and the prospect of fading away in a hospice with Ministers of Health plaguing your last hours with the television cameras."

"Where in Ireland did you come from?" said Till, sipping her whisky.

"Fermoy."

"Fermoy?" Her brain was working slowly, her tongue more slowly still. "That's nowhere near the sea."

"You have the right of it there," said Biddy, puzzled.

"How did you lick the salt off your arms in Fermoy?"

"Perspiration?"

Till began to get the measure of Biddy's conversation. "Should I ring St Charles Hospital for you? They'd probably give more information to a doctor." She met Biddy's mischievous eyes with a smile of her own.

"That would be a waste of time, now," said Biddy. "Seeing as the police have him on a drunk and disorderly charge, and didn't I tell you the other to avoid the shame of it?"

"Absolutely," said Till. "I must tell you about my last lover. He was a journalist, a lovely man but tragic, terribly tragic. Both his children died . . ."

Chapter Twelve

Till sat in the glassed-in veranda of her cottage watching the reflection of moonlight on the surface of the bay. It was mid-August and warm; both doors were ajar and a breeze lifted the hem of the cotton skirt and fluttered it against her legs. Honey, facing sideways, was gazing over open sea.

"Amazing to think that the next land is America," she said wistfully.

Jacky, lying on the sofa in the living-room behind them, his aching leg propped on cushions, turned down the volume on the stereo to be heard over the climax of Mahler's Ninth. "Particularly as we're on the east coast of Ireland," he said.

"What?" said Honey.

"The wrong side of Ireland, precious Honey. To be facing America we'd have to be on the west coast. Kerry, for instance. We're in County Cork."

"Oh." Honey was untroubled. "It's nice sea, which-ever way it's facing."

"Excellent sea," said Till. She was thinking about Ben. She hadn't seen him for months; not since, after lunch with Pandora, she had decided that she would not allow him to see her again. She foresaw a protracted, sporadic, guilt-ridden (on his side) telephone-hanging relation-ship with a certainly painful outcome. She had done the decent thing.

After a few days, of course, she had found that doing the decent thing is only easily supportable if you have plenty else to do, and her life was so empty of men that she had regretted her decision almost daily ever since. To stop thinking about Ben she forced herself to concentrate on the here and now, with the result that she was becoming increasingly irritable with her surroundings. Now, she could hear the voices of Harry and Amanda and Harry's friend arguing amicably over how to fit their baggage into Harry's ancient car. Only by gripping her chair did Till prevent herself from shouting at them to get on with it, to let her do it.

They were twenty yards away on the hard standing at the top of the steep drive leading to the cottage. Soon, they would be leaving to drive to Rosslare for the two-o'clock-in-the-morning ferry back to Wales. Till had been two weeks at the cottage with convalescing Jacky and the children and, when she could forget Ben, was sunk in Ireland's indolence. Most days she woke at ten and spent the morning deciding what time to drive into Youghal to shop. The nearest telephone was a mile away and the nearest habitation – the only other one in sight apart from the ruined castle at the other point of the bay – was a fisherman's cottage two hundred yards back up the track at the foot of the drive.

The track ended at the beach. Once a day Jacky went down to the beach to bathe, with Amanda in anxious attendance. She regarded him as her own property since, months ago, Till had sent her to Nairobi to escort him on the aeroplane back to London and install him in the spare room at Till's flat. In London she had taken him swimming in the local pool, driven him to his physiotherapy appointments, prepared his food. Now he was almost recovered. He would never again be able to lift his right arm directly above his head; in damp weather, his joints ached; his left leg was slightly twisted below the knee and when tired, he limped. His muscles were almost restored and his squint had gone but he still had nightmares and he was noticeably quieter. He refused to talk at all about the accident or the woman who had left him penniless in hospital. He only really laughed with Amanda at childish jokes.

He was no longer a threat in Honey's eyes. She had waited with Till at Heathrow to meet Jacky and Amanda off the plane from Nairobi, feeling as nearly aggressive as her nature would allow. But he had looked vulnerable and wasted when Amanda, strapping and solid by contrast, pushed the wheelchair through the rubber doors from Customs. He was ill from the pain of the long flight after so many weeks in a hospital bed; his beauty had gone. Honey longed to comfort, not confront, and she gripped Till's arm. "Don't say anything to frighten him," she said. "He promised he wouldn't tell the media or Florence. I believe him."

"Because he's ill?"

"It's what I feel." So Jacky, for months, believed that Honey paid his fare home out of kindness. When, finally, she told him her motives, he was silent – disappointed, she thought.

"You could have trusted me," he said. "And now it's a debt of honour. I'll never tell anyone." Once more, she believed him, but she was surprised when she told Till not to be laughed at for being naive.

"That's safe enough," Till said. "If it's a debt of honour, he'll pay."

Honey found this glamorous. She grew fonder of Jacky; when she was not in San Francisco with Ms Fishkind she kept him company. She was glad he was to be with her in Ireland during the next few vital days when she would insert her sperm. As she sat watching the sea her fingertips rested on the large carrying box filled with dry ice which protected the sperm. Yesterday, she had brought it back from California with her. For the first time in her adult life her make-up bag, no longer her first priority, had gone into the aircraft's hold.

"We're off," said Amanda. "All packed and ready." Harry and his friend Rob stood behind her making departing and thank-you noises. Jacky limped from the sofa to hug Amanda though Till had the distinct impression he would have preferred to hug Rob. She would have enjoyed hugging Rob herself. He was shorter than Harry, more muscular, full of sexual self-confidence.

It was quiet after they had gone, so quiet she could hear the sigh and scrabble of the retreating tide. Jacky, back on the sofa, was restless. Two weeks in the Spartan cottage were enough for him. Daily, he checked his reflection in the shaving mirror (thinking each time how extraordinary it was for a woman to live in a cottage without a full-length mirror) and counted the days till he had recovered enough of his looks to try his luck back in London. Meanwhile he lay on the sofa and his agile fingers shuffled and dealt, shuffled and dealt. "Poker, anyone?" he said.

"Not with you," said Till without turning her head.

"For matchsticks?"

"No."

"Do let's," said Honey. "Why not, Till?"

"I only enjoy games with some element of chance."

"But poker . . ." began Honey.

"Not with Jacky."

"Please, Till, he'd like to."

"Dealer's choice? Seven card stud?" said Jacky clearing the card table, setting the chairs.

"I only know the kind where you're given five cards and you change them if you want," said Honey, settling herself in a chair, her box at her knee.

"Then that's what we'll play," said Jacky, desperate not to obstruct his ally. Till sat down at the table reluctantly. Already she wished that the children had not left, or that they had taken Jacky with them. She and Honey alone would have been as good as solitude, but Jacky had to be entertained: he saw silence as a social dereliction.

Till liked her cottage for peace and the few roots it gave

216

her. She was otherwise almost without roots. Her father had been a medical missionary, a failed monk. Her childhood was spent in Kenya, Tanganyika, the southern Sudan, and though she loved it she never felt at home in Africa. It was too big, they moved too often, and she felt like the outcast of a roving herd of animals, soon to be picked off by a predator. But in Ireland she felt close to her mother, otherwise a pathetic woman who loved her husband without understanding him and who fought single-handed the colonial fight to recreate the chintz and Chippendale of an Anglo-Irish household in a succession of battered bungalows surrounded by scrub grass and the eerie noises of an African night. In Africa she was wistful and incongruous: longing for children, brave boys and pretty girls, producing only Matilda; the dates in her head the opening of the hunting season, the Dublin show, Cheltenham week, lost in the backdrop of seasons so broad they ignored her familiar rituals, drowning them in blazing sun and sheeting rain. She longed for the soft drizzle and grey-green tints of an Ireland she never visited but always talked of as home. Till's bedtime stories were about her mother's family, the horses, the nursery jokes and the house she had lived in as a child. The house she described was now long sold. Eventually it was bought by a trainer who had extended the stables and left the house to crumble into yet another Irish ruin. Beside it, he built a large sprawling bungalow with picture windows, painted pink.

Till was glad her mother had never seen it. It was melancholy even for her to drive past the house set in its formal gardens and imagine the nursery games once played behind the glassless windows. It was only ten miles from her cottage which was left to her by one of her mother's many eccentric great-aunts. There were still relations of her mother's dotted about nearby and, every summer, she went to see them, taking Harry and Amanda.

Her mother was buried very far from the winning post at Cheltenham. She lay in a cemetery in Khartoum where she had contracted 'flu and died on one of her trips from the southern Sudan to pick up airmail copies of *The Times* and stores of *patum peperium* and Oxford marmalade sent from Fortnum's. Till had been fifteen at the time.

When her mother was alive, Till had felt superior to her: how could you respect a woman who thought that reading gave you wrinkles in your forehead and stopped you being outside improving your seat on a horse, who thought medicine was no career for a girl and that Till's father was damaging his daughter's innocence by allowing her to assist him delivering babies. With her mother gone Till increasingly felt the sadness of a relationship never developed and irreplaceable. So she came to Ireland every summer and drove the roads her mother had travelled and visited the houses where her mother was remembered as the charming Fitzgerald girl who had won the Ladies' Race at Cork three years running, before her twentieth birthday.

This time, she brought Jacky because Honey wanted her to. Honey worried about lonely Jacky, so often confined to his room, so nearly damaged beyond repair. Sea air is what he needs, said Honey, and company. Till felt the only sea air Jacky would find invigorating blew in the Mediterranean or Caribbean; certainly not in the Irish Sea. Jacky had agreed to come to please Honey.

"It's lovely being so isolated," said Honey. "Nobody even knows where I am."

"Me neither," said Jacky glumly.

"Except Tom Wyatt. He caught me at the flat. Odd thing. Two odd things."

"I'll raise you five," said Till. Each had started with fifty matchsticks and the agreement was that the game would end when one of them was cleaned out. Till was trying to lose.

"What was odd?" said Jacky. "Raise you three."

"The first thing was, he dropped in just after I got back to London from San Francisco this morning, and managed to catch me in the three hours before I left for the airport to fly here. Almost as if he was watching the flat."

"Amazing," said Till.

"Beyond belief," said Jacky. "Are you still betting, Honey?"

"No, I've a terrible hand, I'll pack it in," said Honey. "And the other thing was, he's going to be here tomorrow and the next day."

"*Here?* What do you mean, at the cottage?" said Till. She often pressed the Wyatts to stay with her in Ireland, knowing they wouldn't come.

"No, at a hotel the other side of Youghal."

"Till, are you still with me?" persisted Jacky.

"I'll match you and see you," said Till.

"Don't you always?" said Jacky. "Full house, Kings high."

"Amazing," said Till, folding her three knaves. Jacky shuffled, Till cut, Jacky dealt. "What are the Wyatts doing near Youghal?"

"He's trying to sign an author. Purves, I think her name was."

"Thunderthighs Fay. She used to hunt with my mother."

"And he said they'd come to see us, he and Maggie. He said he so wanted to see the cottage."

"And its contents," said Jacky.

"What?" said Honey. "Do you mean the furniture?" She looked round at the beach-cottage, ill-assorted pieces that she politely hadn't mentioned when she first arrived.

"You, Honey," said Till. "Remember, he's in love with you."

"Oh – no," said Honey. "I'm not sure you were right about that, but in any case he'll have forgotten it by now."

"Dear Honey, I doubt it," said Jacky. "Sex is a very powerful thing. Thank heavens."

"People often say that." Honey looked piqued. "I don't agree. Marcus Aurelius hardly mentions it."

"He hardly mentions money either," said Till, her spirits still further lowered by the prospect of the Wyatts' visit.

"I knew you'd want to see the Wyatts, anyhow," said Honey, "so I encouraged him to come. Tell me again what a Royal Flush is."

Till watched Jacky's pleasant, uninformative expression. "I'll bet all my matchsticks it's what you've got in your hand."

"So I win?" said Honey.

"Hang on, hang on," said Jacky, "we have to bet."

In Ireland, Till usually woke to the sound of the sea. Next day she woke to a babble of voices reminiscent of the crush bar at Covent Garden. She checked the clock. It was only nine: none of her Irish acquaintances would drop in at that hour. She pulled on a kimono wrapper and waddled flat-footed towards the living-room. It was entirely full but the only person she saw was Ben. She immediately ducked into the bathroom and poked ineffectually at her hair, shaking, disoriented. I'm not *prepared*, she thought bitterly, I had no *warning*, how could he do this to me? She woke up slowly at the best of times and liked to spend half an hour pottering about making coffee and groaning gently to herself. She felt equally unprepared for emotional scenes or social obligations. What was Ben doing here? Why hadn't she washed her hair the night before?

Harry appeared in the doorway looking, as only the young can, both exhausted and attractive. "Hi, Ma, I've made you some coffee." He balanced the cup on the side of the bath.

"What the hell's going on out there? Do they have coffee?"

"Don't worry, Jacky's in charge of all that. We three are back because the ferries are suddenly out on strike. Ben and Pandora are here because they were going to cross on the Rosslare ferry too and we met on the quayside, and Ben seemed to think it would be an amusing idea to come on here with us."

"How drunk was he?"

"Fairly, then. He's better now. Pandora's in a blazing rage; Honey's trying to calm her down. And Tom and Maggie Wyatt are here on a social call."

"At NINE IN THE MORNING? IN IRELAND?" Tactfully, Harry closed the door behind him, though everyone in the living-room must have heard Till's outraged cry. She brushed her teeth viciously, pulled at her hair again and forced herself to join her guests.

Ben looked old. Stubble sooted his chin, his eyes were bloodshot and the bags beneath them puffy. He had evidently been up all night and Till thought Harry was being optimistic in assessing his sobriety. He leaned against the wall ignoring the others. Pandora was on the veranda, her back to the company in a distinct pose. When Till came in Pandora didn't turn her body to meet her, merely looked over her shoulder and watched.

"Good morning, everybody," said Till. "Ben. It's been a long time."

"More than eight years, isn't it?" said Ben. Till refused to meet his eyes; she was angry with him for disregarding her appeal to leave her alone, for precipitating what was bound to be an unpleasant scene; she refused to conspire with him against Pandora.

"As long as that?" she said.

"Quite eight years. So that means you don't know why Pandora's standing with her back to us."

Immediately, there was a babble of voices trying to drown Ben's, and Till gathered the Considines were locked in a full-dress row. Usually she enjoyed rows, found them stimulating, but she preferred to avoid this one so she greeted Maggie and turned away from Ben.

"I'm going to say it anyway," said Ben in his deep, penetrating voice, easily overriding the others. "Pandora's standing with her back to us becaue she just made the pilot for a sit-com and the cameraman foolishly – one might even say short-sightedly – told her she had a sexy bum. She's not been out of trousers since and she must be getting a cricked neck, turning her head all the time."

"Do shut up, Ben," said Till. "I'm bad enough at this hour without squabbles."

"Don't talk to Ben like that," said Pandora, still presenting her bottom which was now the focus of many a judicial gaze.

"Till can talk to me how she likes," said Ben. "At least *she* usually makes sense."

"Not in my experience," said Pandora.

"It's a lovely warm day," said Jacky. "Have you seen the garden, Maggie? Tom?"

Tom was standing next to Honey whose leg was resting against her precious box. Social instinct told her that she should provide a descant to Jacky's tune but she didn't want to leave the box and didn't see how she could take it on a casual tour of the garden: worse still, if she did, Tom would certainly offer to carry it for her.

"That would be delightful, Jacky," said Maggie. "A quick turn round the garden before we go. We only dropped in to ask you – all – for dinner tonight. We're at the Rathveen Castle Hotel and the food looks promising. There was a piece on it in the *Observer* colour supplement a while ago."

Till followed them outside. Of all gardens hers was the least rewarding for a horticultural tour. It was long and narrow, ending at the cliffs of the point, containing only overgrown lawn and bordered by dry stone walls covered with proliferating, untended fuchsia. Her bare feet encountered weeds, pebbles and occasional slugs.

Jacky continued with the empressement of a guide to the Versailles gardens. "So simple yet so stunning. A natural garden – emphasising the contrast of deep green Irish grass and the flaming, rampant fuchsia, against the background of the omnipresent sea in the gentle light."

"Such well-established fuchsia," said Maggie. "An idyllic place, Till. I'm so glad we've seen it. What's in this bucket?" Maggie, Tom, Jacky and Till, with Pandora, stiff with rage, bringing up the rear, all looked at a bucket full of recently dead mackerel.

"The fisherman's been out, I expect," said Till. "When he does, I usually take six or so mackerel. They're only twenty-five pence each and absolutely fresh."

"The only trouble is," said Amanda joining them, "Mummy can't cook mackerel, so we have to throw them away, and if we don't remember to take them to the rubbish dump they stink the place out."

"You buy fish to throw away?" said Pandora scornfully.

"He's my neighbour, he's a good chap, I don't mind. I only wish it was less oily. There's nothing one can use it for."

"Surely," said Maggie. "You can have it steamed, stuffed, baked, soused—"

"With white wine," said Pandora, "with egg, butter and herb sauce, baked with olives, with cucumber and sour cream—"

"With horseradish and tomatoes, in pâté, and of course mackerel roes are so useful," said Maggie.

"Not to me," said Till.

"Matilda's better with cod," said Ben from the out-skirts of the group. "Aren't you, Matilda?"

"Go and sleep it off, Ben," said Till.

"Certainly. Are you joining me?"

"*I'm* leaving," snapped Pandora.

"I'm staying here," said Ben. "I want to talk to Till."

"I'm sorry, Ben," said Till, "there isn't room for you and Pandora to stay here. We only have two bedrooms."

Pandora walked away, Maggie followed. "I'll go and get dressed," said Till.

When she re-emerged, the Wyatts and the Considines had gone, Harry and Rob were erecting a tent in the garden, Jacky was lying on the sofa and Amanda was talking to him. Honey and her box were nowhere to be seen. It was an improvement but Till still felt overwhelmed by people.

"Ben took Pandora to find a hotel. He said he'd be back later on," said Amanda. "That was some row they were having. Do we have to go to dinner with the Wyatts, Mummy?"

"We can't, there's too many of us, and I owe them too much already. We'd better have them here."

"Oh God," said Amanda blankly. "I could do my spaghetti, I suppose."

"Surely some of those charming fisher-people have wives who can cook?" said Jacky, waving his arm gracefully in the direction of the beach where some men and boys were mending their nets.

"We'll manage it between us."

"With plenty of drink," said Jacky. "Especially if Ben and Pandora are coming."

Maggie was miserable. Holidays, even very short ones, frightened her. Without a household to run she lost all sense of her own identity and significance; she wandered through the Rathveen Castle Hotel which was running very well without her and tried to decide whether to confront Tom about Matilda. That was the source of the problem. He'd been odd for months, withdrawn, even vaguer than usual; if it hadn't been Tom, who of course was fundamentally happy, one might even have said depressed. He kept asking her to have Matilda for dinner and recently Maggie had found a book of matches in his pocket. It came from the local wine bar; she'd teased him about secret lunches and he'd admitted to lunch with Matilda. Everyone knew what lunch meant. It was either business or the other thing.

Could he be having an affair with Matilda? Everyone else seemed to. What on earth her attraction was, Maggie couldn't see; in that kimono she'd seemed like a lumpy bolster, she had practically no looks, not even the remnants of them, and she was completely unfeminine. Throwing mackerel away, for instance, simply because she was an incompetent housekeeper. Yet there was Benjamin, drunk of course, but that didn't excuse him, in fact it made it worse, insulting Pandora who had done her best for him, been completely loyal.

She plucked irritably at a lop-sided flower arrangement then looked round, anxious in case she had been spotted. None of the staff were paying any attention to her. They were gossiping by the big Gothic windows that could do with a polish. She went on fiddling with the flowers. Tom wouldn't be back for at least two hours: he was lunching with the Purves woman, and why he bothered – he was above dealing with authors now – and there was something distinctly wrong with Candida. Her last phone call had been most unsettling, and here Maggie was, stuck in Ireland where nobody ever went when Tom could certainly have seen the author in London, authors always came to London, and though Maggie had tried to read the Purves book she couldn't see anything special in it, all about animals and surely that had been exhausted by *Watership Down*, so seventies.

She sat in a huge armchair with an unsuitably garish cover and tried not to cry. What should she do? If Tom was having an affair with Matilda it meant she, Maggie, was at fault. She wasn't satisfying him, she had failed. It struck at the root of everything. Her marriage and her life were basically rotten, that's what it meant. She knew what other women would say. Never mind, it's his age, all men do it. For Maggie, that would be too massive an adjustment. She couldn't make it. And dinner tonight, having to feed Matilda and her wretched hangers-on, the arrogant son, the lumpish daughter – actually, Amanda was fining down a little and beginning to smile occasionally. If her mother gave her any guidance she'd be quite a pretty girl – with Jacky twittering along like the pathetic, decadent creature he was, and Honey – Honey was the only decent one. She at least was normal.

She closed her eyes and imagined herself back in the kitchen at Campden Hill.

Ben was asleep, sprawled across the double bed of the second-rate hotel room which was all they could find, so many other people had been stranded by the ferry strike. Pandora sat rigidly upright on the one uncomfortable chair – didn't people ever sit down in hotel rooms in Ireland? – and reviewed the possibilities. Her first rage had passed. She understood Ben was upset by visiting his father, slowly dying in a Dublin hospital; once again, Peregrine had refused to meet him; he had been drunk for three days; probably the ferry strike had seemed a perfect excuse to see Matilda.

She understood it but didn't know how to endure it. Matilda was even worse than the blondes he had finally admitted to because she was more inexplicable and more matrimonial. She couldn't be seen as a mistress, she was so obviously a wife. Ben kept saying he wanted to talk to her. He quite clearly didn't want to talk to Pandora.

She crossed to the bed and watched him sleeping. Earlier she had wanted to pick up a heavy object and batter his face with it, his sneering, unloving, rejecting face, but now she started to undress him, stroking his thick, smooth, olive skin in the process, rubbing her hands in his beard stubble, kissing him. She didn't know what was left to do but if she found something she would do it. Ben was hers. Without her he would disintegrate. Till couldn't afford him. Endurance, that was all. If she could endure she would win. Everything was on her side, and she wanted him because for a reason she could not define she felt he was a significant person. Most of the other people she knew, her own family, were famous but not significant; Ben was. Perhaps as a playwright; but in any case as a human being because he felt things deeply, he was passionate, there was a kind of largeness about him, he tried to . . . she couldn't find words. It was something to do with facing the world and trying to overcome it; he didn't accept what other people accepted and his failures were more grand. Her father was learning the lines for a production of *Lear* and Pandora had been helping him, feeding him cues, and she'd got to know the play well. She hadn't said it to anyone because they would have thought it absurd but she saw Ben as Lear, so much hurt and so wrong.

He moved and groaned in his sleep. She pulled the blankets up over him, filled a glass of water – funny brown colour the water had, even when you ran it for ages – and put it beside him for when he woke up thirsty, and prepared to sleep herself. If endurance would do it, she would have him.

Later that afternoon, Till came back from Youghal with the shopping. The children were still asleep in their tent; Jacky unpacked the food, carolling "gourmet chicken casserole à la Till, what joy!" and Till listened to Honey. "I'm going to insert the sperm tomorrow," said Honey. "I've taken my temperature and it isn't today so I'm sure it'll be tomorrow. If you give me the address of that chemical factory I'll go and get some more dry ice."

"The address is over there. You can't miss it, about three miles beyond Youghal on the Cork road. Are you looking forward to conception day?"

"I'm frightened, but excited too. Are you all right, Till?"

"Why do you ask?"

"Because of Ben. I know you love him, you always

227

have, ever since *Captain Bridge*. His turning up here must have been a shock."

"I don't know what love means."

"You don't have to understand something to do it, otherwise I'd never do anything. I've been selfish, just talking about me and America and the baby and paying no attention to you, just asking for reassurance, and you must get enough of that at work. Tell me what you're feeling."

"Mostly, angry with Ben. I asked him to leave me alone."

"I don't think he can. He's so unhappy."

"At this moment, so am I," said Till. "He disrupts me and disturbs my life and I wish he would go away."

"How long before the ferries are running again?" said Honey. "I don't think Pandora can take much more. They were here for half an hour before you woke up this morning, Till, and I had a good talk with Pandora."

"What about?"

"Lots of things. Ben. God."

"I expect Pandora said she'd met him lately," said Till, but her heart wasn't in flippancy, she felt bruised all over.

"Just to add to the general jollities," said Jacky joining them, "Maggie Wyatt thinks Tom is having it off with Till."

"Oh, are you?" said Honey, interested.

"No. He's in love with you, as all London probably knows except you and Maggie. It wasn't an accident when he caught you at the flat the other day. He'd already rung me every other day before I came to Ireland to find out your movements. That's why he arranged this trip over to meet Thunderthighs Fay."

"Just so long as he leaves me alone tomorrow morning, that's all I ask. Can I have the cottage to myself, Till? I'd like to play some classical music because it may help the child. We don't know, do we?"

"You may very well not conceive first time," said Till.

"I know, Ms Fishkind keeps telling me that, but I have a feeling that I will and that it'll be a girl. Would you mind if I called it Matilda?"

"I'd be honoured, but aren't you going to call it after Ms Fishkind?"

"I am," said Honey.

"Matilda Fishkind Markham. An intricate weave of 'm' and 'k' sounds," said Jacky.

"Shut up, Jacky. Matilda Betsy Markham."

"That sounds like a starlet who only takes off her clothes when it's absolutely necessary for the artistic success of the film," said Jacky hugging her.

"She's never going to be *in* a film," said Honey. "She's going to go to school and then university and she's going to do a proper job so she *never* has to take her clothes off. Why are you making faces, Till?"

"Because I don't think you should decide what she's going to be. I seem to remember another mother doing that for another little girl."

"Listen to the shrink," said Jacky derisively.

"She's right." Honey was downcast. "You will *tell* me when I do something wrong to her, Till? Promise?"

"Matilda will *certainly* tell you. Matilda is the *authority* on other people's lives, aren't you, Matilda?"

Jacky was getting better, Till thought. His little outbursts of natural spite were resurfacing.

"What do you want us to do?" said Harry. Till turned, her eyes streaming from chopping onions, to see Harry, Amanda and Rob lined up with napkins over their arms like butlers in a Hollywood romantic comedy. Her spirits began to lift. " 'You're so young and bee – yootifuhul and I love you soh-oo,' " she sang. Rob looked perplexed.

"She thinks she's singing," said Amanda reassuringly. "It's a good sign."

"I didn't think she meant it," said Rob. "I've never

been called beautiful before." He met as much of Till's gaze as he could reach through the onions and she began to laugh which made her eyes worse.

"This man is a flirt," she said.

"I know. He's famous for it," said Harry. Amanda looked disconcerted and Till hastened to change the subject. She had been getting on so much better with Amanda lately that she was loath to jeopardise the advance. "What I really want you to do is go to the pub for dinner," she said. "Before that, one of you could lay the table in the veranda and do me some flowers for decoration."

"Flowers?" said Rob.

"Fuchsias," chorused Harry and Amanda, and Amanda went on, "I'll do that."

"Another could lay out the bar and wash the glasses. Better use the desk in the living-room and wash them in the bathroom. There isn't space here."

"Yes, ma'am," said Harry.

"Then Rob can help me cook."

"Absolutely," said Rob. She handed him green peppers and tomatoes to chop and he set to work. It was a very small kitchen but he was deft. "I'm so sorry circumstance landed me back on you," he said after a while.

"Not at all. I'm delighted to have you."

"I'd rather got the impression you wanted to be alone."

"Wanted to be without Jacky, certainly."

"Where is he now?"

"Out with Honey."

"And now you've got a dinner-party, which Harry tells me you won't enjoy."

"The fortunes of war."

"Will the tall man and that television woman still be fighting?"

"Probably."

"Harry tells me you and the tall man were very close."

"Chop those peppers, Rob."

"I am. Are you still involved with him?"

"What's that to you, Shorty?"

"I was rather hoping to take you out to dinner, back in London."

Till ran cold water over her fingers and the onion knife, trying not to laugh.

"What's so funny?" he said, not offended, merely curious.

"Aren't I a little old for you?"

"Do you mean, aren't I too young for you?"

"That too."

"We could suck it and see," he said. "I'm not entirely inexperienced." ·

"Neither am I," said Till. She felt much, much better, like an old horse back in the hunting-field, still reliable over fences. "Jacky's interested in you."

"I know, but it's hopeless. I've never been bi. Any more tomatoes?"

"In the fridge."

"So what's your answer?"

"I don't want to upset Harry."

"I didn't intend to include him in the party."

"Call me in London."

Dinner had reached the pudding stage and Till, trying to keep the conversation going, felt she was pushing porridge up Mount Everest with her nose. Apart from herself, only Jacky was still soldiering on. Honey, an earlier ally, had been silenced by Ben's vicious and entirely insincere attack on Marcus Aurelius.

"Shall we move for coffee?" said Till. They had already had cheese, at Jacky's insistence, before pudding. He evidently hoped this small continental gesture would add much-needed distinction to the dinner.

Maggie began to clear the table. "Don't worry," said

Till. "The children can do that. They'll be back from the pub any minute now. Loo, anyone? The men can go outside." Jacky marshalled the men towards the fuchsias and Maggie vanished into the bathroom. Honey went to her bedroom to check on the box and Pandora and Till were left with the coffee.

"He's getting drunk again," said Pandora glumly.

"Mmmm."

"His father's dying."

"I'm sorry."

"Peregrine's snubbed him again."

"Oh."

"And he's still not writing."

"He will. Eventually. About him and Peregrine. You could suggest it."

"OK."

For once in their relationship, Till felt close to Pandora, even sympathetic. But not for long. "I love him more than you do," said Pandora, "otherwise you'd have married him. Let him go."

As that was exactly what Till was trying to do, Pandora's urging was unbearably irksome, almost irksome enough to change Till's mind.

"Shall I carry cups?" said Maggie, breaking the awkward silence. Pandora went to the bathroom and Maggie seized her opportunity. "I know all about it, Matilda, and I must say I think you've behaved very badly."

"Specifically how? What are we talking about?"

"You and my husband. You had lunch together."

"True."

"Why?"

"We met and it seemed like a good idea."

"He said it was to discuss a book you might write."

"Then he should have told me what he was going to tell you," said Till. "Unanimity is all in such matters. Could you take that tray?"

"No, I won't. Not until you've admitted it."

"What?"

"Are you sleeping with my husband?"

"No," said Till.

"You're lying."

"No."

Maggie was nonplussed. It would be far more in character, she thought, for Till to crow. "Has he asked you?"

"No."

"What are you talking about?" said Ben, leaning against the doorpost for balance. "Didn't I hear someone talking about husbands? I can give you an update on Till and husbands. She's sleeping with Pandora's husband, she's sleeping with the husband of some tragic trauma-ridden wife in the Home Counties, but as far as I know she isn't sleeping with your husband, Maggie. I'm sure she would if you wished it as her generosity would certainly be approved by Equal Opportunity legislators, knowing as it does no barriers of race, creed or colour."

"Shut up, Ben."

"People say that to me so often," said Ben, *faux-naif*.

"What's going on now?" demanded Pandora.

"Nothing," said Maggie, taking the tray through and beginning to pour coffee. She didn't know what to believe. She could see Tom through the glass of the veranda. He was talking to Jacky and smoothing his hair against the breeze. She wanted to take a pair of scissors and cut his hair off. The cups rattled in her hand. After all I've done, she thought, and now Ben Considine's laughing at me. There was also laughter outside. Those bloody children are back, she thought, slopping coffee into the saucer as she thrust it at Pandora.

Till grabbed Harry and pulled him into the kitchen, past Ben. "We'll have to play party games. Organise it."

"What kind?"

"Not Consequences," said Ben. Till ignored him.

"*Give us a Clue*," said Till. Harry groaned.

"Must we?"

"We must. FRR."

"What's that mean?" said Ben.

"Family Rally Round."

"How cosy."

Harry organised it, despite a ground-swell of resistance. The only enthusiasts were Amanda, who was good at mime, and Honey who liked games as long as she understood them and who had several times appeared in the television game. Jacky, hoping for poker or at least bridge, pouted. Everyone eventually settled into chairs and Honey took the floor and explained the rules to Maggie who claimed she was too busy ever to watch television and had never once seen *Give us a Clue*.

Honey began to make signs. "Film," said Rob.

"Three words," said Harry.

"Second word – small word – a, an, the – it's *the*," said Amanda. All three were evidently so acclimatised to taking tests that they couldn't not try.

"First word," said Harry. Honey was moving across the room sweeping her arms.

"Cinderella," said Pandora.

"Beauty," said Tom. Maggie looked at him.

"Go home," said Ben.

"*Gone with the Wind*," said Till, who could bear it no longer.

"That's got four words," said Pandora.

"Oh," said deflated Honey. "Sorry. I must have counted wrong. Sorry. Till guessed, anyway. Your turn, Till."

"When isn't it?" said Ben.

"I must go to the loo. Pandora can take my turn," said Till who thought that Pandora would explode if she wasn't the centre of attention soon. When she came back the players had established they were looking for a film title with two words. Pandora was sticking out her bottom and gesturing at her pelvic area for the first word.

"*Rear Window*," said Tom.

"Blind cameraman," said Ben.

"Underpants, bottom, behind, knickers, pants," the company offered. Pandora shook her head and started on the second word. She pointed her forefingers together and moved them till they touched, then moved them away again. "Meeting, fingers, touch, bump, crash." Pandora shook her head again and went on to the whole title. She mimed a romantic scene and parting, rather well, Till thought. She hoped someone would guess soon as she didn't want to keep winning.

Rob looked straight at her. "*Brief Encounter*," he said.

Ben gave a roar. "No," he shouted. "No, that's too much."

"He's right," said Pandora, puzzled. "What is it?"

"I'll kill him," said Ben and pulled Rob out of his chair. "You bloody little *sod*. Who do you think you are?" He was shaking him; Rob offered no resistance.

"Put me down," he said calmly. "I'm not going to fight; you're too old." Till came up behind Ben and pulled the back of his jacket over his face, forcing his arms down.

"Bitch," Ben screamed through the cloth, "that's the limit, you unutterable *bitch*."

"Can someone explain what's going on?" said Maggie collecting cups and putting them in the kitchen out of the way.

"Ben's drunk," said Till hustling him into the garden. Rob followed and she gestured him away.

"Sure you'll be all right?" he said, annoyed, pugnacious.

"Sure," she said and closed the door behind her. She could see Pandora deciding whether to follow them and Honey restraining her. She helped Ben disentangle himself from the cloth. "You're fucking him, aren't you?" he said, furious.

"No."

235

"But you soon will."

"Possibly. More likely just talk about it."

"You must be desperate. That's as bad as Madeline."

"I don't intend to pay."

"Anyone but me, is that it? Anyone but me."

"It's hopeless for us, Benjamin, you know that. Pandora loves you. Call it quits, my darling, please. Why be jealous now? You've never cared before."

"That's because you were mine before. Oh God," he said, "I've made a complete balls-up of everything."

Chapter Thirteen

Honey woke knowing it was The Day. Before she got up she took her temperature to confirm it. She was anxious. Would Till remember she'd promised to clear the cottage? Would she be able to? Honey checked the box, touched it, looked at the dry ice, still covering the two vials of sperm. She took the syringe from her bag, laid it on the dressing-table. There was no sound from the living-room. Jacky was probably still asleep on the sofabed.

It was only half-past seven, ages before anyone got up. She read Marcus Aurelius to calm herself: she could feel her heart thudding in her chest. After today she might never be alone again, but was it fair? Would her child, if she ever discovered how she was conceived, forgive her? Surely it was no worse than many normal conceptions? The ideal picture of a loving couple embracing in their well-decorated, mortgaged bedroom, hoping to make a baby, was touching but out of reach. If she was part of the loving couple, soon she would strangle that love to death by clinging. She knew no other way, she had been taught nothing else and it was too late to learn before it was too late to conceive.

She forced herself to concentrate on Marcus Aurelius, but he seemed distant and male. The hands of the clock weren't moving. She put it to her ear. It was ticking. Why wasn't it moving?

She did stretching exercises, relaxed every muscle in her body, couldn't relax her mind. She took out the instructions for insertion, read them again. "Aspirate the sperm from the vial." What did that mean? Wasn't it something to do with breathing? She looked it up in her travelling dictionary. "Sound with h, consonant blended with this." That made no sense, even when she looked up "consonant". She read the sentence again in context. It must mean "draw up the sperm into the syringe", but why didn't it say so?

Panic seized her. Why didn't she *know* things like other people? She wasn't meant to have a child, that was it, her mother was right. She held her stomach and rocked backwards and forwards. Marooned in the sleeping house, she felt like the child she had been tiptoeing round a hungover Florence in bed with an unpredictable or hostile lover.

By nine o'clock she could stand it no longer and went into the kitchen to make coffee. Inevitably this woke Jacky and soon the smell of toast attracted the tent-dwellers.

The last to join the breakfast table and the post-mortem on the party was Till, with reddened eyes she'd tried to disguise. Crying about Ben, thought Honey, distracted for a moment from her concentration, poor Till.

But poor Till was also reliable, competent Till. By ten o'clock the cottage was cleared of people, ostensibly so that Honey could meditate. Till was counting on the fact that meditation was so dull that no one would ask Honey more about it in case she told them. Till was the last to leave; she was going for a walk. She kissed Honey before she left and Honey hugged her in return, whispering, "Do you think it's OK to do this?"

"Absolutely," said Till. "The Garden of Life is on a pick-your-own basis."

Left alone, Honey was overwhelmed by fear. Marcus Aurelius. She opened him at random. "Dig within," she read. "There lies the well-spring of good: ever dig, and it will ever flow." He and Till were working along the same lines. She put water in a saucepan to heat, closed the curtains in her bedroom ready for the one minute the vial of sperm had to spend at room temperature in a low-light setting (were the curtains thick enough?). She had to draw the curtains in any case otherwise anyone standing outside the front door would see into her bedroom. It was quite dim – dim enough. She checked the temperature of the water. 100°F. It would cool to 98.6. She took the saucepan into the bedroom, took the vial out of the dry ice, checked the other vial was still covered, timed a minute, put the sperm in the saucepan of warm water, turning it frequently, dashed to the record-player to start the Mahler symphony, dashed back to the sperm. After three minutes she removed the vial, dried it with extreme care, lay down on the floor with pillows under her to tilt her hips so the sperm would pool at the neck of her womb, removed her pants, and . . .

"Anyone in? Hello? Till?" called Tom. He was outside the front door. She could see his shadow on the curtain. She inserted the sperm, her concentration jangled, the moment spoilt. Now she had to stay still for half an hour. Would Tom go away?

When Till left the cottage she was thinking about Honey, poor Honey who seemed so vulnerable and dismayed now the moment had come. Often, damaged people made her angry. How could human beings hurt each other so much? Why had Florence, of all people, had Honey, of all people, to mother? Knowing it was an unanswerable question, she still couldn't refrain from asking it. She walked up the track and turned off it onto the cliff path that circled the bay. She would walk over to the far point on the cliffs and walk back on the beach, when the tide had receded a little.

A hundred yards along the cliff, she was stopped by the sound of a car engine. She turned to look: Ben's car. Whichever Considine it was must be prevented from going to the cottage. She ran back, waving. Ben stopped and got out and now all Till could think of was herself. Of all things she wanted to avoid another scene with Ben, but as he approached her she saw he was calm.

"Good morning, Matilda," he said. "I'll walk with you."

"All right." They walked, in single file which was all the path allowed, for several minutes. When they reached the mid-point of the bay Ben put his hand on her shoulder to halt her and they stood side by side looking out at the sea. Two dinghies bobbed inshore; a tanker was framed against cloud on the horizon. The beach was deserted apart from a farmer exercising his horse with a collie at his side. The dog was capering in and out of the shallow water, barking with pleasure. The barks reached them faintly on the wind.

"I'll never love anyone as much as I love you," said Ben, and Till knew she had lost him. With the knowledge came self-knowledge; she hadn't ever, sincerely, intended him to go or thought that he might. She turned away so he couldn't see her crying. It seemed an age she stood with her back to him; it seemed that the path of her life had ended, abruptly, at a rock-face, too sheer to climb, too wide to circumvent.

"I've been talking to Pandora," he began, and though she shook her head violently to stop him he went on. "You can look at me. Please. Look at me."

He was crying too. He hugged her and bent his face to hers and their tears mingled. "Till, I . . ."

"Don't say nice things for me to remember, please, Ben. Leave me some pride."

"You have too much." He stroked her hair, held her tighter. "I can't leave this marriage. I can't."

His words were an echo, probably deliberate, of her words to him during her divorce. "I can't leave the children. I can't," she'd said, thinking even then how futile it was seeking new words for acute pain.

There was silence. Till thought she would never stop crying. Her tears turned to sobs and Ben rubbed her back like a baby. "I've never had a child with you," she said.

"Not Harry?"

"Almost certainly not Harry."

"So many years," he said. "How shall I bear it?"

"Don't drink too much. Be virtuous in good health."

The wind was drying their tears. She moved away from him. "I'd better walk on. I can't go back to the cottage. Honey wants to be alone."

"Any particular reason?"

"No."

"Because by now I expect Wyatt's at the cottage. I met him at the petrol station in Youghal. He was going to get a newspaper then come on up, he said to see you, though he's after Honey, of course."

"Damn," said Till, starting to walk back.

Tom called twice. There was no answer. He could hear music, the bedroom curtains were drawn, there was probably someone still in the house. With his luck it would be Jacky, but it might – it could – be Honey. He tried the door and it opened. Inside, Mahler was very loud. Still no sign of a human presence. He could go into Honey's bedroom, he thought, he could see her bed, even lie on it, touch her nightdress. Blood pounded in his head as he imagined the scene.

He pushed open her door and stepped back, startled. There was someone lying on the floor. Honey was lying there, almost naked, her skirt rucked up and her pants around her knees. He could see her thighs. Fifty years of conditioning told him to step back, close the door, apologise. She could be ill but her eyes were open. They were – oddly – angry. He wanted to comfort and cradle her, touch her, slip his hand up the inside of her thighs. He was unbearably excited.

She fought for calm. It was only Tom; he was embarrassed but, always, polite. If she smiled at him, used all her charm, he would go. She pressed her knees together, clasped her arms round her naked legs, said, "Please go away," and smiled.

The smile convinced him. Honey wanted him to stay. Women often said the opposite of what they meant. Perhaps she had rape fantasies.

He began to take his clothes off, half his mind functioning, that half astounded at himself. She wanted him otherwise she would have moved. His jacket landed on a chair, slipped to the floor. His chest felt tight. Removing his shirt didn't ease that; he unzipped his trousers, dropped them.

"Tom, please, go away, don't do that," she said more urgently. "I'm meditating."

"No, you're not." He could see her pubic hair, blonde, curly, thicker and less straggly than Maggie's. He wanted to take off her shirt, lick her skin, excite her as he was excited. He was naked now. Still she didn't move. He smoothed his hair, knelt beside her and buried his head in her lap. He could smell her; the sweetness hurt his chest. She wriggled away, keeping her knees lifted. He followed. "I love you, I want you, I must have you," he said hoarsely, desperate for other and better words to release the intolerable pressure inside him.

"Go away! Leave me alone! For God's sake, Tom—"

"I can't, I can't, I'm going to come, I must—" he groaned, and fell across her. She couldn't move. Frustration, rage seized her completely and she began to scratch and slap him. Her thighs were wet. He had come, pumping his superfluous sperm over her, perhaps mingling it with the sperm of Ms Fishkind's Caucasian male. All her accumulated hatred for men who demeaned her, ignoring her wishes and imposing their will on hers, erupted in a flurry of violence. She scratched his face and back, tearing the skin; she thumped his ears with her delicate bunched fists. He did not respond and gradually she realised that his blood and skin were packed under her nails. With a squeal of revulsion she began to pick at them, the nails of each hand digging deep to scour the other.

He still didn't move. Her rage ebbed and she wriggled away, panting and heaving to shift his solid weight. Finally, she understood. He wasn't breathing.

She leaped to her feet, imagining the sperm trickling uselessly down her vagina, down her legs, wasted, all her efforts wasted. She ran to the front door, appalled at the notion of being alone with a cooling corpse. "Till!" she screamed. "Till! Anyone! Help!"

Down on the track, Till and Ben heard her. "Damn and blast and bloody hell!" said Till, thoroughly cheated of her parting from Ben, straining to run up the steep drive, Ben soon overtaking her. He drew the curtains. Till was on her knees beside Tom. His face was tinged with blue. No breath. "Get an ambulance!" She cleared the airway, tilted his head back, breathed for him. No pulse. Thump, thump, thump, she began external cardiac massage. "Ring for an ambulance. Go, Ben, there's a telephone at the post office on the main road." Breathe, breathe, breathe. "Wait for them there and bring them back as quick as you can." Thump, thump, thump. "Tell the hospital it's a heart attack. GO, BEN!"

"I hope he's *dead*," said Honey savagely.

Till was taken aback, not at the sentiment, but at her expression of it. "At present he is," she said, "and likely to stay that way. I haven't been a real doctor for years. Hell, that sounded like a rib."

"You've broken his rib?"

"It often happens," said Till soothingly, still reacting to the Honey she expected. "Don't worry, it's more important to get a heartbeat."

"I wasn't worrying," said Honey. "Break some more."

Till put the question of Honey's behaviour out of her

mind. Breathe, breathe, thump, thump, the rhythm took her over. It was only minutes before his heart restarted and little longer before he breathed for himself, but by then Till was shaking with breathlessness and shock. She wiped away the sour taste of his saliva and turned him over into the recovery position, noticing as she did so the raw scratches left by Honey's nails.

Honey had gone into the bathroom. She was washing herself clean of Tom, starting on her nails then scrubbing the skin of her thighs with a brush. "Help me," called Till. "We must get his trousers on. If he goes in the ambulance mother-naked it'll be all over the hospital and Maggie's sure to hear."

"Let her," said Honey brushing her teeth for good measure. "Let her know he's just like all the others, then maybe she'll stop – looking down on me, treating me like she's the one who gives everything—"

"Patronising you."

"That's it."

"Please help me with his pants. I can't manage him by myself. For me, Honey, not for Maggie."

"What do you care?"

"Why hurt people when you don't have to?"

Honey went back into the bedroom and looked at Tom's inert body. It seemed to her massive, ugly, the flesh of his back and buttocks leaden and unfinished, like dough spilt on the coir flooring. "I want to hurt him," she said. "I can't forgive it and I won't. I've never encouraged him or led him on and he *intruded*."

"That's what men do," said Till. "They have to. Otherwise there'd be no babies."

"Shut up!" said Honey. "Don't tell me what to think and what to feel. I've left that behind, I'm free of it, I'm – I'm—"

"Emancipated," said Till. She was already desolated by the parting from Ben, anxious for Tom. It was all she could do not to snap at a Honey who, having for twenty years tried to make Till tell her what to do and what to feel, chose this moment to end her discipleship.

"I'm emancipated," said Honey.

"Good; please help get his trousers on."

"So long as you understand I'm doing this for you, not for him."

"I don't care if you're doing it for Marcus Aurelius," said Till, heaving Tom's dead weight while Honey inched his underpants up his legs. They were laundry-white, courtesy of Maggie, whose misery Till refused to contemplate. "Get his balls in," said Till impatiently.

"I don't want to touch them."

"Hold him up then."

"I'm not strong enough."

Till didn't sigh. She propped Tom's hips over her knees, tugged at the underpants, felt for the pulse in his neck. It was weak but perceptible. "Trousers," she said.

"You frighten me," said Honey. "You're like a machine. Don't you ever feel anything?"

Till felt like shutting Honey's head in a door. "Trousers," she said again. "Ben came to tell me he and I were finished."

Honey fetched the trousers. Her anger had banked down: years of devotion to Till, deep affection, forced her to respond. "He won't be able to keep away," she said. "Or Pandora might die."

"You're overdoing the heartlessness," said Till. Honey was disconcerting her.

"I prefer you to Pandora. If you want Ben, why shouldn't I wish Pandora dead?" Honey was tugging at the waistband of Tom's trousers, trying to fasten them. "Ugh," she said. "Tom's got tons of hair on his legs and none on the top of his head and he doesn't even buy his trousers large enough, he's so vain, and I thought he was a kind man. I thought he was one of the few kind men I'd ever met."

"He is kind. Just human, ageing and wistful."

"Lustful?"

"No, wistful. You were his dream of youth."

"Shows how much he knows. It's not only my inner thighs that have gone now. I can't turn my neck without it going crêpey. And he made me read that awful book."

"What awful book?" Till's head began to ache and she could feel tears pressing behind her eyes. Mahler was still thundering in the other room, approaching yet another unsatisfactory climax. Honey had put the record on continuous play; Till saw it as a metaphor for Honey's life, Ben's, perhaps her own, and went into the other room to turn it off.

Honey followed her. "That awful book *Mucus*. He said it changed his life and I took hours, *days* reading it and then I gave it to Ms Fishkind and she said it was garbage. Why didn't you tell me that, Till? Why didn't you? England just laughs at me because I can't spell or read properly. The whole country, even you, laughing. Tom gave it to me as a joke, like Marilyn Monroe."

"What?"

"Me, like Marilyn Monroe, not as famous of course or as beautiful. But STUPID! IGNORANT!"

"You're not ignorant," said Till. She knew Honey was anguished, partly felt it, but wanted Ben so much and was so devastated by the stark vista of life without him that not all her training and her innate desire to subordinate her own interests to those of others could force more than automatic reassurance. "You have the wisdom of the heart," she said limply.

"Wisdom of the heart? I like that. Who said that?"

Almost everyone, thought Till. "Hugh Walpole," she said wildly.

"Hugh Walpole? Was he a great writer?"

Hysterical laughter curdled in Till's throat at the prospect of starting Honey on yet another futile paper-chase through hundreds of thousands of Walpole words. "He was good but not that good," she said

246

temperately. When would the ambulance come? She checked Tom again. Better to leave his shirt off. Think of an explanation for the scratches. Honey's nails, professionally tended, tungsten-hard, had gouged deep. Over the sea she could hear the ambulance siren. With the ambulance, Ben would come. Then he would go, back to the baby Pandora would produce from her recently acclaimed pelvic area.

"Good morning to you, and where's the patient?" said an ambulance man outside.

Jacky hated Ireland. It was damp, dull and hideous. The only houses with any visual appeal were either ruined or decaying, the shops contained nothing that any sighted person would wish to buy; Till's cottage was uncomfortable, her cooking indifferent; there was no demand for gigolos among any of her friends. If he hadn't owed Honey so much, emotionally and financially, he would have been on the first plane to Heathrow. And, of course, he was living free, even if he was sleeping on a sofabed in cotton sheets and drinking instant coffee.

He limped beside Amanda along yet another beach (seaweed-smelling, pebbly, deserted) hoping that Honey was conceiving immediately. Otherwise she might insist on returning to Ireland and want him to accompany her. Meanwhile he had to listen to Amanda, an adolescent girl so commonplace that she would win an award for it if awards were offered, and to whom, after all her help, he felt obliged.

Ahead of them, Rob and Harry were skimming stones across the grey, undistinguished sea. "And the thing is," said Amanda, "I'm sure Rob likes me, because, for instance, last night in the pub he talked to me for ages and Harry was quite jealous."

"Ummm," said Jacky, thinking that Rob would be interested in Amanda when the Rio Carnival came to Youghal.

"Do you think I'm attractive, Jacky?"

"Very," said Jacky with manly conviction, studying the curve of denim on Rob's buttocks.

"More attractive than Mummy?"

"Of course," said Jacky.

"I think she rather resents it," said Amanda. "It can't be easy for an ageing woman to have a daughter younger than herself."

"Even more difficult to have a daughter older than herself," said Jacky, the pain in his leg eroding compliance. Amanda wasn't listening.

"And my whole life is before me and she's made such a mess of hers."

"Poor Till," said Jacky, entirely insincere.

"Ben Considine fancies me too."

"Ummm." The seaweed beneath their feet gave way to a heap of dead jellyfish. Jacky picked his way round them.

"I actually considered having an affair with him, you know, but he's too old."

"Did he ask you?"

"Not in so many words, but I could tell from the way he looked at me. A woman knows."

"Of course," said Jacky. "I'm a bit tired. Do you think we could go back?"

"Back to the car? We're supposed to stay away from the cottage for a while yet."

Back to the world, thought Jacky. Let's go back to civilisation. Away from Ireland.

Chapter Fourteen

Trafalgar Square was closed to traffic for Honey's memorial service. Even though it was a bleak day in January, crowds stood soaking in persistent rain from a ponderous grey sky, listening to the service relayed through loudspeakers, and not all of them were celebrity-spotters. Most had come because Honey had touched their hearts with her beauty and become part of their memories, like long-ago Christmases and faded holiday snapshots, a reminder of happier times. They took the only opportunity open to them to recognise the passing of a character from the folk-history of a nation which cherished fewer and fewer heroes.

"A Service of Thanksgiving for the Life and Work of Honey Markham", said the posters on the railings of St Martin-in-the-Fields. Florence had worded the posters and chosen the guests: there had been vicious squabbling over tickets for seats inside the church, which Florence enjoyed, when she forgot to be bereaved.

Now she sat in a front pew supported by Leo Pardoe on one side and her latest lover on the other and reviewed the situation. If Honey had to die so young – the thought forced an involuntary but useful gush of tears – then she could not have died more profitably if Florence had stage-managed it herself.

Four months ago Honey had unaccountably decided to make one last public appearance at the opening night of a season of her films at an art cinema in New York. It was a slow news day and the cinema's manager had connections: her arrival at the airport the previous day made the local news. Next morning, she walked out of the St Regis and vanished. The opening night celebrations and question-and-answer session were postponed and the cinema manager summoned Florence. Lacking a beautiful actress, he could at least use a distraught mother. Florence appeared, coast to coast, appealing to the American people to give her back her daughter. The American people were perfectly prepared to give her back but unfortunately none of them, including the New York police, could find her, though her rifled handbag turned up, complete with passport, in Central Park. Florence stayed in New York for three weeks and was shown a series of unidentified dead women. No Honey. Then a policeman made a grisly discovery in an apartment not far from Central Park. Attending the scene of a shotgun suicide – male – he routinely searched the apartment and found two walk-in cupboards full of female bodies.

Most were beyond visual identification; two were wheeled out on trolleys for Florence. She already knew she had a good chance of seeing Honey, whose ring and bracelet had been among the pathetic heap of belongings found in a drawer of the apartment. She hardly looked; she was squeamish and almost fainting from the mortuary smell. It was Honey, she was nearly sure. She fainted in good earnest.

Video sales of *Captain Bridge* and other hasty re-issues of Honey's films soared. Florence returned to England and surprise. She was the only executor of Honey's will. At first touched by Honey's trust, she quickly became suspicious. The estate was massively depleted. Soon after Honey's return from her first visit to San Francisco that year, she had sold her house to Madeline, and the money had gone. Her broker had been selling steadily that year: that money, also, had gone. Over a million pounds had simply disappeared.

Florence's instinct was to make a monumental hullabaloo but her second thought, her natural wariness, prevailed. Perhaps that poor body hadn't been Honey; perhaps Honey had chosen to disappear. Meanwhile the estate was swelling with royalties and Florence was doing nicely on chat shows as a bereaved Madame Arcati. For once in her life she was discreet. She told nobody, not even her lover, of her suspicions. In October in Golders Green she allowed the coffin containing Jane Doe to glide into immolation as smoothly as an ice-dancer. When the curtains swished together and the body had gone, she broke down and wept tears of rage and loss. Her current lover, a retired bank manager, was moved by her devotion to her child and comforted her with gin. She was profoundly disturbed, chiefly by the knowledge that Honey had finally eluded her.

She was furious for weeks. Then, arrangements for the memorial service absorbed her. The manner of Honey's death had elevated her from a personality into a myth. At Christmas, as usual, the nation watched *The Daughters of Captain Bridge* and, when Honey smiled, the nation reached for its Kleenex. The service was to be an outlet for popular feeling.

Looking round at the famous faces inside the church, remembering the crowds outside, Florence felt justified. Her only reservation about the service was that Till was to speak. She couldn't very well have omitted her. Everyone who had worked on *Captain Bridge*, down to the electrician's boy, had a seat inside the church: Vernon, Ben and Pandora were reading. Till was well known to be Honey's best friend. But experience had taught Florence that allowing Till free rein to express her views about anything was inviting irritation if not disaster, and she only asked her to read any uplifting sonnet of her choice. Till had insisted that if she took part at all she must be allowed carte blanche. Now Florence watched Till bitterly. The wretched woman had some-how managed to cobble together what remained of her looks, buy an expensive black coat and a very clever hat, and arrive escorted by Jacky, easily the best-looking man in the church.

The television vicar cleared his throat with professional inaudibility and announced the hymn, "Jerusalem the Golden". The congregation stood. At the second line, "with milk and honey blest", Florence broke down. Leo Pardoe comforted her in mime and the bank manager nudged her with a hip-flask. Till left her pew and moved to stand beside the vicar at the lectern.

"Who art, with God the Father, And Spirit, ever blest," sang the congregation, and sat down, coughing and shuffling.

Till gripped the lectern. Honey's death had devastated her and she was not yet recovered. She looked at the congregation, at the rows of Pardoes, at Tom Wyatt, greyer than ever, aged and diminished by his heart attack and Maggie who wore the preoccupied air of one who had invited fifty people to a buffet lunch after the service. Pandora was leaning forward in her seat. She looked anxious for Till, like a prompter without a text. Perhaps she feared Till might talk about Ben. Till's eye moved away from Ben, then back. He looked tired. He was watching her. Had he noticed the coat and the hat? Jacky had chosen them, recklessly spending altogether too much money, Till felt, although she could afford it. She had been included in Honey's recently remade will: "To my friend Matilda Livesey, enough money to buy a red Ferrari, or any sports car in a colour of her choice, to drive in perpetual felicity". An odd bequest. Honey couldn't reasonably have expected Till to receive it until she was well past driving.

The congregation was shuffling; one of Honey's stepsons was looking at his watch. Both the stepsons, with their wives, were present and trying not to show the pleasure they certainly felt at the early reversion of her trust fund. Vernon looked sober, and sad. Possibly he had been fond of her; possibly her death foreshadowed his; probably both. Madeline, with the Wyatts, was smiling, but then Madeline's face smiled without her. Jacky looked appropriate.

Till began. "We are here to remember Honey, Sarah, Markham. We all have different memories." Ben grimaced. Till wondered if he was rejecting her platitude or recalling something entirely different, perhaps the awkward night he and Till had spent twenty years ago, in bed, trying to find any sexual activity Honey enjoyed. "I don't believe Honey will ever die," she went on.

Florence flinched.

"She won't ever die for me. Although the manner of her death was appalling, horrible –" those in the congregation who knew Till braced themselves for some enormity, possibly a detailed account of the autopsy report "– that doesn't matter now. It certainly doesn't matter to Honey. What remains is what she hoped for, what she wanted to achieve. I'd like to describe to you what Honey would be doing if she had lived."

Florence had turned an unappealing shade of suffused puce.

"She wanted a baby, she wanted to learn, she wanted – simple as it sounds – to be free. And that is how I imagine her, somewhere in America, perhaps in a beach house in Santa Monica or walking beside the sea, pregnant, counting the days until her baby comes, quoting Marcus Aurelius to the seagulls, and smiling."

She stepped down from the lectern and went back to her pew; Jacky stood gracefully to receive her. For the rest of the service she sat in numb misery. If she could have negotiated with death, there was only one member of the congregation she would not have traded for Honey.

Afterwards they milled round in the church porch, on the steps, waiting for the police to clear a way through the crowds for car and taxis. Florence hissed at Till. "Bitch!" she said. "Bloody bitch!" Till was taken aback but, because she valued Florence's opinion so little, not upset. She and Jacky moved away, stood apart from the rest. She saw Ben approaching and controlled her impulse to walk away and evade him, unwilling to let him see how much he affected her. "Matilda," said Ben, stopping very close to her.

"I'll just –" said Jacky vaguely, and left them together.

"That was a very limp eulogy, for you," Ben said.

"Honey's outside my range. She needs a watercolourist. I do satirical etchings."

"Can I come up and see them sometime?"

"No," said Till flatly. She could feel, under the pain of Honey's loss, the nagging hurt of Ben's.

"Perhaps I could see Amanda, then?"

"Touch Amanda and I'll cut your cock off."

"Because of me?"

"Because of Amanda. I mean it, Ben."

"I know. My play is coming along."

"Don't tell me. It's about a father who can't communicate with his son."

"Wrong, for once. It's about you."

"It won't work, then. I'm not a heroine, I'm a subplot."

"Not to me. I should have seen it long ago. Not to me."

"Matilda," said Pandora tucking her arm into Ben's. "I loved your speech; it made me cry. Are you coming to lunch at Maggie's?"

"I was going to, but I'm not feeling up to it now. I'll take a taxi home."

In the taxi on the way to Ladbroke Grove she held her hands out in front of her and watched them shake. She forced herself to think about Florence. Why was she angry? But the question held no interest and her mind slipped back to Honey and futile suppositions. If Honey had stayed in her hotel, if she had not been so compliant, if she had not been so beautiful . . .

Outside her flat, Biddy Keefe waited with Othello.

"'Tis grand you look, sure and you could pull a man of your choice. Was it a fitting service?"

"Very fitting."

"Did himself hold together?"

"He read marvellously. From Wordsworth."

"He was destroyed entirely at the news."

"I know." Till had spent hours with Biddy and Vernon over Christmas.

"Both your precious lambs are inside so I'll not be coming in and disturbing you but if it's takeaway and telly you want tonight then I'm your person. Any time."

"I know. Thank you, Biddy."

"And I'm sorry for your trouble."

"I know." Till watched woman and dog amble towards the council flats then went up her own front steps and opened the door. There was a typewritten letter for her with an American stamp and a San Francisco postmark. She held it, unopened, her brain grasping at once the overwhelming news it contained and the source of Florence's anger. She hesitated to read it. Perhaps she was wrong. While she didn't read it, she could hope.

Amanda was lying on the sofa, Harry playing a Chopin ballade on the piano, cursing when he missed the notes. They were surprised to see her. "You're early," said Harry. "How was it?"

"Better than I expected," said Till, turning the letter between her fingers.

"I'll get some milk for your tea. We're right out," said Harry.

When the door closed behind him Amanda swung her legs down and sat up, watching her mother closely. "What's happened? What is it?"

"Nothing."

"Yes, it is. Did you see Ben at the service?"

"Yes."

"That's what upset you, then," said Amanda. "When I'm your age, I hope I'll eat men like him for breakfast."

255

Mother and daughter grinned at each other and Till decided. "If I tell you something, will you swear never to tell anyone else?"

"Are you going to tell Harry?"

"No. Only you."

"Only me in the whole world?"

"Only you. But you must never tell, not when you're drunk or in bed with a man you're trying to impress. You mustn't hint or nod or wink. Swear."

"I swear," said Amanda. "Shall we play the rest of the 'mole' scene from *Hamlet*, or are you going to tell me?"

"Come and read this," said Till. She tore open the envelope. The letter was typed, with handwritten postscripts.

"I have a wordprocessor which corrects spellings! My baby is due the second week in July. Please write and visit me SOON. I meant to tell no one in England but there is not enough salt in my food here without you, dearest, best Till. I worked it all out by myself (with help from film plots). I am called Felicity Cousins. I used her birth certificate to get a passport. I don't think she'd mind, do you? Wasn't I lucky that poor murdered girl stole the ring and bracelet? I am growing. Best love, Felicity (Honey).

P.S. I will never, *never* cum bak, yu must cum to me and I wil tell yu all abote how I dide it, it was copmlicaytid.

P.P.S. I am not so stewpid."